CW01623157

Defining Gravity

Genevieve Mckay

Copyright©2017 Genevieve Mckay.

This book is a work of fiction. Names, characters, places, and incidents are either the product of the author's imagination or are used fictitiously, and any resemblance to actual persons, living or dead, business establishments, events, or locales is entirely coincidental. All rights reserved. No part of this book may be reproduced, scanned, or distributed in any printed or electronic form without permission. Please do not participate in or encourage piracy of copyrighted materials in violation of the author's rights. Purchase only authorized editions.

Acknowledgments

Huge thanks to my fabulous editor Jinxie Gervasio who always laughs and cries in the right places.

And massive appreciation, in no particular order, to Heather Stewart of Sweet Water Stables, Helen Cartwright, Helen Yeo, Jennifer Warburton, Joanne Uhrig of Dressage on the Go, Mariko Brown, Marti Oltmann, Tam Paulin, and Emily Pelletier of Generation Farms for being the first readers. Your help was invaluable!

Fabulous cover design credit goes to *Cover Design by James, GoOnWrite.com*

Interior design credit goes to the wonderful folks at Polgarus Studio.

And last, but not least, many thanks to Messenger, who is the funniest, bossiest, most clever horse in the world. Thanks for putting up with me all these years, buddy.

Chapter One

"More punch, Astrid?"

Thomas Ling's impeccably chiseled face loomed close, near enough that I could smell the delicious, spicy cologne clinging to his skin. The sky behind him had turned a vibrant shade of pink, the sun dipping low toward the horizon in a dreamy, leisurely way that left me feeling as if I'd stepped through a looking glass and into someone else's spectacular life. A surge of excitement shot through my chest; electricity rippling up my arms as if every nerve ending was awake.

"Sure," I said as casually as I could, as if boys handed me drinks all the time. I wiped my damp palms on my dress and arranged myself awkwardly on the grass with my knees to one side, surreptitiously brushing at the bits of grass embedded in my calves.

His fingers were warm against mine as he handed me my glass half full of red liquid; Mr. Ling's signature punch. It was a tangy mixture of blood orange and spices his father concocted for every gathering the Ling's held. And believe me; despite being the most socially inept person on the planet, I'd been forced to attend a lot of Ling parties.

"Wow, what's in this?" I said, wincing as I took a sip. My last two drinks hadn't tasted this strong. The punch burned with a cloying sweetness that coated my tongue and made my nose tingle.

Thomas laughed quietly, tossing his head back so a thick lock of black hair fell across his forehead. I wanted to reach out and touch it, smooth it back into place. "Sorry about that, this batch might be a little stronger than the last one. Quinton just added a little more fun, that's all."

"Oh," I said, awareness dawning. This was more than Mr. Ling's signature punch. Had the other drinks been spiked, too? My father would kill me if he found out I'd even so much as *tasted* alcohol, even by accident.

Thomas winked and laughed again. "You're one of us now, Astrid. Welcome to the dark side, but don't tell my parents, right?"

"Right," I said slowly, setting the glass down on the grass beside me. I wondered how I'd know if I was already drunk. "Of course."

I looked up into his shining eyes and felt my anxiety melt away. I'd loved Thomas since childhood with an irrational, burning passion that couldn't be extinguished despite the obvious fact he barely knew I existed. I went to Sacred Heart Academy with him and his sister Susan, but that was where our similarities ended.

Thomas was older than me; he'd graduated last week and was off to University in the fall. He was practically a god at Sacred Heart, and I was the kid who ate lunch alone in the library every single day, and whose father sent her to a so-called "health spa" every year instead of summer camp. The only reason Thomas knew my name was that his father worked for WorldCor, my dad's exploratory mining and development company, so I'd been a mandatory invite to every party the Ling kids had ever thrown.

Tonight, though, things seemed to finally be falling into place. I had optimistically worn one of the dresses my stepmother Marion always tried to foist on me and my unruly black curls were actually behaving for once. The full-piece bathing suit I'd worn underneath, just in case I felt brave enough to swim, squashed all my curves into just the right shape for my dress to cling to.

"I'm glad you came, Astrid," Thomas said, his eyes never leaving mine. "You look beautiful."

My intelligent reply died an instant, happy death. I smiled idiotically, a warm glow radiating out from my belly until I was practically on fire. *Thomas Ling just said you were beautiful!* I grabbed my glass and took a nervous gulp just to have something to do with my hands. The liquid flowed smooth down my throat like warm honey.

"Well, enjoy the party," Thomas said after a long, embarrassing pause where I just stared dreamily at his perfect lips. With a wink, he sauntered off to mingle with the other guests.

"Oh, there you are." Miranda flopped down on the grass beside me, looking frazzled and uncomfortable, red hair falling loose from its braid. Crowds weren't really her thing and she'd only come because I'd begged. "I was looking all over for you."

"Here I am," I said happily. "Isn't this the best party?" I slipped my sweaty sandals off and pushed my toes in the lush, cool grass.

Miranda raised her eyebrows and shrugged. "I suppose if you like this sort of thing. Was that Susan's brother talking to you?"

"Yes," I said. "It was Thom-as Ling." Even his name was beautiful, each drawn-out syllable full of promise. I hugged my knees to my chest in delight, thinking of his fingers brushing mine when he'd handed me the cup.

Miranda peered into my face and frowned. "Are you okay, Astrid? You look kind of funny. You know he was just being polite, right? There's no way he actually *like* likes you."

The bubble of happiness surrounding me didn't burst; it deflated slowly like a leaky balloon, leaving me shivering despite the warm air.

I tugged the hem of my dress down to cover my too-thick thighs and struggled to find some good thoughts. The counsellors at Windy Shores, the high priced fat-camp my father sent me to once or twice a year, were always going on about emphasizing the good and ignoring the bad. But that was much easier to do in the safety of my own room when there weren't other people around.

Miranda stared at me, her green eyes wide with concern. "Don't be upset, Astrid. I didn't mean to be rude. You look great, really, but you have to admit you're no cheerleader. Thomas is way, *way* out of your league."

"Of course, I know that," I said quickly. I bared my teeth in a painful smile to show her I was fine. "I'm just not his type."

"Good. Because you know I love you no matter what you look like. You're really smart and you have *such* a great personality. You just need to be realistic."

I willed myself not to be offended. Miranda and I had been

friends for years, ever since she'd come to Sacred Heart on scholarship and we'd started on the archery team together. We'd gone to the BC Winter Games last year and had both medaled; I took Gold and she had the Silver. We each had our future Olympic careers mapped out. Miranda had a reputation for being blunt and bull-headed; not many of the other kids on our team liked her. But I knew she had a soft heart underneath.

"Come on," Miranda said, throwing an arm over my shoulders, "let's go for a walk and clear your head of all things Ling."

"Sure, I guess." I clambered to my feet, stumbling a little as I tottered upright. All those glasses of punch, whether they'd been spiked or not, now sat heavy in my gut; my stomach gurgled ominously and I took a deep breath to calm it. I set my half-finished glass next to my purse and discarded sandals and followed Miranda barefoot over the thick carpet of grass toward the lake.

The Ling's weekend house was a huge modern mansion, bristling with metal and glass, overlooking a secluded edge of Horne Lake. The first thing they'd done when they'd bought the property was to take out the scrubby pines and dense underbrush and replace it with a flawless carpet of green that went right down to the edge of the water. There, they'd left a few gnarled old cedar trees and it was from one of these that a group of boys were taking turns swinging far out over the lake suspended from a long rope.

One of them grasped the thick line in both hands and, without hesitating, leapt into the air, cutting through the sky like an arrow, head thrown back and toes nearly skimming the water.

His arms strained against the rope; shirtless, suntanned body riding a steady arc that seemed to go on forever. He reached the end of his sweep and hung there suspended, silhouetted against the sunset like a beautiful painting, before flying rapidly toward the shore and dismounting perfectly with a light spring to the ground.

I sighed, suddenly full of an inexplicable longing to be anyone rather than myself. That boy looked so comfortable in his own skin, like he didn't have a care in the world and was exactly where he belonged. I wanted that feeling more than anything, for my fat, clumsy body to rise free, effortlessly from the earth.

"I wish that was me up there," I spoke out loud without thinking.

"What, with Robert?" Miranda said scathingly. "Isn't he that weird Mexican kid who used to eat his pencils?"

"No," I said, embarrassed. "Not *with* him. I mean, to be so free and sort of, well, beautiful, like that."

Miranda shot me a strange look. "Robert's not beautiful," she snorted. "You don't really want to swing on that dirty rope. Everyone would be watching you and you'd probably fall off. You're not exactly coordinated."

I turned slowly to stare at Miranda as if I were seeing her for the first time. Unfamiliar anger blossomed in my chest. Maybe it was the alcohol or maybe it was the memory of the few moments of giddy happiness I'd felt earlier, but suddenly it was like someone else took over my body. Before I could change my mind, I turned away from her and marched toward the lake.

"Astrid, what are you doing?"

I barely heard Miranda's warning voice, my bare feet

practically moved of their own accord across the cool grass. I almost couldn't believe this was *me*, walking boldly up to a group of shirtless boys; strangers most of them. Something wild and reckless had taken hold of me.

"Could I try, please?"

The boys looked up one by one, eyes skimming expertly over my extra curves, assessing and dismissing in a split second. The boy who'd just finished swinging, Robert, raised a questioning eyebrow and tossed his hair out of his eyes. Then Quinton Anderson, one of Thomas's teammates from the Sacred Heart lacrosse team, quirked his winning smile at me.

"Sure thing, short stuff, if you think you can handle it. You brought your bathing suit?"

"Yes," I said, fumbling at my dress strap and glad Miranda and I had worn our suits underneath our clothes just in case anyone miraculously invited us to swim.

"Oh no you don't," Miranda said firmly, reaching my side and glaring at the circle of boys. "You're not thinking straight, Astrid. I'm calling my mom and we're going home right now. We have archery practice first thing in the morning and the tournament on Sunday."

An uneasy twinge shot through my belly. The sun was fading fast and I *did* have to be at the range early. What was I doing here with all these strange boys who were probably laughing behind my back?

"Chill out, Granny," Quinton said to Miranda with an unpleasant smirk. "If Fat Camp wants to swing then she gets to swing."

I froze, the hated nickname hung suspended in the air

between us, sharp and ugly. Nobody ever called me that to my face. Ever. It was always half-hidden, a name buried in whispered laughter following me down the hall.

"Dude." Someone coughed. "Not cool."

"Right. Sorry, uh, Astrid, right? That just slipped out. You know we're kidding anyway. You still want to swing?"

I want to melt into the ground, I want to be pretty, I want to not be an awkward cow. I just nodded and said, "Yes, I want to swing."

Miranda shook her head. "I don't believe this." She crossed her arms over her chest. "Fine. One swing and then we go. But you keep your clothes on."

Someone pushed the thick rope between my fingers. I looked down to where the sharp twisted fibres bit into my skin, not sure what to do next. Quinton stepped up beside me, leaning in so close I could feel his breath on my cheek.

"Okay, let's show you how to do this."

Suddenly, I was excited again; thinking only about flying.

"It's easy. Put your foot in the loop and hold on tight with both hands. You have three swings out over the lake before you have to jump off or you'll land in the water. Okay?"

"Okay," I said breathlessly, a flicker of fear twisting in my belly. My foot fit perfectly into the loop, the sharp fibres, worn smooth with use, were soft against my bare skin.

"Then, go. And watch out for the tree."

Quinton gave the soft spot between my shoulder blades a shove and I sailed out over the lake, wind whipping through my hair and my heart thudding a million miles a minute.

Fear was replaced with exhilaration. It wasn't anything like flying in an airplane; instead, I was a bird, lifted high above the world so nothing could touch me. The feeling was almost as good as shooting; that perfect, still moment when I anchored my bow string tight against my cheekbone and time slowed down until there was nothing else in the world but me, my breathing, and the target.

The rope reached the end of its arc and gravity took over, pulling me backwards with electrifying speed until I hung suspended over the group on the shore, their upturned faces indistinct in the growing dusk. I closed my eyes, leaning way back to abandon myself to the rush of speed taking over again.

On the second swing, I opened my eyes. I didn't want my turn to end, but Quinton had said I had exactly three swings before I had to stop. I wouldn't make a fool of myself by landing in a heap at his feet or anything. I turned to face the shore and just then, the rope made a soft popping noise and sort of stretched between my fingers as if the woven fibres were unraveling from the inside. My heart gave a lurch of fear, but I tightened my grip and focused on the shore. I was almost there.

"Look out!" Someone yelled from the bank.

I glanced up to see one strand of the yellow rope above my head spinning in the air, unwinding faster and faster toward my hands. I twisted in an effort to hold on and that's when the tree came up to meet me. There was no way to avoid it. I hunched sideways and crashed into the rough bark shoulder-first, the impact jarring my whole body and making me cry out. I still didn't let go of the rope, so I was far out over the water when the fraying strands finally broke and I plummeted into the lake.

I hit the water like a cannon ball and plunged straight to the shallow bottom where I lay half-buried in muck. I held my breath and stared up at the shimmering surface of the shallow lake, stained pink by the sunset, wondering if anyone would notice if I just stayed down there forever.

The water churned and rough hands grabbed at my arms, fingers digging deep into my skin. There was a wrenching, popping feeling in my shoulder and I cried out, inhaling buckets of murky water.

I kicked wildly, but the hands didn't let go. They dragged me out of the water and dumped me, choking and crying and clutching my shoulder, onto the soggy bank.

"Are you okay?" voices asked all around me. "Should we call the ambulance?"

I could hear Thomas calmly ordering everyone to stand back and give me room.

Quinton's face hovered next to me. "Do you need me to give you mouth to mouth, Astrid?"

There was laughter in his voice. I was supposed to say something witty, but instead I heaved and puked up a stomach full of punch and dirty lake water right on his bare feet.

"Awesome!" Someone laughed. "I got that on video. Nice one, Astrid."

I rolled over on the grass, closing my eyes and trying to stay as still as possible. Everything hurt: my whole right side where I hit the tree, my burning lungs and throat, my hands from where the rope had burned them. I felt like I'd been run over by a bus.

"Look at her," someone whispered loudly. "Fat Camp snapped the rope right in half."

"Shh," a girl's voice cautioned, "that's not nice."

I stopped breathing in my effort to disappear. How ridiculous did I look lying there in a muddy heap with my hair plastered across my face and my sodden dress hiked up around my thighs? I could practically hear the pictures of my miserable-self flying, right then, from phone to phone, from party to party, school to school until the whole world saw me exposed and there'd be nowhere to hide.

"Astrid?" Thomas whispered. I cracked open an eye to see his beautiful face looming over me. There was genuine concern in his eyes but something else too; maybe anger. He draped a blanket carefully over my shoulders, his fingers lightly brushing across my skin. "Don't move. We've called the ambulance. You're going to be fine."

"Okay." I gulped, fighting back tears of humiliation. Just when I'd thought Thomas might actually be interested in knowing me better, something like *this* had to happen. He must think I was a complete idiot.

"Listen," he said quickly, shooting a look upward at someone standing behind me. "You can't tell anyone about the punch, Astrid. Quinton could lose his place on the team if he gets in any trouble and my parents would kill me if they knew we were drinking. You understand, right?"

He looked into my eyes intently, his perfect brow crinkled unhappily.

"Um, okay," I whispered. It wasn't like I was the type of person to go around blabbing anyway. I liked to keep my head down and stay out of trouble. And of course, my dad could never find out about it, either.

"Great," he said, breaking into a relieved smile. "That's my girl. I owe you, Astrid. Maybe we'll see you around this summer. You play badminton or something, right? We should play a game sometime."

"Archery," I murmured. "I'm an archer." But he didn't hear me. He'd already turned away.

A high-pitched scream exploded next to my ear, followed by words firing rapidly in Cantonese too fast for me to comprehend. Susan and Thomas's mother was having one of her famous meltdowns. I didn't blame her; not only was she a very strict, conservative lady, but her husband worked for my dad, which was guaranteed to be a stressful way to make a living. I could only imagine how Mr. Ling would attempt to explain me almost dying at his kid's party.

"Ma, calm down." Thomas's usually smooth voice rose angrily. "Dad already called the ambulance. Of course, we weren't drinking. It was just an accident."

There was another bout of yelling in Cantonese followed by Thomas's raised voice.

"How should I know about the punch? Am I supposed to guard the drink table all night? Maybe someone smuggled something in. Maybe she brought a bottle herself. I don't know, I'm not a babysitter."

A spurt of helpless indignation rose in my chest. All I could do was lay face down on the grass and try not to mortify myself further. I started to shiver and pulled my head underneath the blanket, curled inside like a turtle in its shell.

I must have passed out because the next thing I knew the jostling and barking orders of the EMT's woke me up.

"We're going to lift you onto a stretcher," a man's voice said very clearly in my ear. “It might hurt.”

I yelped when they lifted me onto the board, but it was a relief to be inside the privacy of the ambulance. The last thing I saw before the doors slammed shut was Miranda’s pale, terrified face peering in at me. Her cheeks were blotchy with tears and I wished she would ride with me, but before I could call out to her she’d disappeared into the crowd.

Chapter Two

The ride to the hospital was very anticlimactic. They didn't even turn the sirens on. The ambulance guy who rode with me told me a few lame jokes to try and cheer me up. Then he bundled me under a heavy blanket and went on filling out his paperwork. He didn't ask questions and I was able to just lie there sniffling and feeling sorry for myself.

The nurse who checked me in at the hospital was not sympathetic at all. She had bottle-red dyed hair and stared down at me over a pair of tiny glasses, narrowing her eyes suspiciously as she took down my information.

"We need to X-ray your arm," she said brusquely. "But there's a line-up right now, so you'll have to wait. Get out of those filthy, wet clothes and put on a gown."

She turned her back on me abruptly, marching from the room without saying anything else. I whimpered miserably and, clutching my hurt arm to my chest, painstakingly shimmied out of my ruined dress. The muddy, wet bathing suit clung to my skin like glue and it took all my strength to peel it off and crawl into the thin blue pillow case thing that she'd called a "gown."

Finally, I could lie back on the bed, exhausted.

The room they'd wheeled me into on the rolling cot was a private room, which was nice. The waiting room I'd been taken through had been packed full of people. Some had just looked sick, but one man had a bloody bandage wrapped around his head and wild rolling eyes that scanned the crowd suspiciously. When his eyes locked on mine, I'd turned my head and pretended to be sleeping until we'd reached the safety of my room.

It wasn't until my X-rays were done that anyone showed up for me, and then it wasn't my dad but my step-mom Marion who appeared at my bedside.

"Astrid," she said quietly, reaching a hand out to smooth the muddy, tangled hair back from my forehead. She looked down at the smear of dirt on her hand and wrinkled her nose in distaste. "I came as soon as I could. Poor girl, are you hurt?"

Her kindness undid the cold knot in my throat and I started to blubber, trying to tell her everything that had happened. But before I could get a coherent word out, that same grumpy nurse banged into the room with a clipboard in her hand.

'The doctor will be in shortly," she said, eyeing Marion with a frown. "In the meantime, I'm supposed to go over some literature and let you know that there are support groups available to help underage drinkers. The Young Addicts group has been particularly helpful in managing difficult teens."

That stopped my crying. I gaped at her with my mouth open, shaking my head when Marion shot me a questioning look.

"There must be some mistake. Astrid is far from troublesome. And she would never drink," she answered in her soft, firm voice.

The nurse pursed her lips into a tight line. "Yeah, that's what they all say. This young lady smelled clearly of alcohol. She was barely coherent when they brought her in. There was a fire down on First Street tonight and some of the firefighters were injured. Those men were real heroes who could have been brought here faster if an ambulance hadn't been tied up driving to a house party way out on Horne Lake road to deal with a spoiled, drunk teenager who fell into the lake."

She paused to pull herself together. "I will leave you some pamphlets to read and let you and your husband decide how to best handle your daughter. Hopefully, for her sake, you do something before it's too late."

She swept out, leaving me and Marion staring at each other in stunned silence.

"It's not true," I whispered urgently. "Marion, I swear I only had a few glasses of punch, that's it. I didn't know it was spiked. I'm not an addict. I've never had a drink before in my life. You can't tell my dad."

"Astrid." She faltered. "You know how your father feels about drinking, after what your mother—"

I didn't want to hear it. My mom had been the worst kind of alcoholic, the kind that abandons her family and then slowly kills herself one drink at a time. My father was rabid on the subject of alcohol. I'd never even seen him sip a beer and our condo had always been a drink-free zone. He would literally kill me if he thought I'd broken his most obsessive rule.

The door opened and a grey-haired doctor breezed into the room, all smiles. Brown eyes sparkled behind his glasses. He wore his long white lab coat over jeans and on his feet were a pair of bright yellow running shoes.

"Ladies," he said with a smile. "I looked at the X-rays and the good news is that there is nothing broken. The bad news is that you've injured that shoulder quite badly; there's a lot of soft tissue damage. You're going to have to keep your arm in a sling for a few weeks and then take it easy for the next two months while you go through physiotherapy. That shouldn't be too much of a problem for a pretty young girl like you; spend the summer shopping at the mall or lying around on the beach. Doctor's orders."

"What?" The word felt sharp in my mouth.

His smile fell as he took in my suddenly stricken face. He turned to where Marion sat equally frozen on the plastic chair beside my bed. Her skirt, jacket and even her hair were the same unassuming taupe as the walls. If it weren't for a slightly warm splash of pale, pink lipstick she could have been another piece of furniture.

My chest was so tight I couldn't breathe; it was like drowning all over again. I counted the months rapidly in my head, not able to believe the disaster unravelling in front of me like a long, dark road. I'd been so busy feeling mortified that I hadn't even thought about what would happen tomorrow or the next day. Now, the utter awfulness of my situation sank in. I would miss the tournament on Sunday and the entire first part of summer training camp. I had a summer full of competitions planned. Worst of all, my dad had planned a trip for just the two of us to see the archery at the Nadaam Festival in Mongolia in July. He would lose his mind when he'd found out what I'd done.

I sank into my pillow, my whole body shaking so hard the

bed rattled. I put a hand over my mouth to keep back the sobs but it was no good. I choked and snuffled, tears running down my face.

"She's an archer," Marion said quietly, reaching over to put a hand on my good shoulder. "She has a whole schedule of training and competitions coming up. Is there really no way she can compete this summer?"

The doctor frowned and shook his head. "I honestly don't think so, not without doing long-term damage. The physiotherapist might have a different assessment after a week of rest, though. Don't make any big decisions until you've seen him first, right?"

After he left, I could practically see the wheels turning in Marion's head. "Astrid, your father flew out to the Vancouver office this afternoon, but he'll only be gone a few days. You have to stay here at the hospital tonight for observation, and I'll leave you at Hilary's place for the weekend. I think it's wise for me to break the news to your father gently before you come home; give him time to adjust. All right?"

I nodded gratefully. Some people complained about having awful stepparents, but Marion was fantastic. She was always on my side, or as much as she could be in the face of my father's contempt. She might come across as stuck up and prissy, but she'd been nice to me since the moment she entered our lives. Over the past four years, she'd become a necessary buffer between me and my dad's ever-increasing anger.

Archery was the only thing my dad liked about me and I wasn't sure what he'd do if I couldn't compete.

"Marion," I whispered tearfully, finally gaining control over my voice. “I am so sorry. I’ve wrecked everything.”

She took a deep breath. “Astrid, no matter what your father thinks, you’re not an Olympic athlete yet; you’re a child and children do foolish things. Your father will understand. Eventually.”

I slumped back on my pillow, not thrilled about being called foolish and a child in the same sentence. Still, it had been pretty childish to have drunken so many cups of that stupid punch. Why on earth hadn’t I realized right away that the drink was spiked? Mr. and Mrs. Ling might be as strict and straight-laced as they came, but Thomas was certainly no angel, even though he looked like one. I’d overheard plenty of stories about him from Susan. Why hadn’t I used my head?

The whole party came flooding back to me. I vaguely remembered someone laughing about taking a video of me vomiting all over Quinton’s feet. I’d bet there was more than one video. I’d bet that every one of my classmates had their cell phones out taking pictures or videos.

“Oh no, I left my purse and phone at the party, and my shoes.”

Marion reached down beside her chair handed me my purse. “Miranda and her mother dropped your things at the hospital front desk. The nurse gave them to me when I arrived.”

“Miranda,” I said weakly, remembering her blotchy face when I was being taken away in the ambulance. “She didn’t want to come in and visit?”

Marion shook her head. “She was very upset, Astrid. She said she had to get up early to get to practice. There’s the tournament on Sunday.”

"Right," I said numbly, "of course."

There was a soft tap on the door.

"Is it all right if we come in?"

"Of course, Syun." Marion rose smoothly to meet them at the door. Mrs. Ling inched into the room, her teeth bared in a tight, anxious smile. She scanned the room nervously and frowned when she saw me lying in bed. Susan and Thomas trailed in reluctantly behind her.

Susan's eyes held a mixture of concern and excitement; she studied the room with interest, most likely filing away all the gritty details so she could share them on her blog later. Susan had never been mean to me in school, even though she was easily one of the most popular girls our age, but she loved drama and I doubted she was going to miss an opportunity to write a good story. She had a wicked sense of humor and I cringed thinking about what she might already be writing about me in her head.

Thomas didn't even look at me when he came in. He glared at a spot on the floor and ignored everyone, his arms crossed over his chest.

"We came to see if you needed anything, Astrid," Mrs. Ling said nervously. "We wanted to make sure you were okay. Your…your father isn't here?"

She peered apprehensively around the hospital room as if he might be hiding under the bed or stashed in a closet, ready to leap out and serve her with legal papers. As if my dad could stand to be in a room for more than two seconds and not announce his presence to everyone.

"No, he flew out today," Marion reassured her. "I'm sure he'll understand that it was an accident, Syun. It's very nice of you to come with the children. We appreciate it."

"Thomas and Susan were very anxious to see Astrid," Mrs. Ling said. "Weren't you, Susan?" She gave her daughter a little shove in my direction.

"Yes, mom," Susan said. Her eyes flicked up to meet mine and one side of her mouth curved into a wicked smile. She let her curtain of black hair fall forward to frame her face and discretely rolled her eyes in her mom's direction, making me laugh despite my embarrassment.

"Hey, Astrid," she said in her soft, clear voice. "I'm glad you're not hurt. Everyone was worried."

I sincerely doubted that, but it was nice of her to say.

"Sorry I broke your rope swing," I said finally.

"Oh," Mrs. Ling gasped, clutching her purse strap between her hands so hard I was sure it would tear in two. "Don't think about that. It was time to take it down anyway. What matters is that you're okay. Don't you have something to say to Astrid, Thomas?"

Thomas stood woodenly behind his sister, eyes trained on the floor. A faint blush of colour stained his cheeks. Susan had told me once that their last name meant Ice in Chinese and that's what I thought of at that moment, watching him stand like a frozen prince, expressionless and cold.

"Thomas!" his mother hissed, glancing at Marion in embarrassment.

"Fine," he said through gritted teeth, as if the word was poison. His gaze settled on my injured arm, not meeting my eyes. "I'm sorry you were hurt, Astrid."

A spark of anger flared in my belly. It was partly his fault I was here; if it hadn't been for that punch I might have stayed safe on the shore instead of trying anything risky.

"Thank you, Thomas." Marion moved to my side. "Astrid needs her rest now. But thank you for coming."

Susan shot me another smile and winked. "I'll text you later, Astrid."

Thomas said nothing. He just followed his mother out without another backward glance.

"Those kids appear to be growing up a little wild." Marion sighed. "I can see Syun has her hands full. Still, it was nice of them to come."

"She forced them to come," I said, unable to keep the bitterness out of my voice. "She just doesn't want to get sued for negligence." I closed my eyes and turned my face abruptly to the wall, fighting back tears.

"Well, get some rest, sweetie. You'll feel better in the morning." Marion kissed me softly on the cheek and left the room, shutting the door quietly behind her.

That night I dreamt of drowning. I writhed under the water, desperate for air, but this time there were no helpful rescuers pulling me to the surface. Instead, a pair of cold, heavy hands gripped my throat, pushing me downward, squeezing the life slowly from my body.

No, I shouted in my head, *I'm not ready to die!*

I kicked out frantically and my assailant loosened his hold enough for me to slither backward a few inches. As the hands reached for me again, I saw the flash of a familiar ring: a gold square topped with a huge ruby.

No! I screamed again and this time the sound was loud

enough to wake me up.

I sat up panting, tears streaming down my face, my arm and side throbbing with pain. The image of my father's choking hands still hovering before me in the air.

Chapter Three

The next morning Marion was there bright and early to collect me. The nurses had set up a sling to keep my arm pinned tightly to my chest, but there was nothing they could do to hide the awful bruises that had blossomed on my face and one side of my body overnight. I'd taken medication for the pain, but my whole right side throbbed as I hobbled toward the door like an old lady.

"I've spoken to Hilary's mother," Marion said in her no-nonsense voice. "I'll drop you off at their house on my way home. You can stay there for a few days until I've filled in your father and let him have time to process the situation. I've packed your overnight bag."

I nodded gratefully. I felt a little guilty leaving Marion to deal with my dad's temper on her own, especially when I was the one who'd messed up, but she never seemed to mind his explosive yelling fits like I did. They terrified me.

We drove in silence until we reached the Ahlberg's gate. Marion punched the familiar code onto the little pin pad and waited until the black metal gates swung slowly inward before rolling up the driveway. Hilary's house was about a hundred times the size of our million dollar condo. She lived in a sprawling log and rock home with huge windows that ran from the floor up three stories to a vaulted ceiling. They even had a man-made waterfall and fish pond in their entrance way. As much as I loved Hilary's house, I loved her parents even more.

"Oh, Astrid," Hilary's mother said as soon as she saw my face. Her eyes widened as she took in the sling and the livid bruise that ran from my right cheekbone all the way down into the collar of my shirt. "Come inside, Ronald is making cookies and you're just in time to add the chocolate chips."

Mr. Ahlberg ran his business from home, but when he needed to de-stress, he liked to bake things. His job must have been pretty stressful because the house was always overflowing with more delicious food than one family could eat. Every weekend they'd take Rubbermaid tubs full of dessert down to the church soup kitchen and help serve homeless people. They were actually pretty religious, but not in an 'in your face' sort of way. They basically just tried to love people and not hurt them. It's hard to fault that.

"You, too, Marion. You haven't lived until you've tasted Ronald's cookies. They practically melt in your mouth."

Marion recoiled slightly, clutching her purse with both hands and wrinkling her nose delicately. "No thank you, Linea," she said quickly. "And I'd appreciate if Astrid didn't have too many, either. She's watching her carb and sugar intake. Astrid, I'll pick you up in a few days."

"Thanks again," I said weakly to her retreating back. I hoped Dad wouldn't be too hard on her.

Hilary's mom wrapped me in a careful hug so she didn't re-injure me, and this time I didn't worry about holding back my tears. I never had to hide how I felt here.

"I'm so sorry about your injury, sweetie. We're all so proud at how hard you've worked; this is just a minor blip in your career, though. You'll be back better than ever in no time."

I groaned. Last year, I'd come home with an individual gold medal in archery from the BC Winter Games, which was a province-wide competition for young talent. My dad had left aside the chilly politeness he reserved for me and had looked at me with new regard, as if he'd just woken up to find a brand-new, exciting, daughter living in his house. He'd gone on and on about how I was destined for the Olympics; he'd even gone so far as to surprise me with the trip to Mongolia for this July. I'd always wanted to go there. My dad had one of his mining offices in Ulaanbaatar, but I'd never in a million years dreamed he'd take me with him. He usually spent as little time with me as possible.

The gift had been a surprise; the first nice thing he'd ever planned for me on his own. We'd gone out to dinner at a fancy Greek restaurant to celebrate my birthday; just the two of us. We'd sat across from each other while he talked about all sorts of things. His eyes had shone with pride and excitement when he'd handed me the envelope holding the tickets. My heart had lit up from within like a firecracker, feeling we were going to be a real father and daughter at last.

One silly mistake and, in the seconds it took me to crash down into that lake, my brief friendship with him was over. If I couldn't compete then I'd killed both our dreams in one stupid move. He was never, ever going to forgive me.

Hilary slid down the hall from the kitchen in her socked feet, coasting across the polished wood floor without stopping until she'd skidded sideways into her mom and added herself to our hug.

"Come on, Astrid," she murmured, "don't be upset. Marion said you probably only have to rest for the summer and then you'll be back in training. You'll have hardly missed any time at all. And we'll come up with something else fun to do."

Her huge blue eyes were wide with compassion. She'd coiled her waist-length blonde hair into a bun on top of her head and wore some sort of modern ballet type costume with tights, gauzy skirt and purple legwarmers that only she could have pulled off wearing. Hilary was pretty much the opposite of me; she was thin and athletic and was always bubbling over with confident enthusiasm while I hovered in the background like her dark, hulking shadow.

Everyone who met Hilary was instantly charmed. People were constantly telling her that she should be a model or an actress, but she never seemed to let all the compliments go to her head; it was like she didn't care what people thought of her at all. She'd gone to Sacred Heart with me for a year before she'd started homeschooling and we'd somehow stayed friends. Sometimes I wondered if she was only nice to me because of the religion thing; like maybe it was her duty to befriend losers like me. But for some reason she genuinely seemed to like having me around.

"Thanks, Hilary." I sighed. "But there *is* nothing better than Archery; it's literally the only thing I'm good at. Besides, Dad already paid for training camp this summer plus my ticket to

Mongolia. I'll bet he won't be able to get his money back for either of them. He'll never speak to me again if that happens. I'll be grounded for life."

"Oh"—Hilary waved her hand in the air dismissively—"he'll get over it. He'll stomp around and be mad for a week then find something else to obsess over."

"Hilary," her mom warned. "That's not very respectful."

"Sorry, Mom. He's always so mean to Astrid and he never says anything nice. He's always grumbling like a big, angry warthog, don't you think?"

Hilary's mom didn't answer, but the corner of her mouth twitched into a smile. She ruffled her daughter's hair and pushed us both gently toward the kitchen.

"What I think is that it's time for you two to get some cookies."

I wasn't about to argue with that.

* * * * *

Later that night, when Hilary and I were tucked into the two double beds in our favourite ocean-themed guest room, we talked seriously about what I would do if I couldn't practice or compete. My whole world had been balanced between school and archery for the last three years. I lived, breathed, and slept for shooting. My bow had a place of honor hanging on my bedroom wall, and I spent more time at the range than I did in my own home. No matter what the doctor thought I needed, I knew I'd go crazy lying around our cold, empty condo doing nothing.

"What about horses?" Hilary hung half out of bed, her head

hanging over the edge so she looked at me upside-down, long blonde hair pooling on the floor.

"What about them?"

"You could start riding with me. It's lots of fun. Take lessons, win lots of shows, make your dad happy, you know the drill."

I laughed. "Yeah, that sounds easy. Considering I've never sat on a horse in my life. Besides, aren't riding lessons expensive?"

"Does it really matter? Old Money Bags can afford to pay for a few lessons, can't he?"

I giggled. Hilary made up the best nick names for everyone. "Oh, he has money all right, but it's pretty hard to get him to pay for anything unless you practically beg. He didn't buy me a new bow until I started winning with the old, crappy one."

"Well, there you go. You don't even need your own horse. Take lessons on a school horse to see if you even like it."

"Hilary, I'll be lucky if he doesn't throw me out of the house or ship me off to military school once Marion tells him what happened. There's a reason I'm hiding here until he cools off. I'm pretty sure my dad is not going to give me anything except a headache from all the yelling. Plus, you missed an obvious flaw in your plan. I can't use my right arm at all. I think you need both hands to ride a horse, don't you?"

She grinned at me wickedly. "Not if you ride with Claudia, you don't. She's going to have you on the lunge line working on your position for months. She's not even going to let you touch the reins until she's sure you're not going to wreck her horses."

I shook my head doubtfully and reached down to check my phone for the millionth time. Miranda hadn't answered any of my texts yet. I knew she would be furious with me for missing the tournament this weekend, but it was strange that I hadn't heard from her at all since the accident.

"I'm not athletic like you, Hilary. I'm too fat to sit on a horse."

Her smile dropped and she pulled herself upright, twisting around in bed to stare at me seriously. "You know that's not true, right, Astrid?" she said in a quiet voice. "You're absolutely perfect just as you are. You can do anything."

I blushed furiously and looked down at my empty phone screen. I made a point of never talking about my weight with Hilary. She'd gotten really mad the first time I admitted that my dad had sent me to fat camp. It had been a little scary; she'd gotten this strange look on her face and then she'd actually had to go into another room and pray until she was calm enough to not call my dad right then and yell at him. Even though she looked like a porcelain doll she was actually tough as nails inside.

"Wait here," Hilary said suddenly, breaking my concentration. She leapt out of bed and swept out into the hall. In less than a minute she was back, this time with a stack of books in her hand. She piled them onto my bed before bouncing back to her own.

"Here. You can do some studying tonight before we go to the barn tomorrow. My lesson's right after church so we have to get up early. I've set my alarm." She rolled over and crawled under the covers, her face already twisting into a yawn.

"Night," she added sleepily before burying herself in a pillow.

"Okay." I sighed, feeling slightly abandoned. As long as I kept busy talking or doing things I could keep my overwhelming sadness at bay. But as soon as I was on my own that sick, anxious feeling came rolling back in. I lay on my back, staring up at the beautiful ocean scene painted on the ceiling. Those smiling dolphins should have cheered up anyone; but tonight they just made me feel more depressed. I texted Miranda again.

Hey, it's me. Is your phone working? I guess you heard the news. Just rest, rest, rest for me this summer. I can't believe I had such a stupid accident. It totally sucks missing the tournament.

My word bubble popped up at the bottom of the screen and I stared at the phone, willing her to answer. Nothing.

After a while I sighed and set the phone down on its face. I idly flipped through the books piled on my bed and wondered how my life had suddenly become so complicated.

At least going to visit a horse barn tomorrow was better than being stuck in the condo with my enraged father. I would humour Hilary because she was my friend, but I was pretty sure that horses were not going to be my rebound sport. I loved archery too much to abandon it for prancing around on a large, stinky animal.

Most of the books she'd handed me were just full of dry, boring text with tiny black and white pictures to look at, but finally I found one that was a little more interesting. I set the other books on the floor and pulled my covers up to my chin, shifting around until I found a position that wasn't so agonizing to lie in. The book was titled "The Mighty Lipizzaner" and had a photo on the cover of a white horse standing right up on its hind legs; rider sitting motionless like a statue on top. The rider wore a weird, pointy hat and shiny boots and a coat like Elton John might wear. The horse was stunning, even to my unpracticed eye.

"Wow," I whispered, flipping pages. Was this really what Hilary did when she went to the stable? I knew she had a grey horse named Jerry, but she was involved in so many different activities that it was hard to keep track. I didn't remember her saying anything about doing all this leaping and springing in the air, though. Surely she would have mentioned *that.*

Levade, corbette, capriole. I thought sleepily, reading the captions under the photos of horses rearing on their hind legs and leaping. *Sure, I can see myself doing that while I wait to heal.*

That night I didn't dream about drowning. Instead, I was on a shining white horse galloping across a grassy plain. I had my bow in my hand and, for that moment, my heart was light.

Chapter Four

I woke up before Hilary's alarm went off to the pinging of my phone.

Miranda! I lunged for it and turned off the volume before it could wake up Hilary. Eagerly, I peered down at the screen.

Yes, it does totally suck...for the whole team. Your accident was definitely stupid.

My heart plummeted. Maybe I was misreading her text, but she sounded like it was my fault the rope broke. I decided to give her the benefit of the doubt; sometimes texts sounded harsh when they weren't meant to be.

I know, right? I guess the rope was just old. I missed you at the hospital. Good luck at the tournament.

I waited a long time for an answer but finally gave up. She was probably getting psyched up for the competition. Unlike me, Miranda was a hard core athlete. After practice at the range she usually went to the gym to do cross-training on Saturday mornings and sometimes even after school. She was always working on sculpting different muscle groups to improve her form or working on her cardio. I knew it kind of bothered her that I'd come home with the gold at the BC Games when the only exercise I did was lift my bow while she knocked herself out with training and only got a silver.

Still, she'd always been a good friend and teammate, and I felt sick that she was disappointed in me.

* * * * *

"Good job, Hilary. Now, let's ask him for one more lengthening down the long side. That's it, sit deep and encourage him to work from his hind end. He needs to step upward *into* your gentle, supporting hand. Nice! Working trot and tell him he's a superstar. That's enough for today; we're going to end it on a good note. Give him a pat and let him have a nice stretchy trot and then time to cool out. Great work, you two."

I sighed, pinching the bridge of my nose to stop the throbbing headache that had taken up residence behind my eyes. Every part of my body ached; I was overdue for a pain pill, but I needed to find water to wash it down. Sitting for so long on hard bleachers was not the best thing for my battered body. And I'd already had to sit through the morning service at church that the Ahlberg's had dragged me to. But at least those seats had been padded.

Leaning my good elbow on the edge of the polished wooden railing, I tilted my head upward to study the glass chandeliers hanging from the high wood-beamed ceiling of the cavernous indoor arena. The bits of dangling glass danced in the low light, lighting the arena with a golden, otherworldly glow. Watching Hilary ride in circles was about as exciting as watching paint dry, but at least the arena we were in was something spectacular.

Walking into it was like entering a cathedral; the air was a few degrees cooler than outside and even the air seemed heavy with hushed expectancy. I felt like it was disrespectful to talk above a whisper; like being in the big library downtown.

Hilary, dressed in tight pants, tall boots, and looking like Ralph Lauren model, beamed at me from across the arena and I gave her a half-hearted thumbs-up. I'd sat through her lesson for the last forty-five minutes and it hadn't been at all like in The Mighty Lipizzaner. Jerry, groomed until he shone like silver in the low light, had walked for a long time then done some prancing and then ran in circles until both he and Hilary were damp with sweat, but there had been none of the leaping and acrobatics I'd been hoping for. He was beautiful to watch, for the first five minutes, but after that I was bored and incredibly sore.

Hilary's coach, Claudia, stood in the middle of the ring, her knee-high black boots coated with dust. She was wearing the same type of tight pants as Hilary, only hers were black instead of cream. Tight pants were another reason to add to my list of why I did not want to ride horses.

"Good job, Hilary, even though he's relaxing he needs to stay in that rhythm," Claudia said as Jerry trotted by; his neck stretching down and out, and his reins loose on his sweaty neck. Puffs of dust rose from his footfalls and Claudia took a wheezing breath before turning her head sharply and putting a hand over her mouth. An awful cough nearly doubled her in half and it sounded like she was gasping for air. The small chocolate coloured dog who'd been sitting at her feet the entire lesson looked up anxiously, standing to put its little front paws on her leg and letting out a few high-pitched yelps.

"Are you okay, Claudia?" Hilary brought Jerry to a walk and watched her coach anxiously.

"Just a tickle in my throat." Claudia pulled upright and took a deep, wheezy breath. "Nothing to worry about." She gave the dog a reassuring scratch on its head and smiled weakly at Hilary.

I couldn't tell how old Claudia was, but she was beautiful in a majestic sort of way; you could easily imagine her being a queen back in the middle ages. Her long, silver hair was pulled back in a bun at the back of her head, she was slim and athletic, her body alive with coiled energy. As if she worked out every day and was just waiting to leap into cartwheels or run a marathon at a moment's notice, just like Miranda. She gave Jerry a pat on the shoulder and strode from the arena toward the barn, the little dog following in her wake.

"Wasn't he amazing?" Hilary said, riding a puffing Jerry over to where I was sitting. "He's really starting to be able to sit and use his hind effectively now. And did you see how he was really thinking about everything instead of just reacting?"

"Um, yes?" I guessed just as Jerry shook his head and snorted, blowing horsey nose slime all over me, spattering my shirt and my arm sling with goo. "Oh my god, Hilary!" I squealed, lurching painfully to my feet. "Tell me he did not just DO that!"

"Calm down." She frowned. "Stop talking about God like that and stop jumping around. You'll scare Jerry. The bathroom's upstairs in the lounge; the door is just outside the arena to the right. Go get cleaned up and meet me back by his stall. Then we'll talk to Claudia about lessons. You must be so excited to try it out."

"Yeah," I muttered. "Ecstatic." Holding my dripping hand in front of me I limped out of the arena into the barn aisle and stomped up the stairs. The door opened to a large wood paneled room that almost looked like an apartment. Heavy leather couches were arranged in front of a huge picture window that overlooked the arena below.

"Wow," I whispered, pausing to admire the set-up. Then I remembered I was coated in slime and marched to the open bathroom door. It took me forever to make sure every last drop of horse spray was scrubbed off me and my sling, and that my clothes were free from any potentially embarrassing stains. My hands were shaking by the time I was done. I really needed to take a pain pill and fast.

I limped back to the viewing room, hoping to find maybe a water cooler and a paper cup. There was an entire high-end kitchen in one corner with a stainless steel fridge, microwave and a Keurig machine sitting beside a tower of carefully arranged mugs on the slate counter. There wasn't a water cooler and I wasn't sure if barn water would be safe to drink. Feeling like a thief, I cracked open the fridge and was relieved to see two full cases of bottled water. I pulled one out and fumbled in my pocket for the bottle of medication. I gulped down a pill and chased it with half a bottle of water.

I knew it would take a few minutes to kick in. I sank down on one of the leather couches and leaned back, closing my eyes and taking a deep steadying breath. Gradually my body relaxed, the edges of the pain dulling and then receding into the background until it was just a distant ache. I opened my eyes, staring at the room around me.

Well, it's certainly more impressive than the club house at the shooting range, I thought, gazing from the polished hardwood floor up to the high-beamed wooden ceiling and immaculate leather furniture. It was really like a small apartment. There was a small wooden dining table across from the bank of heavy leather couches and one wall was full of wooden lockers. Everything was immaculate and smelled like lemon cleaner.

A flash of white from the arena below caught my eye; and I pulled myself up a little. Another horse and rider had come into the ring and were now moving in circles at the far end of the arena. This horse was so white he glowed like there was a light illuminating him from inside. He had dark eyes and pink nostrils. All he needed was a delicate, spiraling horn coming from the middle of his forehead and he could have passed for a perfect unicorn.

This horse moved forward in way that was completely different from Jerry. Each step hung suspended in the air so that the animal appeared to be floating; muscles coiled and powerful neck arched. The rider sat motionless; I couldn't even see how she was asking the horse to do anything. Suddenly the animal was prancing in one place without going forward. Still moving, it leaned all its weight on its powerful back legs until it seemed any minute it would rise up and sit on its haunches in a levade, just like in the book.

I leaned forward eagerly, holding my breath, but instead of leaping it merely propelled itself forward again, this time into a flat, boring gait more like Jerry's. I sighed and sank back into the chair, strangely disappointed.

"What took you so long?" Hilary had Jerry tied in the middle of the barn aisle and was polishing his face with what looked like a car-washing mitt when I finally made it back downstairs.

"Sorry, I was watching that other horse; the white one. Who was riding him?"

"Oh, that was Claudia with Quarry. He's her old Grand-prix horse. He's pretty much retired now, but he still knows all the right moves. She just rides him for fun now."

"Huh," I said, struggling to remain disinterested. "He moves a lot differently than Jerry. He arches his neck and looks all light and bouncy."

Hilary frowned at me and threw a protective arm around Jerry's neck, giving him a squeeze. "Like I said, Quarry is a Grand prix horse, Jerry is just a baby and we've only started schooling seriously. He'll get there someday."

"Right," I said quickly. "I wasn't knocking Jerry. He's great. It's just that, if I *did* decide to ride, then I'd like to do what the other horse did in there."

Despite her irritation that I'd insulted Jerry, Hilary's face split into a grin. "Um, *yeah*. So would every rider, Astrid. Quarry and Claudia were short-listed for the Olympic team back in their day. She's been studying with every world class dressage rider she could for the last twenty years and has competed all over the world. That's why she's the best of the best. You don't get that way overnight, you know."

"Sorry," I said. "I didn't mean to sound rude."

Hilary shrugged and gave me a smile. She was always so good natured; not much fazed her for long.

"It's okay, you'll learn. I'll put Jerry away and then you can help me brush and tack up Marcus for Claudia to ride next. I'm helping her out while her working student, Liza is away in Germany with Cole."

I trailed Hilary slowly down the aisle, still limping even with the pain meds on board. I was exhausted and couldn't wait to just get back to her place so I could crawl into bed and sleep.

The inside of the barn was just as stunning as the rest of the facility. Running alongside the indoor riding ring in an L shape was a wide concrete aisle lined with rubber mats so the horses had something soft to walk on. High beamed ceilings ran overhead with more chandeliers that cast a golden glow on everything. Opposite the arena sat rows of polished wooden boxes filled with soft wood shavings for horses to live in. Hilary called them 'stalls' but with the vertical bars running from the wooden panels up to the ceiling that made them look awfully like horse cages to me.

Hilary put Jerry back in his stall-cage and then brought the hugest creature I'd ever seen clopping down the aisle toward me. The horse was massive; chocolate brown with a black fringe of thick hair hanging half way down his neck and another tuft of black hair hanging roguishly between his ears. It was so long it covered his eyes. He had black markings that made him look like he was wearing dark knee socks on all four legs. His feet were like dinner plates. Hilary handed me his leash to hold for a second and I stood there, gazing upward in awe.

"Astrid, meet Marcus. He's a gentle giant."

"Um, hello horse?" I gulped, staring up at the whiskers on the bottom of his chin.

She expertly clipped him to the ropes attached to the wall and unhooked his cotton leash and hung it up on a hook. "Here," she said, handing me a small, round rubber brush with nubbins on the bottom. "This is a curry comb. You use it like this, in a circular motion, to give him a massage and bring all the dirt up to the surface of his coat. Claudia wants the horses to be spotless before anyone rides them. It's one of the rules here."

Thankfully my pain meds had finally kicked in fully. The curry comb was awkward in my left hand and brushing Marcus wasn't easy because I made sure to stand as far away from him and his giant feet as I possibly could. With my good arm stretched out I worked the brush slowly in circles along Marcus's back and sides the way Hilary showed me. From what I could tell, he was enjoying himself. He kept curling his lip into the air when I reached certain spots and leaned as hard as he could into the brush. He didn't seem bothered every time the brush fell from my clumsy fingers onto the floor, either.

Hilary handed me a comb and told me to brush the hair falling over his neck, what she called his mane, as gently as I could without breaking any strands while she did his tail and went over his body with a soft finishing brush. I ran the small, metal comb through Marcus's mane as gingerly as I could until the black hair was lying nice and flat along his neck.

A series of sharp barks sounded at my feet and I felt a pair of little paws patting at my jeans.

"Down, Cappy." Hilary laughed. "Astrid just tell her to get down when she's being annoying. That's Claudia's dog, Caprice. She's a little needy."

"It's okay," I said, stroking the fluffy little head. Her hair was curly and so long I couldn't even see her eyes; just her grinning teeth and lolling pink tongue. "What kind of dog is she?"

"A miniature poodle with a bad haircut. She hates the groomer so Claudia always waits too long between trims. She's way overdue."

Clopping hooves started up the aisle toward us and I turned to see Hilary's teacher, Claudia, leading the beautiful white horse, Quarry. Marcus made a happy, chortling noise under his breath and I wondered if horses could recognize one another or if they even had friends. I'd never been allowed to have a pet, not even a goldfish, so I wasn't really sure what animals thought about.

"Almost done, Claudia," Hilary sang out, slipping a saddle onto Marcus's broad back.

Claudia didn't look so intimidating up close, her green eyes held a calm warmth and intelligence. "You must be Astrid," she said with a smile. She had a faint foreign accent I couldn't place. "Hilary told me about you. Would you mind holding Quarry for me, while I get Marcus to the ring?"

"Um, sure," I said tentatively, taking the soft cotton leash in my good hand. If the horse decided to take off, there wasn't much I could do about it. But staring at the beautiful white creature I'd seen earlier, I didn't think there was much chance of him bolting; he radiated a feeling of quiet confidence. Quarry was not nearly as massive as Marcus. He had much smaller feet and delicate little legs. He had such a soft, kind expression on his face that I found it impossible to feel scared. He nuzzled my sling gently with his velvety muzzle as if he knew I was hurt.

"I think he likes me," I said wonderingly, meeting Claudia's smile.

She nodded. "That's a big compliment. He's very particular

about who he makes friends with. He'd be very happy if you and Hilary would give him a bath and take him out for some grass. Put him away when he's dry and we'll talk more about your lessons."

I shot a look at Hilary, but she was making herself very busy fiddling with Marcus's bridle.

"You told her I wanted to take lessons?" I asked incredulously as soon as Claudia led Marcus out of earshot. "You know my dad's never going to go for that. I don't even *like* horses, Hilary. Besides, I'm in a sling, silly. I'm pretty much useless."

Hilary looked miserable. "I'm sorry, Astrid. I thought you'd like it once you got here and, honestly, there's just a bunch of older ladies riding at the stable right now. Everyone our age left when Claudia stopped focusing on showing. And Liza's in Germany right now getting some international experience so it's just me. I love Claudia and I love spending my weekends at the barn, but it does get a bit lonely sometimes. We'd have fun."

It was hard to stay irritated when she used *that* logic.

"Okay, I'm not mad," I said diplomatically, rubbing my good hand gently down Quarry's silky white face. His fur was soft like velvet and he smelled nice, not like a horse at all. "I'll think about it."

In my head, though, I knew it wasn't for me, despite the fact that Quarry was one of the most beautiful creatures I'd ever seen. There wasn't any point in starting something new when I'd be back at archery soon anyway. I had to stay focused. Plus, besides Quarry, the horses were too big and dirty, and I didn't see much point in going around a ring in endless circles.

Chapter Five

The next night, Marion showed up at Hilary's to take me home. I'd known my vacation with the Ahlbergs couldn't last forever, but I'd somehow convinced myself not to think about home at all until the moment her tires crunched up the driveway. Then the dread hit me like a punch in the gut.

The Ahlbergs followed me to the door as if they were sending me off to war.

"Call as soon as you can," Hilary said, squeezing my hand for good luck.

"Remember that you can come stay with us whenever you like, dear," Mrs. Ahlberg said, giving me a last, careful hug.

"Do you think if it would help if I called your dad and spoke to him?" Mr.Ahlberg asked hopefully. "Maybe we could have you all over for dinner."

"No, it's best to let Marion handle him. Thanks for everything, you guys." I took a deep breath and walked toward Marion's waiting car.

Marion's fingers tapped nervously on the steering wheel as she drove, but she didn't say much until we'd pulled into the underground parking lot beneath our building. She shut off the ignition and turned to face me.

"I'm not going to lie to you, Astrid. Your father is not happy. He's agreed to wait until we hear from the specialists before making any long term plans. But in the meantime, you're going to be grounded. You'll stay home from the range. No T.V. and no computer, or phone. He's very disappointed."

"Did he even care at all that I was hurt?" I couldn't keep the bitter note from my voice.

Marion was silent for so long I didn't think she was going to answer. "Astrid, if he didn't care then he wouldn't bother getting angry. He wants what's best for you, but he doesn't always show it. I know that's hard on you."

I slid awkwardly out of the passenger seat and slammed the door behind me, limping quickly toward the elevator so Marion couldn't say anything else. She had a blind spot where my dad was concerned; she couldn't see how little he liked me at all.

We rode the spacious, wood-paneled, elevator upward in silence. Nothing was going to make this first meeting with my dad any easier. The best thing to do was to get it over with as fast as possible. When the doors opened on the top floor, I stepped out reluctantly and moved aside so Marion could unlock the front door with her pass code. Ours was a penthouse condo so we were the only people living on the entire floor; everyone else lived downstairs. Even though my dad complained that the place had cost a fortune and it had been written up in architectural magazines as a modern marvel, it was nothing like the warm and welcoming splendor of Hilary's home. Ours was full of cold, polished white floors, expensive furniture that was too uncomfortable to sit on, and glass tables that scratched if you so much as touched them.

We did have a 360-degree view of the horizon, though. On one side, the ocean stretched out across the island-strewn Salish Sea all the way to the mainland. The city sprawled beneath us on the other side. The amazing view was the one thing I loved about our condo. When I woke up early for practice and the sun was peeking up over the horizon turning the buildings and mountains into gold, I sometimes felt like the luckiest person in the world.

Tonight, I did not feel lucky at all. "Hey, Dad," I said tentatively, my heart thudding in my chest. I stepped inside and slipped out of my shoes.

No answer. He was seated in an upright armchair in the living room with a copy of the Business Examiner held up about five inches from his face. A shiver of fear rippled down my spine. It was a bad sign. I slid a few steps toward the sanctuary of my room, holding my breath; maybe I could slip by unnoticed.

"Stop!" He thwacked his paper open onto his knees and glared at me with undisguised rage. "Sit over there," he said through gritted teeth. "Sit there and think good and hard about how you've disappointed not only this family, but your team and your own pathetic self. I'll let you know when I'm ready to speak with you."

He jabbed a finger toward the arm chair across from him and snapped the paper back up in front of his face, returning to reading as if there was no doubt I'd obey him instantly.

"Go." Marion gave me a small push toward the chair, and then disappeared toward the kitchen from where I knew she'd be listening.

Sinking painfully into the deep leather chair, I prepared myself for the worst.

"Leave your phone on the table. You won't need it for a while," he said, not looking up.

I reluctantly pulled my phone out of my pocket and set it on the glass end table. It was my only link with the outside world. How would I call for help if I was trapped here in this condo?

I sat as still as I could, trying not to fidget, covertly watching my dad for signs of what he was planning. With him you almost never could tell what he was thinking; it made him a great poker player and business owner but a really lousy father. Over the years, though, I'd learned to look for subtle clues. He still had his shoes on, something normally forbidden in our house, and both feet were pressed flat on the floor, not crossed at the ankle, which meant that he was at his most high-strung; ready to leap up and yell at any second. His thick fingers dug so hard into his paper that he'd crumpled the edges. He normally kept a years' worth of pristine Business Examiner copies in boxes in one of the spare bedrooms so he could go back and study investment trends. The fact that he was destroying one now did not bode well for me.

And then there was the throat clearing. When he was especially mad, my dad made a series of rumbling, choking sounds deep in his throat which was like a train engine coming to life, building steam until his anger could erupt on whoever was closest to him. He was making them now.

I had a sudden image of him simmering like a volcano, cheeks red with repressed lava and black smoke billowing out of his ears. Despite the danger, I laughed nervously under my breath.

As soon as the tiny sound left my mouth, I regretted it. My father stood up abruptly, tossing the paper aside so the pages scattered across the floor. He loomed over me like an angel of death.

"You think this is funny!" he roared, as I shrank back in my seat. "You think this is some sort of joke, young lady? Well, I can assure you that it is not. Your little stunt this weekend made me a laughing stock among my employees. Imagine a daughter of mine, smuggling alcohol, of all things, into a party full of school children."

He held up his hand as I opened my mouth in shocked protest. "You will have your chance to apologize later. Right now, you're going to listen to what I have to say until it sinks into that thick, fat head of yours. Do you understand?"

I froze, stung by the insult and by the hatred in his voice. There was nothing for me to do but nod. If I played along it might be over quicker.

"You've hurt your stepmother and me deeply; you've lost our trust. Not only that, but your foolish stunt has hurt your career and impacted your teammates who have worked so hard. Worst of all, you cost me a great deal of money that I can't recoup. If there's one thing I can't stand, Astrid, it's losing money."

He paused then sat abruptly in his chair again, his voice ominously quiet. "Bottom line: I will not tolerate any of your mother's influence in this house, Astrid. I made a vow when she died that I would stamp out every last rebellious trace of her in you. These last few years, you have focused on your studies and at the archery range, and I began to hope I'd succeeded, but this...this destructive streak has clearly raised its head again. It will not be tolerated. Astrid, you're fourteen years old—"

"Fifteen," I whispered, almost against my will. "I'm fifteen."

He stared at me blankly, his gaze shifting to the livid bruise on my cheek. He frowned and shook his head as if to clear it. When he spoke again his voice was softer.

"Fine. That makes it even worse, then. You're growing up fast; you look more like your mother every day."

He got a strange, far-off look on his face and I knew he wasn't really seeing me in front of him; he was seeing my mother. She'd been an alcoholic before she died and she'd been in and out of treatment a lot. I didn't remember any of this, I'd been six when she passed away and my father had removed all traces of her from the house, but I remembered him raging about her after she died. I didn't even have one single photo of her. All I remembered was how she'd cuddle me before bed and how she'd made this crazy-good banana bread with chocolate chips. I also knew I looked exactly like her; something which drove my dad crazy.

He'd never been exactly warm and snuggly, but he hadn't been so mean when I was little, either. I'd thought about it a lot and had come to the conclusion that he'd really, really loved my mom and watching her slowly drink herself to death had broken him inside. I do remember that it was right after she died when he'd stopped carrying me around on his shoulders or joking with me or walking me home from school. It was like she took the best pieces of him with her when she died, and left behind the angry, bitter part. When I think about it like that, as if he were a tragic character in a story, I'm almost sad for him. Almost.

He leaned back in his chair and closed his eyes, marshalling his thoughts. When he looked up again his expression was cold.

"The next step is to decide what to do with the situation you have created. You obviously can't be trusted unsupervised so, until we have a final verdict from the specialists, you will remain grounded in this house until I tell you otherwise. Understand?"

"Yes, sir," I whispered.

He narrowed his eyes at me. "You can put any thoughts of our trip to Mongolia out of your head. Luckily, for you, I was able to get a refund. Depending on what the doctors say, we might still be able to salvage your career. If not, then you'll have to get a job to pay me back the money I've invested in your training."

"Yes, sir," I murmured again. So far this was going better than I expected.

"And, of course, you will have to make an apology to the entire Ling family for making a scene and ruining their party. And, for exposing their children to alcohol."

I should have held my tongue, but there was something in the automatic way he assumed I was guilty that caused a spark of anger to ignite.

"I'll apologize for almost drowning," I whispered, fixing my gaze on the carpet, "but I did *not* bring any alcohol to their party. It's the first time I've ever drank and it was an accident, or at least a mistake."

My dad said nothing. I risked a glance up and saw him staring at me with an irritated look on his face. I suddenly realized that he knew very well I hadn't smuggled anything to the party. It was just him testing me, playing with me to see where my boundaries were, how far he could push me. It was a sick thought.

"Lose the attitude," he said, but his voice lacked any fire. "Fine. You'll apologize to the Lings for causing a scene. We'll let them deal with their own delinquent children. For now, you'll go to your room, stay there, and think about what you've done. I don't want to see your face until I decide what to do with you. Get out of here."

I leapt up, making a beeline for my room and silently congratulating myself for surviving round one, when he cleared his throat loudly behind me.

"One more thing," he drew his words out slowly so they hung in the air, "since you obviously don't care about your career, I have given away your spot in the summer training camp to someone who deserves it."

I stopped dead, biting my lip to keep back the words swarming to get out. The doctor had said to wait and see. I might be able to do *some* of the camp this summer. Why had my dad gone and given my spot away? I could feel him watching me closely, so I merely nodded.

"Yes, sir."

I walked carefully to my room and shut the door tightly behind me before I dared to even breathe. As unfair as it had been, I still felt like I'd gotten off too easy. I'd been expecting much more screaming and waving of arms. I'd even wondered if he'd finally snap and *hit* me. Marion had been right to give him a few days to cool out before bringing me home. Maybe I'd get lucky and he'd send me far away to boarding school so he wouldn't have to see me at all anymore.

As I turned to the bed my gaze fell on the empty space over my bedroom door and my heart gave a painful lurch.

My bow, my beautiful competition bow was gone. Only my old, battered, wooden practice bow was there, looking lonely on its hook.

I couldn't believe it. All the sadness and frustration building up inside of me erupted suddenly into a flood of hysterical tears that wouldn't stop. I threw myself down on the bed, jolting my already screaming body. I buried my face in my pillow and gave loose to all my misery. *I hate him,* I sobbed, *he only wants to destroy my life. I hate him.*

I couldn't stop shaking. That bow had been with me for nearly two years and losing it felt like a piece of me had been violently ripped away. Living in the same house with someone who would do something like that to me was like living with a serial killer. I had no idea what he'd take away next.

I sat up, suddenly afraid. Now, as I looked around the room more closely, I noticed other things missing: my laptop, the framed photos of me and Miranda winning at the Winter Games, my medals and trophies, even the silly souvenirs on my desk that I'd collected over years of competition. It was as if he were trying to erase the entire last few years of my life; the years where I'd finally been a winner. The magnitude of the act terrified me.

It was a relief when I finally cried myself to sleep.

Chapter Six

The chiropractor, the osteopath, the physiotherapist and the sports massage therapist all agreed—I was not going to be shooting in the next two months. I'd be lucky to be back to my old self by the time school started.

"It's that pulling motion," the physiotherapist told me sympathetically. "It's unique to sports like archery and puts a lot of strain on the rotator cuff. When you damage that area, it not only takes a long time to heal but you also need to build up those muscles properly again. If you start shooting too soon, you risk doing permanent damage. If you focus on cross-training for now and take six months off shooting to heal, you're going to come back better and stronger than ever."

I gulped and stared down at the floor, too scared to look at my dad. He'd insisted on coming to each of my appointments to hear the verdict for himself and I'd seen his face getting redder and redder with rage. I wished so much that Marion could have come with me instead.

"Well, that's it then," he said with finality as he'd hustled me to the car. "You're done. Finished."

He didn't say anything else. Just jammed the key in the ignition and squealed out of the parking lot.

I sat as still as possible in my seat while he drove like a street racer, slamming the brakes inches before hitting another car and cursing at every red light. I kept my face turned to the window, willing myself to disappear. I didn't pay attention to where we were going until we'd pulled into a familiar parking lot in front of a squat, brown building. A hand-carved, wooden sign posted out front read Edith Chapel Memorial Archery Range. The land and building had been donated just for the junior program about five years ago. This place felt like a second home to me.

"Get out," my dad ordered, shoving open his door and slamming it behind him.

I sat still in shock, struggling to hold down my breakfast. I couldn't believe it. He was going to barge in there and make a scene and drag me in with him.

"Move it," he barked, yanking my door open and pointing to building.

Numbly, I obeyed, my clumsy feet stumbling after him up the pathway to the front door, my cheeks already flaming with mortification.

Luckily, he'd chosen a time when there was hardly anyone there. I'm sure he'd have preferred the range to be packed full of people, but in the middle of the day there was just a volunteer manning the office, my coach Earl and a handful of shooters. And, of course, Miranda.

"Oh my gosh, Astrid!" she said, as soon as she saw my bruised face and my sling. "You're here. Are you okay? I was so worried."

Her eyes widened with concern. "Sorry I didn't text you much. I've been busy practicing."

I shot a quick look toward my dad, unsure if he was going to yell at me if I talked to anyone, but he was already marching toward Earl, not paying attention to me at all.

"I'm grounded and he took my phone and internet," I whispered quickly. "How was the tournament?"

She looked down at the floor, her cheeks flushing a dark red. "We tanked, but don't worry about it. I'm so glad you're okay. Oh, Astrid, I'm so, so sorry about everything. I feel terrible. When your dad offered me the spot, I couldn't turn it down. And it wasn't like you could use it...." Her words died as she saw the confusion on my face. "He didn't tell you, did he?"

It took a few seconds for the realization to dawn on me.

"Summer training camp," I said, stung by her betrayal. "Did he give you my bow, too?"

Her face paled. "Of course not. I would have never—"

"Astrid!" My dad bellowed, before she could finish. "Get over here."

"I'm so sorry, Astrid. I never meant to hurt you," Miranda whispered quickly as I limped over to where he and Earl were standing.

"Don't you have anything to say for yourself for letting down your coach and the entire team? You'll be lucky if they even take you back this winter."

"I'm sorry," I whispered miserably, wishing I could sink through the floor. I was still thinking about Miranda taking my spot at camp. I knew her parents couldn't really afford to send her, even with the partial scholarship she'd earned, and that it was a great opportunity for her...but still, she was supposed to be my best friend. After a long silence, I risked a quick glance upward.

Earl was the kindest, most good-natured man on the planet as far as I was concerned. He was the best coach, too. He was a big guy, bigger than my dad even, and had an unfortunate pair of bushy eyebrows and matching red sideburns that stood out about an inch off his face. He always wore the same green t-shirt and a baseball cap with an archer on it. As a coach, he knew how to push us hard, but he always emphasized fair play, teamwork, and staying positive. Now his face was dark like a thundercloud and he'd balled his fists at his sides. His anger wasn't directed at me, though; he was staring at my dad.

"Mr. Kendrick," he said quietly. "Astrid has been a star member of my team for the last two years, long before she started winning medals. She has shown a level of maturity and kindness far beyond her years, and has always strived to help those new archers moving up the ranks. We teach here that it's okay to make mistakes as long as you learn from them and move on. If Astrid can't practice this summer then she can teach, or assist as a camp counsellor or volunteer in the office. Bottom line is, she's a member of this team and we support each other no matter what."

My face must have lit up with hope, which was a mistake, because as soon as my dad saw that, he'd already made his decision.

"And that's the kind of weak-livered babying of children that got her in this mess in the first place. She doesn't deserve to be given a pat on the back and a free ride. She needs to see the seriousness of her mistake. I'm sorry, Earl, but, if that is your way of handling bad behaviour, then I'm going to have to rethink Astrid's place here. When she proves to me that she's fully repented her behaviour then I'll consider when and if she can return. You'll have my answer in the fall. Astrid, get in the car."

I shot an apologetic look at Earl before turning to follow my dad, but inside my heart had felt a small stab of hope. My coach and the team still wanted me, no matter what my dad wanted to believe. And, if I could think of a way to get back to the range, then I was going to take it.

I must have looked too optimistic because, once we were in the car, my dad started ranting and didn't stop until we'd driven all the way across town and reached our underground parking lot.

"If you think you're going to be rewarded for being an idiot by getting to spend time fooling around at the range with your friends all summer then you are sorely mistaken. You will get a job, but it's going to be one that I chose for you, and it's not going to be fun."

Back at the condo I was, thankfully, once again banished to my room. I flopped down on my bed exhausted. Too tired and worn out, and sort of hollow-feeling to even cry, I stared blankly at the ceiling wondering for the millionth time why I had such a crazy father.

It wasn't the first time he'd made scenes in public. He was forever arguing with waiters or ticket attendants or screaming at other drivers. There had been one whole season when he'd been banned from coming to tournaments after he'd gotten in a fist fight with one of the other dads. He'd been warned multiple times about heckling my competition, and even some of my teammates, from the sidelines.

Thank goodness he spent three quarters of the year travelling. WorldCor had offices and mining sites in eight different countries. It was always such a relief for everyone when he was away.

* * * * *

That night I was summoned to the dinner table to eat with my dad and Marion. Filled with dread, I dressed as neatly as I could and made an effort to tame my curls, hoping to stay as small and unnoticeable as possible.

It wasn't any use; as soon as I sat down my dad started to simmer. "Imagine, Marion," he said between rapid bites of food. "Imagine trying to reward a mistake by offering someone their dream job. Imagine if that's how I conducted business in my office."

Maybe you'd have fewer people quitting if you stopped shouting at them and said "good job" once in a while, I thought bitterly. He was always complaining about unreliable employees who stole his equipment and skipped out to work for other companies. I was smart enough not to remind him of this out loud.

Marion nodded at him encouragingly, her eyes wide, like he was saying something fascinating. When he paused in his rant, she cleared her throat hesitantly. "Well, you *were* saying a summer job is the perfect thing for Astrid right now. Linea told me today that there is an opening at the stable where they keep Hilary's horse. It wouldn't be very glamourous and the hours are long. It's an entry level position, cleaning stalls and equipment, but it does offer a good wage once she's fully mobile. It will be volunteer hours until she heals, but then it will be paid. She'll get to learn on the job."

My dad grunted, shoveling food in his mouth like it was the most important thing in the world, but I could practically see the wheels turning in his head. On one hand, he didn't like taking other people's advice; he liked to come up with ideas on his own. On the other hand, having me clean poopy horse stalls for the summer was exactly the type of punishment he'd had in mind. He also had a love-hate relationship with Hilary's family. Mr. Ahlberg had started his own multi-billion-dollar business from scratch and was, what my dad liked to call, a self-made man. On the other hand, they were pretty heavy into the religion thing, which my father most certainly was not. Still, I knew he thought Hilary was a good influence on me.

After a long struggle with himself he dropped his fork and picked up his napkin, wiping the steak-juice off his face.

"Well, it will keep you out of your stepmother's hair anyway."

Marion and I shot each other a quick glance and she shook her head ever so slightly. I hated when he called her that—*step*mother—as if she had no connection to me other than the fact that I was a passing annoyance in her life. I loved Marion ten times—no, a million times more than I loved him, whether she was related to me by blood or not. And I was pretty sure that she loved me, too.

"Astrid's aunt has a ranch," my father said out of the blue, startling us both. "She raises expensive Quarter Horses; sells them for a fortune. It's back-breaking work, but she's a hard-working woman. Hard work builds character. This might be just the thing to whip you into shape this summer, Astrid."

I stared down at my plate, pushing my asparagus around in circles. I'd forgotten that my Aunt Lillian had horses. I hadn't seen her since I was ten years old when she and my dad had a falling out. When I was very little she'd actually moved down to the Island to take care of me right after my mom died; when my dad was too full of rage and sadness to look after himself let alone me. It hadn't lasted long. She'd visited for a while after that, but now she lived on the mainland and we only heard from her on Christmas and birthdays.

I sighed. Deep down I'd hoped Marion could convince my dad to let me work at the range, but it was clear he was not going to let me do that until he'd had a while to cool down. He was always happier when he'd just come back from working overseas so that would be the time to approach him. In the meantime, even if I had to clean horse stalls, at least I'd get to be around Hilary.

As if reading my thoughts, my dad reached over to poke my good arm sharply with his fork. "Don't think this is going to be a chance for you to slack off. I'll be monitoring your performance closely; any shenanigans and you'll be packed off to boarding school so fast your head will spin. Do you understand?"

"Yes, sir," I said quickly, staring down at the dents and the green spatter of sauce his fork tines had left on my arm. "I understand."

Chapter Seven

On Monday, two good things happened. My dad flew out to the WorldCor mining site in Belize first thing in the morning without saying goodbye, and I woke up feeling less sore than I had since the accident. It had been the longest two weeks of my life, but today the sling could start coming off for short periods.

I stretched my arm out gingerly, wincing when it was only half-way extended. The physiotherapist had given me all sorts of exercises to start once the pain was not so bad, but for now I was just glad I could leave it hanging by my side once in a while instead of keeping it penned in close to my body. It felt strange, as if it were not really a part of me anymore. I experimentally picked up a small paperback, but even that caused a twinge of pain to ripple through my shoulder. Still, it was progress and nothing could dampen my mood today.

Marion was back from driving my dad to the airport and was humming to herself as she moved around the kitchen, emptying the dishwasher. Even though she'd never admit it, I could tell that a weight lifted off her shoulders as soon as he was gone.

"Granola and fat-free yogurt," she said happily. "I added blueberries as a treat."

"Yay," I muttered, wishing I was having pancakes at Hilary's house. Still, the granola was not half bad, and Marion and I pulled stools up to the kitchen counter and had our breakfast and coffee together while we chatted about random things.

"I'm dropping you off at the barn after lunch so you can have a visit with Hilary and get an idea of what will be asked of you when you start work on Thursday."

"Okay," I said, wishing I wasn't being shuttled around like a child. It would be nice to actually be in charge of even the tiniest aspect of my own life once in a while. But, seeing Hilary again would be a welcome change.

"I'm also giving you your phone back. It's for emergencies only, mind you. Your dad took the data package off your plan, so you only have it for phoning and texting. Use it wisely, understood?"

I understood; knowing him, my dad probably had some creepy way of monitoring my phone use so I would have to be careful about what I said and who I called.

I powered up my phone and checked for messages. I didn't really expect to have any, but to my surprise there was one from both Susan and Thomas.

"*Hope you're feeling better, Astrid,*" Susan had written. "*Don't worry about Thomas being all weird at the hospital. That wasn't about you; he feels really bad. He had a huge fight with our parents earlier that night and he was still mad. Talk soon, S.*"

Huh, I thought, *that's interesting.*

"*I really hope you're okay, Astrid,*" Thomas wrote. "*I messed up.*

I hope your dad wasn't too hard on you. I know how he can be. He yelled at my dad for over an hour, but at least he didn't fire him. Let me know if I can do anything to help. See you around this summer."

I slowly set my phone down and ate a spoonful of granola. My very first text from Thomas Ling was a little disappointing. I'd always envisioned him pledging his undying love to me, but an apology was a good start. At least it showed that he cared about what I thought.

I pocketed my phone without answering them. I was glad they'd texted, but I wasn't ready to answer back yet. I wasn't sure if I was still mad at Thomas or not.

* * * * *

The spring sunshine was in full effect when we drove up the imposing driveway to Mud Lark. Even Marion was impressed.

"Wow, Astrid. This is quite the place. I had no idea. I'm not sure this was quite what your father had envisioned."

Instead of saying goodbye to me in the car like she normally would, Marion actually got out and came with me to the entrance of the barn. She hovered there, peering inside the large open door. "It's so clean; it's hard to believe it's a place to keep animals."

Caprice came trotting down the aisle toward us; she'd had her hair newly trimmed and looked more like a show poodle and less like the scruffy beast I'd seen last week. She ran straight up to Marion and bounced up and down, tongue lolling in excitement.

"Don't jump up, Cappy," I said, bending down stiffly so I could hold the little dog's collar. "Sorry, Marion. She's really friendly."

To my surprise, Marion was smiling. She reached out and petted the dog with the tip of her fingers, only shrinking back when the poodle started licking her hand.

"That's okay," she said, moving back to the car to grab her sanitizing wipes from the glove box. "I had a dog once...."

"Astrid!" Hilary appeared from the tack room, holding a dirty cloth in one hand and a bar of orange soap in the other. She had a smudge of dirt along one cheek. She was so excited she practically danced down the aisle toward us. "Hi, Marion, this is so great you got Astrid this job. Would you like to meet my horse Jerry?"

Marion pulled herself up straight and backed quickly away; eyes fixed on Hilary's dirty hands. "That's quite all right, dear. You two go on and have fun. Astrid has lunch money for both of you when you're ready to order something from town. Try to make healthy choices, girls."

Hilary grabbed my good hand in her sticky one and dragged me down the aisle to the tack room. "Here, sit down." She pointed me toward one of the wooden trunks lining the wall. There was a pile of saddle pads on top and I sat down gingerly. "Tell me everything."

While she disassembled complicated bits of leather and cleaned them, I filled her in on everything that had happened since I'd last seen her. Her face clouded as I told her about the scene at the range and she had tears in her eyes when I said that my bow and all my trophies and even pictures had been taken.

"That man is not right in the head, Astrid. He's really mean. It was just an accident and he's making it sound like you're this hardcore druggie or something. I mean, giving your spot away at camp and yelling at you in front of your teammates is just not okay. I wonder why Marion puts up with him; she's so nice, even though she's a little weird about the whole germ thing."

I shrugged but didn't say anything. I'd often wondered the same thing myself. Marion seemed to genuinely love my dad in a way I couldn't comprehend; she'd never say anything bad about him or disagree outright with him. Whatever it was, I just hoped she'd stay with him long enough for me to finish school and escape to a place as far from home as possible.

The door opened and a pudgy, middle-aged lady stumbled in, her cheeks red with exercise and brown hair flying in a halo around her head. She set her saddle heavily on a rack and then plopped down on a trunk opposite me, puffing as though she couldn't quite catch her breath. "No stirrups," she panted, as if that was an explanation. "Forty-five minutes of trot without"—she paused painfully—"stirrups."

Hilary winced sympathetically. "It's like an ab and thigh workout from H.E.L.L.," she explained to me, spelling out the letters for hell because she thought it was a swear word. "It's an exercise Claudia uses to build core strength, but until you're used to it, it really kills."

The lady groaned and slumped against the wall. "I'm too old for this."

"You most certainly are not, Pender," Claudia said, appearing in the doorway. Caprice pushed past her and leapt up beside me, lolling her tongue and panting hot dog breath into my face. "George Morris is in his seventies and is still going strong. I'm sure he could easily jump an entire course without stirrups. You just have to go around in circles on the lunge line."

"But it hurts," Pender whimpered.

"Yes." Claudia nodded, turning back into the barn with a small smile. "No pain, no gain, my dear."

I spent the afternoon helping Hilary with the few barn chores I could do. Cleaning tack wasn't too hard once I figured out a system. The horse's bridles, saddles, and random pieces of leather had to be cleaned until they shone after each ride. The bridles had to be taken apart so the individual pieces could be cleaned and then put back together and hung on the hooks just so. The washer and dryer ran non-stop with loads of dank saddle pads and dirty leg wraps, caked with sweat and gross horse hair. It seemed like a lot of trouble to make everything so clean when it was just going to be put back on a dirty, stinky animal the next day.

Hilary didn't see it that way. "Riding can be seen as either a sport or as art, or maybe both. But, either way, both sport and art require discipline in order to succeed. Taking care of your horse and your equipment is part of that discipline. There are a lot of fancy barns out there where riders just show up for their lessons and don't even take the time to form a relationship with their horses at all. Grooming them and taking care of them helps to strengthen the bond between horse and rider."

"Huh," I said thoughtfully, dabbing at a dirty, wet spot on my sling. I was going to need a special one for the barn that was okay to get dirty. I had another week of wearing it, at least, and it was going to start stinking like a horse pretty darn fast.

"Claudia's place isn't like that, though. Everyone has to catch their own horses, brush them and tack them up themselves, and they have to at least make some effort to know their horses' likes and dislikes. She never caters to spoilt or stuck-up clients. Ever.

"This barn used to have a waiting list a mile long to get into," Hilary went on. "So even the spoilt princess-riders would fall over backward trying to do whatever Claudia said so that she'd agree to teach them. But since, well, you know, Claudia stopped showing; or taking her clients to shows, things sort of got a little quiet around here.

"Oh," I said, looking up with interest. "How come?"

Hilary shrugged. "Her health, I guess. She doesn't really talk about it, but it's obvious that she's not a hundred percent well. The only reason she gave is that she wanted to downsize her client base and concentrate on what was really important. Cole was livid, of course, he lives to compete and he'll need rich sponsors if he wants to make it to the Olympics someday. I think he blames her that he has to work so hard all the time.

"Anyway, there are just a few boarders left here and then some clients who trailer in for their lessons. Claudia really is still the best coach out there."

"Are all these pictures of Claudia?" I asked, tilting my head back so I could study the many-framed photos lining the upper half of all four walls. They mostly showed gleaming horses posing with their winning ribbons; riders grinning into the camera, but there were action shots, too.

"Lots of them are, but there are also a bunch of Cole and the rest are her students. See, there's Quarry there; look how dark he was then. He started out as grey as Jerry."

I moved closer so I could see the dark dappled young Quarry dancing through a variety of arenas all over the world; I could almost see him age from picture to picture as he grew thicker, more muscled, and his coat lightened until he gleamed like snow.

The rider on his back changed, too, her face thinning and the look of pure joy and excitement shifting to narrow concentration. I knew that look; when new archers arrived at the range they wanted to learn everything about the sport and were overjoyed just to hit any target, even if it wasn't their own. They were undisciplined and erratic. But gradually, if they stuck to it, their shots would slow down, flowing from their bodies as naturally as breathing. They'd take fewer shots, but those would be more accurate. They'd be quieter, solemn almost, as their inner and outer selves became aligned in one still purpose.

That was the same expression I saw on Claudia's face, like she'd gone deep inside herself and was riding from that place of stillness, where everything was a bit magical. I wondered how long it took to reach that when working with horses.

"Hilary," I said thoughtfully, "why do you work here? Your parents could just pay for lessons, couldn't they?"

Hilary looked up, surprised. "Oh, I love spending time here," she said. "And besides, I don't like making my parents pay for everything when I'm perfectly capable of helping out. They've already done so much for me. Buying Jerry wasn't cheap and they pay to keep him in this wonderful place. They don't even care if I show or not, as long as Jerry and I are happy. My friend Allison kept her horse here and she didn't care about showing, either; but her parents did. They made her move to this snotty barn down island where the horses don't even get to go outside in the winter. Not ever. She hates it there, and so does her horse, but she has to stay put since they're paying the bills. I'm just grateful my parents wouldn't ever do something like that to me."

"Yeah, you are totally lucky to have your parents; they're amazing. I can see my dad pulling something like that; not Marion, though, she would listen to me."

We worked quietly for a while, cleaning and oiling the bits of leather until they shone. It took me a while to figure out how to clean with only one properly working arm, but soon I developed a system where I held onto a piece of leather with the fingertips of my right hand while I cleaned with my left. It was clumsy and awkward, but in the end I got the job done.

At lunch we ordered pizza and, as soon as the food arrived, Pender appeared again out of nowhere with two immaculately dressed ladies in fancy breeches and spotless clean polo shirts bobbing in her wake.

"Ooh, pizza," a platinum-blonde lady dressed in maroon drawled, "you naughty girls are having a treat without us."

"You can have some, Ally," Hilary offered to the blonde. "It's Astrid's treat today."

"Well, you have excellent taste then, thank you, Astrid." Ally turned to smile at me. "I'm Ally. I own that glorious Hanoverian, Severus, you've probably already admired him. He's a looker, isn't he? He cost my husband a fortune to buy, but he's worth every penny. My goodness, did you get that injury from riding? You look awful."

I stared at her blankly, unable to follow any part of her conversation until the question at the end. "Um, no," I shook my head. "I actually don't ride."

All three ladies gaped at me in horror. "Don't ride?" the red headed woman said, eyes wide with astonishment. "How can you *stand* not to?"

I didn't have a polite answer, but luckily Pender saved me. "Well, are we going to eat this pizza or watch it get cold?" she asked bluntly, staring longingly at the box.

That was the signal for the three of them to dive on our pizza, even though Ally kept moaning between bites that she was watching her figure and really could have just one more, *teeny-tiny*, slice. It was a lie, though; she was probably Marion's age, but both she and the red-head, Sadie, looked completely perfect: make-up painted on as if it were airbrushed, brows plucked, and bodies lean sculptures without an inch of fat. Only Pender looked like my idea of a regular mom with her light wrinkles, disorganized hair, and messy clothes.

Sadie ate her pizza in tiny, neat bites, her pointy fox-like face studying me when she thought I wasn't looking. She had strange blue eyes, set off by her deep tan, and when she spoke at all it was with a slight accent.

After lunch, Hilary and Pender turned the horses out into the pastures and we watched as Claudia taught lessons to a steady parade of outside riders. One by one, immaculately polished trucks towing expensive horse trailers stuffed with immaculately dressed horses pulled up and unloaded. Some riders came with an entourage of family, friends, and grooms. Some people came alone.

All of the riders and most of the horses had better clothes than I did. The gleaming animals sported jackets and matching boots, and some even wore hoods that covered everything but their eyes. It was bizarre.

Hilary disappeared to the ring to catch the end of a lesson she wanted to watch. I sat on the little patio outside the feed room door soaking up the sunshine after the dark coolness of the indoor arena and giving my arm a change to hang down without its sling on, when a large, shiny red truck bounced down the driveway towing a silver trailer. The trailer window hung open and a speckled horse stuck its nose out and called shrilly in my direction. He sounded upset; his little eyes rolled wildly and he pulled impatiently against the rope holding his head.

The trailer disappeared behind the barn, but I could still hear the horse calling and his hoofs stamping on the floor. Curious, I stood up and stretched slowly to work out the kinks in my stiffening body. I carefully fitted my arm back into its sling and headed toward the parking lot. By the time I got there, the spotted horse was unloaded and had been tied to the side of the trailer. A boy wearing tight pants and tall leather boots was running a soft brush over the animal's sides. He had his longish black hair tied back in a pony-tail and his profile looked strangely familiar. I stopped, studying the horse he was brushing with interest. He was about the same size as Quarry, but his whole coat was speckled with dark spots on a white basecoat. Except on the top of his butt, where it looked like he was wearing a white blanket. He twisted around so he could look at me and made a low *huh huh huh* noise under his breath.

The boy turned and gave me a polite smile and then stopped and stared more closely. "Astrid?" he asked uncertainly, looking down at my sling. "Is that you?"

I frowned and then suddenly, it hit me, I *knew* this boy. He'd witnessed my shameful accident up close and personal. "Oh, hey Robert," I said casually, as if I didn't remember it had been him who'd inspired me to swing on that stupid rope. He'd probably been one of the guys who had hauled my sorry body out of the lake, too. I felt heat rising steadily up my neck until I was sure my cheeks were tomato red. "Um, how are you doing?"

"Fine. But I should ask how *you're* doing, that was quite the accident. Are you okay?"

"Oh, sure," I waved my good hand in the air dismissively. "It was nothing. So, is this your horse? I didn't know you rode." That was an understatement, the only thing I knew about him was that he was good with rope swings and, according to Miranda, he may have eaten some pencils at some point.

"Uh, yeah, I've been riding since I was a kid. This is Artimax. I just bought him, actually, but I'm not sure what Claudia is going to say. He's not exactly traditional dressage horse material."

"Oh," I said blankly. The horse looked fine to me; he certainly was a pretty colour.

"All tacked up, Rob?" A dark-haired man who must have been his father sauntered around the front of the truck, smiling. "You have to be at the ring in two minutes."

Robert looked at his watch and frowned. "Sorry, Astrid, I've got to get this guy ready. I'll see you around, though."

"Sure, okay. See you."

I watched as Rob disappeared through the outer door of the arena before I walked quickly inside to find Hilary. I found her in the aisle brushing a tall, red horse with big ears and wide, inquisitive eyes. The horse snorted and drew back a little as I approached, gaze fixed on my sling in horrified fascination. He snorted again and banged an oversized front foot on the ground.

"It's okay, Ferdi," Hilary crooned, "stop being such a baby."

She grinned at me. "This is another of Claudia's horses, Ferdinand. He's only four, but I don't think his brain has caught up with his body yet."

The horse snorted again and I retreated a few steps backward so I wouldn't scare him. "Hilary, you didn't tell me that Robert Harris rode here. He was at the Ling's party when my, you know, *accident* happened."

"Oh, Rob, right, I forgot he went to Sacred Heart. He's really nice and he's an amazing rider, too. He was leasing this superstar eventing horse, Vincenzo, for the last few years, but I'd heard the owner sold it. I wonder who he's riding now."

"Um, he said he bought a new horse, but he wasn't sure if Claudia would like it. It has spots."

"Spots!" Hilary said, gaping at me. "Okay, I have to see this. Sorry, Ferdi, we're going to cut your grooming a little short today. I'll make it up to you tomorrow. Come on, Astrid."

I trailed behind Hilary as she put Ferdinand in his stall and then marched upstairs to the viewing room to flop down on the big leather couch.

"Oh, I see what you mean. It's an Appaloosa cross of some sort."

"A what?" I laughed at the strange name.

"Appaloosa is a breed of horse with spots; they're used in western riding more than english. They're not really known for their dressage moves. I wonder what possessed Rob to buy him?" She squinted down at the horse, considering. "Well, he's nicely put together, anyway. Look at that deep chest and those massive hindquarters. He's tall, too, and really powerful. I wonder what he's crossed with. Claudia has her poker face on so she's waiting to see how he moves before passing judgement."

Hilary fell silent while Rob swung himself in the saddle and Artimax strode off across the ring in a ground-covering walk.

"Huh," she said after watching him trot and canter around in both directions. "Well, what do you know, he's actually a really decent horse. I'm not sure what the judges will think, but I guess we'll find out this summer."

We watched them for another half hour before my phone chimed; it was Marion letting me know that she was on her way. My shoulders sagged with relief; my day had been fun, but I was glad it was over. I was exhausted.

Hilary and I walked slowly together through the barn, saying hello to the horses who were still locked inside.

"Why do the horses have to stay in their cages so much, Hilary? Wouldn't they rather be running free?"

"They're not *cages*, Astrid, they're stalls, and they don't mind being locked up as long as they get to spend some time outside every day. The horses that are being worked get turned out after they're ridden. Their stalls are like their bedrooms."

I raised my eyebrows but didn't argue. I'd spent enough time banished to my own room lately to know that it really sucked being locked up. Not being able to come and go as I pleased got old really, really fast. And my room was a lot bigger than a horse's stall. Still, I guessed that these horses were well-loved, which was more than I was at the moment.

Clopping hooves sounded behind us as Rob led a sweaty, puffing, Artimax back down the aisle toward his trailer. I moved far to the side to let them past, still leery of being stepped on or knocked over, but Hilary stepped right up and held out her hand for the horse to sniff before reaching out to scratch him behind the ears.

"This is your new guy, hey? He's cute," she said to Rob. "What did Claudia think of him?"

"Oh, Hilary, you didn't think I'd be prejudiced over a few spots, did you?" Claudia appeared behind us holding a grocery bag full of books. "He's a good, solid, horse with lots of potential. Besides, Rob already loves him so it doesn't matter much what I think." Her mouth curled into a smile and she sent him a wink.

"Here, Astrid, these books are for you. You can start your education from the ground for now until you're able to ride."

I opened my mouth to protest but she held up a hand to stop me. "When you visit my barn, you follow my rules. Every member on our team is expected to have a love and sympathy for horses and to put their welfare first at all times," she said firmly. "You will heal and then you will ride. For now, you will work and you will study. I've marked which books to read first. I've also included a few pages of homework assignments in there. I expect your work handed to me on Thursday when you get here to work. I'll expect you at six-thirty sharp."

"Six-thirty in the morning?" I winced, glaring reproachfully at Marion who had just parked her car and was heading toward us.

"She'll be there," Hilary said brightly. She took the bag from Claudia and pushed it into my hand. "See you Thursday, Astrid."

* * * * *

When we got home, Marion made me go directly to the guest shower so I could scrub the barn smell off. She set a basket of flowery body washes on the shower bench and even made me throw my clothes directly into a laundry bag that I had to seal up and take right to the machine when I was done. I guess she hadn't thought ahead to me tracking barn dirt into our pristine condo when she'd lined up this job for me. I'd been surprised she hadn't laid out towels in the car for me to sit on so I didn't damage her leather interior.

Choking on my own overly floral smell, I sat down on my bed to look over the books Claudia had saddled me with. To my surprise they weren't really about riding at all. On top was a battered kid's book titled "Know your Pony!" which was full of diagrams describing the different parts of the horse. There were charts listing all the different horse breeds in existence and labelled pictures of riding equipment. I guessed that was the book Claudia meant for me to read first.

The other books weren't about riding, either. There was one on horse psychology and one about horse body language and communication. The next one was about how to give a great horse massage and the last one was about yoga stretches for horse riders.

Two sheets of paper fluttered out of the last book. *Astrid,* Claudia had written in neat loopy letters, *here's your first homework assignment. Please hand it in on Thursday when you come to work. I've started off easy on you. Begin reading these books and familiarize yourself with any of the basic yoga stretches that don't interfere with your injury. Study hard, and pay attention; there will be homework every week. Welcome to our team, Claudia.*

I sighed and looked down at the second page, a typewritten questionnaire with some horse sketches near the bottom.

Describe your current riding goals as well as your future riding goals.

Describe the way horses have affected you personally.

Write a paragraph describing what makes horses happy.

Write down two yoga stretches that you enjoy most. How will they help with your riding goals?

Please correctly label the horse anatomy drawing below.

Please correctly label the parts of the skeletal system of the horse.

Please correctly label the musculature system of the horse.

"Fine." I sighed. At least it was an open book assignment; I had two days to find all the answers before I started work on Thursday and it would give me something to do while I was hiding in my room.

I flipped through Know your Pony! half-heartedly, mostly looking at the pictures until my stomach started to growl. I wandered out to the kitchen, feeling the untold luxury of not having to be afraid of walking around in my own house without having to dodge angry death-glares from my father.

Marion was in her office; I could hear the keys of her laptop tapping away as she worked on one project or another. She had her own travel consulting business, Universal Travel, which catered to the type of people who had to travel for business, but who would much rather stay home. She'd started it all by herself when she was young and now she had twenty employees working under her. That was how she'd originally met my dad. He was one of those guys forced to travel to all sorts of exotic locations, but who hated noise, strange food, and people who didn't look and think exactly like himself. Marion had booked him an itinerary down the coast of Africa that managed to make him feel almost like he'd never left home. He'd joked once that he pretty much *had* to marry her after that miracle.

But once she'd married him, she stopped going to the office and instead, let her staff handle most of the clients. She basically was my dad's personal assistant now, which I considered a real step down on the success ladder. But she seemed happy enough, and I guess at least she got to work from home. Which, given her fear of germs, crowds, and human contact, seemed like the safest place for her to be.

I made a plate of crackers, cheese and pickles to take to my room and, to celebrate the fact that my dad was not there; I added some strawberries and about half a wheel of brie as well. I would have liked to have added a piece of chocolate, but junk food, along with anything fun, was not allowed at our house. Fruit and cheese was as wild as it got in this kitchen.

I took the heaping plate back to my room and set it carefully on my bed. Before my banishment, I would have never been allowed to eat in my room, and especially not in bed, but even my dad had to admit that I had to eat *somewhere.* I still had to be careful; knowing him he'd probably send me a bill to replace the duvet if I dropped so much as a single strawberry.

I studied the essay questions again while I ate. At least I could get the personal parts over with quickly. I had touched a horse maybe four times in my life and two of those times had been at Mud Lark in the last couple of weeks.

I don't really have any riding goals, I wrote down, *because horses are quite big and I would most definitely fall off if I were to ride one. Sports, except archery, are not my thing. If, by some miracle, I became a rider then I would want to do the levade and the capriole like they do in the Spanish Riding School. Everything else looks boring, and also seems to be hard work.*

Horses have not affected me personally, except when Jerry sneezed all over me. Also, Quarry has the most amazing eyes I have ever seen. He looks like a wise, old person. I think I would like to know more about how horses think and feel before I climbed up on them.

I actually *had* visited my aunt's ranch in the interior once; one Christmas back when I was a kid, the same year my mom had died. I could hardly remember that visit; just a faded image of my boots crunching on snow, eating delicious gingerbread at her huge kitchen table with a pair oversized dogs lying expectantly at my feet and horses, an overwhelming sense of horses. I wondered if I'd ridden any then.

I hadn't seen my aunt since she and my dad had their big falling out. Now she just sent me birthday and Christmas cards stuffed with twenty-dollar bills every year. But she never included anything personal in those cards, certainly nothing about horses, just her messy signature scrawled at the bottom.

I know some horses like being brushed and they definitely like snacks. I don't like them being locked up in their stalls. I think they'd rather be out running free on millions of acres somewhere.

I looked down at my notebook with a sigh. Everything I'd written was the truth but I couldn't hand this in to Claudia; she was my new boss after all and she'd probably be insulted that I'd said she locked her horses up. I would have to make something up later.

I stuffed the questionnaire between the pages of a book, flipped over on my back and stared unhappily at the ceiling. My arm ached without the support of its sling; I couldn't get comfortable and the pain made me restless. I'd read every fiction book in my room since I'd been grounded and I didn't think Marion would agree to take me to the library while I was still on house arrest. I had no computer anymore and no television. What on earth was there in a world without archery?

Suddenly, I rolled out of bed and walked to the far corner of my room, reaching up with my good arm to pull my old, battered bow down off the wall. I held it in my left hand, feeling the familiar weight of it between my fingers, glossy wood warm and comforting. In one swift move I brought it up level, holding my left arm straight as if the bow were strung and I was about to shoot. The fingers in my right hand twitched reflexively next to my side, eager to perform. I held the bow like that, pointing at my imaginary target until my arm began to shake.

Chapter Eight

The next day I woke up before the alarm and rolled carefully out of bed, only wincing a little bit. I stretched my arm out tentatively and was relieved to feel a slight lessening of pain. It was getting better every day. I was pretty sure I'd be back to my old self by the end of the month, no matter what anyone told me. My practice bow was still lying on the bed beside me, right where I'd dropped it the night before. Tentatively, I reached out to brush the polished wood with my fingertips, remembering how I'd felt back when I'd first held it; back before I knew anything.

Even the first time I'd touched it, the bow had felt like it was an extension of my body, fitting my hand like it had been waiting my whole life to complete me. Archery had been something I'd tried in my first year of secondary school because it was compulsory at Sacred Heart to try every extra-curricular activity at least once. I'd had no illusions that I might become good at it. But, from the moment I held that battered bow in in my hand I had been better than good. I'd been great. Maybe the ghosts of my parent's Scottish ancestors had been hovering over me, guiding me, but that first day of practice felt like I was coming home. Not having archery in my life was like severing a limb. A huge piece of me was missing.

The condo seemed completely empty when I crept down the hall to the bathroom, which meant that Marion was either still sleeping (unlikely), or was doing her online Tai Chi lessons, or had left for a rare visit to her office. Driven by her horror of germs and people, Marion had managed to find an online Tai Chi group of like-minded phobics who all practiced together in the sanitary safety of their own homes. There was an instructor and everything and the whole group was broadcast on a giant viewing screen set up in the corner of her workout room. "It's almost as if they're really in the room with me," Marion had said convincingly.

Tai Chi was supposed to be sort of a martial art, but they didn't really do any fighting that I could see. I thought they looked a little silly, moving through the exercises in slow motion, but she always came out of her work out room looking happy and relaxed, and I guess she deserved to find her happiness where she could.

Today, though the workout room was dark, Marion's bed was empty; neatly made and looking as if it hadn't even been slept in. I was blissfully alone.

The blinds were already open in the living room and the world was just coming alive, sun creeping up and tinging the blue mountains with pinks and golds. The ocean stretched out in a motionless plateau until it touched the mainland. It was a view I never got tired of. No matter what was happening in my life, it never ceased to remind me that I was only one small part of a vast world. My life with my father might be close to unbearable now, but someday I would be old enough to leave this house and make my own way in the world without someone constantly looking over my shoulder and judging me.

I made a cup of coffee—something Marion let me do but my dad never would—and took it onto the patio outside. The air was cold; the sun hadn't reached our side of the building yet, but it was fresh where it touched my face and tasted salty like the ocean. I inhaled deeply, feeling immediately more alive than I had since my accident. I stayed out there as long as I could until I started to shiver and then slipped reluctantly back inside.

Before the accident, I would never have had to wonder what to do with my day. I would have spent my summer mornings getting up early to practice. Since last year, I had been allowed to take the city bus myself across town to the range instead of having someone drive me. Miranda and I even had our own keys to the gates that circled the outdoor range and we'd often meet there early before anyone else arrived. We'd bundle up and walk through the woods with our bows slung over our shoulders and challenge each other to hit harder and harder targets until our arms gave out.

Now, I was aimless, cut adrift.

I dragged the books Claudia had given me out to the living room and curled up in my favourite armchair to study. I was good in school, too good for most peoples' tastes, really. I knew how to study subjects I cared nothing for and write in a way that made my teachers happy. It also didn't hurt that I had a near-photographic memory. I finished the anatomy charts easily by just copying them directly out of the books and fixed up my essay questions so that I sounded like a good employee.

I flipped through a section on horse anatomy; it was interesting to learn that the horse had originally had multiple toes instead of a single hoof millions of years ago. I might have been less afraid of being stepped on if they had paws instead of solid foot-stompers; but probably not.

After an hour of reading, I gave up with a sigh. I didn't want to be cooped up inside today. I wanted to be at the one place where I was happy, doing the only thing in life that mattered. I wanted my bow. I stood up restlessly, pacing the edges of the room, an uneasy feeling keeping me from sitting still. I wandered down the hall, peeking into Marion's empty office and then into their bedroom to make sure she was really gone.

Where would he have hidden my things? I asked myself. Maybe he gave my bow away, but what about my photos and all my souvenirs. He wouldn't have just thrown them out, would he?

I pushed open the door of the first unused guest room, which was nothing at all like the fabulous themed guest rooms at Hilary's house. This was just a white room with a bed with a flowered quilt, a nightstand, and some bland paintings of European cities hanging on the wall. I opened the closet door, hoping to find boxes, but it was empty except for our old, broken vacuum and a few suits and dresses hanging in garment bags on the rail.

Nothing. I moved quickly on to the next room, hurrying just in case Marion was on her way back. It was a bit ironic that we had two guest rooms when we never had any guests. There was a bed in here, too, but the room was mostly used for storage. This was where my dad kept his old boxes of magazines and newspapers. He'd been on the verge of becoming a hoarder until Marion suggested the storage unit down town. Now he only kept a year's worth at home in a few tidy boxes in the corner. I ignored the magazine crates and slowly slid open the closet door.

Aha, this would be a perfect place to hide my stuff.

Here were stacked boxes of random things, extra small kitchen appliances, and linens and old towels. Most of the boxes had been labeled with their contents in Marion's neat hand writing but, way at the top of the stack, was a large brown box without any writing at all. It tilted to one side, looking like it had been stuffed in there hastily.

I stood on my tip-toes to carefully pull it down. I had to inch it off the pile with one hand and then caught it awkwardly as it fell, yelping as a sharp corner hit me in the chest. I managed to somehow hang on, stumbled, and dropped the box clumsily on the bed. As soon as I opened it I knew I'd hit the jackpot. There were my pictures and trophies and a few souvenirs from various tournaments. I sat down on the bed with a lump in my throat, running my fingers over a small trophy, overwhelmed with sadness that my dad would try and take this stuff away from me.

Suddenly, like a kettle on a hot stove, my sadness boiled into rage. "Where is it?" I muttered, feeling reckless and crazy, "what did you do with my bow?"

I reached into the closet and hurled the nearest box to the floor, sending the contents flying. I threw the next and the next one, ignoring the sound of breaking glass, hardly able to see through my choking tears. There was no sign of my bow.

A thick photo album shook loose from the pile and toppled over on me, striking my sore arm with a thwack. I cried out, clutching my arm and sucking in my breath until the pain was manageable. I gave the album a frustrated kick and then knelt down suddenly to look at it more closely.

"Mom," I whispered, settling on the floor and pulling the book into my lap. I ran my fingers over the picture, tracing the angular planes of her face. She was beautiful. I slowly flipped the page, staring in awe at the dozens of photos I hadn't even known existed. There were pictures of my mom and dad and me, even some of my Aunt Lillian taken at various birthday parties. Most of them were from when I was really little; as I became a toddler and then a small child, there were fewer and fewer.

I could see my parent's faces changing as I flipped through the photos, too. They looked happy and carefree when I was small; most of the time they were smiling and laughing or making faces at the camera. In the later pictures, they smiled less and by the end the handful of photos were of me by myself. In the last photo of my mom, she looked like she'd aged a dozen years—her face was lined and her eyes were puffy and bloodshot.

I flipped a page and was surprised to find a picture of myself as a little kid, seated on a short, black pony. I was grinning into the camera and had both my hands wrapped in the pony's mane. The woman standing beside me was Aunt Lillian. I wondered if the photo had been taken at her ranch. She had an arm around my shoulders and one hand on the pony's bridle. She was smiling as hard as I was.

The final photo in the album nearly made me drop the book. It was a photo of my mom, her face gaunt and pale; she was clearly sick at that point. It had been taken outside and my dad stood a few feet behind looking off down the street at something else. But the most surprising thing was that beside her, smiling quietly into the camera, was Marion. *Marion? But she didn't even know my mom.*

"Astrid, what are you doing?"

Marion stood in the guest room doorway her hands on her hips, surveying the mess I'd made of the room. She looked upset. And angry.

I shoved the photo album back into the closet, hoping she hadn't seen it and clambered to my feet trying desperately to think up some sort of explanation for why I'd torn apart their guest room. "I'm sorry Marion." I sat down hard on the bed and burst into tears.

Without saying a word, she came to sit down beside me. She gingerly picked up the photo of Miranda and I with our medals; the glass had been shattered. I must have accidentally broken it when I was throwing things around.

"I wanted my bow." I sniffled, hating how childish I sounded. "I can't believe he really gave it away."

"Oh, Astrid," she said, giving me a delicate hug. "I don't think he gave it away. He was very angry after your accident and I know he makes rash decisions sometimes, but he really does love you."

"No, he doesn't," I said thickly through my tears. "He hates me. He sees my mom every time he looks at me and he hates me just as much as he hated her."

"Sweetie, your father loved your mom very much; he just couldn't handle watching her addiction consume her. He stuck with her right until the very end, you know. He wouldn't have done that for someone he didn't love. Their relationship was complicated, but very much real."

She paused, thinking her words over carefully. "Astrid, even if he *did* get rid of your bow, you can always get a new one, someday. I know that's not what you want to hear right now, but if you really love archery then you're going to have to be brave and fight for it. Don't let your dad boss you into thinking that you don't have any choices here."

It was the closest I'd ever heard her come to saying anything negative about him. I sat up a little straighter and accepted the Kleenex she handed me from the box on the nightstand.

"Marion," I said slowly, choosing my words carefully, "did you know my mom? I thought you and my dad met years after she died."

She didn't answer right away, just reached up and smoothed a curl back from my forehead. "Astrid, this is really a story for you and your dad to discuss together one day. But I will tell you that I did know your mom; she was a wonderful woman and I know she'd be very proud of you."

She stood up abruptly, clearly finished with our conversation. "Now, get this room straightened up while I make us lunch. It looks like a hurricane passed through."

Chapter Nine

Getting up early to go to work was such a relief. Even though I wasn't thrilled to be an unpaid barn worker, I was excited at the opportunity to escape our lonely, suffocating condo. Marion was kind, but she was usually busy with work and didn't have much time for me.

I pulled on jeans and put a hoodie on over my t-shirt. It was so nice to be able to put on clothes without having to bite my lip with pain the whole time. My arm didn't exactly work properly, but at least it didn't get in the way so much. I left the sling off, tucking it into my backpack just in case I needed it later.

Marion was up with our granola already set on the counter when I arrived in the kitchen.

"I hope you don't mind if I packed you a lunch," she said with a smile. "We can't have you eating takeout every day."

"Sure," I said, trying to sound grateful, although I would have much rather eaten pizza than whatever healthy lunch she would have come up with. She was the tofu and sprout type. I would have to get up earlier to make my own lunches from now on if I wanted to find something that wasn't completely fat and flavour free.

The ride to the barn was light and happy. Both our moods seemed to be buoyed up by the early morning fresh air and the absence of my father.

"Have a good day," Marion sang out. "I'll be here to pick you up at five."

She seemed eager to get away and I wondered what she was going to get up to all day by herself.

The big front doors of the barn were already open and I made my way quietly down the aisle, stopping to touch Quarry's soft white nose as I went past.

"Good morning, big guy."

His huge dark eyes surveyed me calmly, warm and gentle; his soft breath caressed my hand and, impulsively, I gave him a quick kiss on the nose.

"You must be Astrid," a voice said from behind me.

I turned around guiltily, embarrassed to be caught doing something stupid on my first day of work, but the girl behind me had a friendly smile.

"You've already made friends with Quarry, I see. He's my favourite, too. I learned everything I know from him. I'm Liza, by the way."

"Nice to meet you," I said formally, shaking her outstretched hand awkwardly with my left one. She looked a lot like Hilary, tall and blonde, with her hair pulled back into a glossy bun. She was wearing the requisite tight pants; these ones were brown plaid. Was looking like a fashion model a pre-requisite to riding? "You were in Germany, right?"

"Yes," she said, her smile dimming. "I was supposed to be gone another month, but I came home early. I flew in last night;

I still have jet lag, but I couldn't wait to see the horses again."

There was a loud banging sound halfway down the aisle. *Bang. Bang. Bang.* As if one of the horses was kicking its stall apart. I jumped, and even Quarry flattened his ears and shook his head in irritation.

"What was that?" I gasped.

"Darn, she's at it again." Liza turned and strode down the aisle until she reached the stall across from the tack room. "Folly, you stop that. Behave!"

A copper-colored horse I'd never seen before loomed behind the bars, one wild eye rolling. She was so big she seemed to fill the entire stall with her menacing presence.

"They had to sedate her to get her on the plane," Liza said. "I guess it's worn off now. She's pretty claustrophobic; she needs to get outside before she hurts herself. We'll feed her breakfast in her paddock."

"They let horses on planes?" I asked, but Liza was already marching toward the tack room. She returned a moment later with a leather halter and a lead rope that had a brass chain on the end.

"You'd better stand far back, Astrid," Liza warned. "When she's in this type of mood, she can be dangerous."

She didn't have to tell me twice, I backed down the aisle to stand in the open doorway where I could watch from a safe distance.

"Easy, Folly," Liza murmured as she carefully slid open the stall door. "Easy girl. There's a sweet girl. You want to get out and stretch your legs, don't you."

There was another muffled bang and an irritated squeal from

inside the stall, but Liza didn't back away. She disappeared inside. Everything was quiet and then suddenly, the morning exploded in a fury of sound and color as Folly burst from the stall squealing and kicking her hind legs out, dragging Liza behind her.

"Folly, no!" Liza jerked hard on the chain looped over the big horse's nose and backed her up quickly until her copper-coloured butt was up against the wall. "Just WALK, Folly," she said sternly, giving the chain another snap.

The horse shook her head angrily, but didn't explode again. She pranced beside Liza as if her feet were on springs. She looked like a winged horse barely contained by the laws of gravity, as if any moment she might launch into the air and disappear.

I followed behind at a safe distance. Liza walked Folly to one of the closest paddocks and led her inside. Folly looked around with her head high and her wild eyes rolling. She snorted, the sound cracking from her nostrils in a very unhorse-like way. She was nothing like the quiet, kind horses I'd met so far. She was a dragon.

She struck out suddenly with one front foot, narrowly missing Liza's knee cap and Liza gave her another series of quick snaps with the chain until she backed up again and lowered her head. Still holding the lead rope, Liza backed herself out of the gate and shut it so it was between her and the big horse. Then she leaned forward quickly, unbuckled the halter and stepped back. She was just in time. The horse whirled and kicked out with both hind feet, hooves splintering pieces of wood off the gatepost right where Liza had been standing.

Folly took off in a ground-covering series of leaps and bucks that took her halfway across the pasture and then she spun around, heading back toward us in a flat-out run. I didn't think she would stop when she reached the gate; I envisioned her plowing over Liza and then mowing me down as well, but at the last minute she swerved and kept running and running until her brassy coat was dark with sweat.

Liza watched her with a grim expression on her face, both hands twisting around the leather crown piece of the halter. Finally, Folly broke into a trot and then a walk. She dropped her head down and began to graze, ripping out the short grass in her pasture like she was channeling her rage into every bite.

"Well, thank goodness that's over with," Liza said, her voice shaking. "That went pretty good, don't you think?"

I stared at her incredulously. "Pretty good? She nearly killed you. She's terrifying."

"Oh, that's nothing," Liza said with a wave of her hand. "You should have seen her in Germany. She nearly killed one of the grooms; she picked him up by the neck and threw him against a wall. That's why she's here. Cole bought her dirt cheap and then sent her home to see if his mom could do anything with her. Typical Cole, running to Claudia to fix his mistakes."

"Is that why you came home early?"

"Yes, well, sort of," Liza said with a small smile. "I was ready to come back, anyway. I missed home and there's only so much Cole I can take at one time. There was a lot of ego flying around that place."

"Cole is Claudia's son? The one who is going to the Olympics?"

Liza snorted. "He *thinks* he is, anyway." She guiltily put a hand over her mouth. "I shouldn't have said that. Come on, let's get the rest of these horses fed. I'll show you our routine and you tell me what you can and can't do with your arm. I know all about injuries and you don't want to push yourself too fast or it won't heal properly."

She waited for me to nod before she continued. "The horses get fed their hay first before their grain. They all get supplements with their grain and soaked beet-pulp, just like we take vitamins with our breakfast."

She led me to a huge white door at the end of the barn and slid it back with a rumble. Inside, was an immense room filled with row upon row of green, leafy hay bales, stretching backwards as far as I could see. By the door, there were four plastic carts on wheels with handles for pulling, and beside them was a huge pile of what looked like discarded fish nets.

"We fill the hay carts in the morning with breakfast, lunch, dinner, and night feed. They get their meals fed to them in hay nets so they don't eat too fast, except for lunch, which they sometimes get fed outside in their paddocks. When the weather is nice, they often don't need a lunch because there is enough grass to eat outside. There's not much out there for grazing right now, but it's enough to keep them nibbling and happy."

I nodded again and, after putting my sling back on just in case, I followed her to the pile of tangled nets, wondering how I was ever going to remember all of this.

"I'll show you the chart when we get to the feed room, but for now all you need to know is that the nets are colour coded. You put one large flake in the red nets and two large flakes in the blue ones. The chart will tell you who gets what for which meal. It's pretty simple."

It sounded far from simple to me. I picked up a red net awkwardly and tried to figure out which end was up. It was like a closed mesh bag with a long loop of rope at the top like a drawstring.

Beside me, Liza expertly clamped a wedge of hay between her knees and quickly dropped a net over it, closing the drawstring so the flake was captured inside. She dumped it in the closest cart and started on the next one.

It was next to impossible to do with two hands, let alone one. Somehow, I managed to trap a flake between my knees and work the net slowly and laboriously over the edge. By the time I actually had the drawstring closed, half the flake had disintegrated on the floor and I was forced to scoop it all up with my good hand and stuff it messily inside the bag. I had one bag done for every six that Liza did, but she worked cheerfully in silence and didn't roll her eyes at me or anything, so I just kept plodding along at it. Liza started on the heavier nets with the two flakes and let me finish the light ones. Finally, we were done and we pulled each cart together to the big feed room and parked them against the far wall. The last cart we pulled down the aisle and Liza hung each bag up for the horses in their stalls, telling me to watch closely how she did it so I could do it myself once my arm was better.

"You have to hang them high enough so they can't get their hooves tangled in them, but low enough so they don't have to stretch up to eat," she explained. "Then you loop the ends of the rope like this so they can't pull the bags off the wall." She demonstrated some complicated looking knot and smiled at me expectantly.

"See, easy, right? So now let's get their grain."

If I thought the hay was complicated, then the grain was a million times worse. Each horse had a bucket half-full of what looked like cold, grey mush mixed with an arsenal of grains and powders.

"Ew, Liza, what is this? Do they really eat this stuff?"

"Sure, they love it," Liza laughed. "See, this is what it looks like before it's soaked." She showed me a handful of dark grey pellets. "It's what's left over after sugar beets are squashed and processed for humans to use for sweetener. You add water to the pellets and they fluff up to more than double their size."

To go with their soaked beets, each horse got pelleted grain, and a variety of different powders and potions designed to optimize their performance. Each bucket had to be stirred together with a large wooden ladle like a magic brew. Then Liza had me toss a few carrot pieces into each bowl.

It reminded me of the different protein shakes, bars, and powders that Miranda was forever experimenting with to give her an edge over the competition. Our coach Earl always shook his head at whatever new concoction she showed up to practice with. I wondered if all this stuff really made a difference to the horses at all.

I followed the chart carefully and did all the mixing and stirring, and then Liza let me feed Quarry his grain while she did the other horses. He nickered gently when I slid open his stall door and hovered politely beside me as I awkwardly dumped the bucket into his rubber feed tub. I stayed in his stall and stroked his soft shoulder while I watched him eat. He didn't seem to mind me there. His lips sifted deftly through the feed until he'd picked out all the bits of carrot, crunching them happily before going back for the rest.

As soon as he'd licked the bowl clean he turned to his hay net with a satisfied sigh.

I slid the stall door shut behind me, feeling more peaceful than I had in a while. There was something about Quarry that made me relaxed and happy. I wandered back to the feed room and Liza met me with a smile.

"We won't clean the stalls until we turn the horses out after breakfast. I don't think you'll be much help in that department anyway, so we'll wait until Hilary gets here. For now, I'll fill the water buckets and you'll scrub the grain tubs."

There was a back door to the feed room that led to a little concrete patio area outside. She helped me carry the empty grain buckets out into the sunshine and handed me a scrub brush. "The hose is right there. You just scrub them all clean and then line them up to dry in the sun. Everything gets done once a day. This is also where we hose down any hay that needs to be rinsed. Thankfully, we don't have any horses here right now that need their hay soaked. That is a royal pain in the winter, believe me."

I sat on a wooden stool in the sunshine and slowly scrubbed the buckets with my left hand. I was getting pretty good at using it after all this time. When they were clean, I stretched my legs out in front of me and inhaled deeply, caught up in the sounds of birds singing and the steady sound of horses munching behind me. No wonder Hilary liked spending time here. It was a beautiful place.

As if I'd conjured her, Hilary appeared behind me.

"Astrid! How do you like your first morning of work?"

"Better than I expected," I admitted with a smile.

"I told you. Just wait until you get to ride."

I made a face at her but didn't argue. There was no way to convince her that horses were too big and intimidating (not to mention, smelly) for me. Especially after I'd seen the performance Folly put on earlier. I had a new respect for how powerful and dangerous they were.

As soon as they were done eating breakfast, Hilary and Liza took the rest of the horses out to pasture with me following them as best I could.

Hilary and I walked side by side with Jerry prancing along on the end of his lead rope, his eyes bright with excitement. "All right, you big goof." Hilary laughed, swatting his shoulder. "We're just going to your boring old pasture."

"He's only six," Hilary said to me, "he's a warmblood and they mature a little slower than some breeds so he still has baby-brain."

"Okay, what's a warmblood?" I laughed. "I would think all horses have warm blood."

"Ninety-nine and a half degrees." Hilary laughed at her own joke. "But Warmbloods are a breed, not a temperature. Jerry's a Swedish Warmblood, actually. So his great, great, grandparents came from Sweden, even though he was bred here in Canada."

"Ooh, fancy," I said, as she reached the pasture and led Jerry in, slipping off his halter and setting him free. He apparently didn't care about his fancy pedigree; the first thing he did was drop down into the dirt and roll around with his feet in the air, itching his back like a dog with fleas. Then he leapt up, farted loudly and took off across the pasture, kicking his heels in the air.

"Yes, very elegant." Hilary laughed. "All horses care about is having enough food, company and exercise, and someone to brush and entertain them."

Once all the horses were out, Liza and Hilary started cleaning the stalls while I hung out and kept them company as they worked. Normally, the boarders didn't start showing up until after nine on weekdays and the outside riders started arriving after lunch. Claudia liked the horses to be fed early so they had time to enjoy a quiet breakfast before they had to work.

All together there were twelve stalls in the barn, but only eight of them were full. Quarry, Marcus, and the gangly young horse, Ferdinand, all belonged to Claudia. Pender had a plain brown horse with long ears named Rabbit, the big black horse named Severus was Ally's, and Sadie had an exotic-looking cream-coloured horse with blue eyes named Riverdance that Hilary said had once been a famous bullfighting horse in Brazil.

After Folly and Jerry's stalls, all the rest stood empty, which I thought was strange since Hilary had said there was a waitlist to get in here. Liza didn't have her own horse; she rode Claudia's horses or sometimes one of the outside client's horses.

I really liked Liza; she was nice and easy to get along with. She told me she'd worked at a few other barns before she came to Mud Lark, but that Claudia's stable was hands down the best place she'd ever been. First of all, the facility was top-notch, the horses were treated like gold, and Claudia was the best instructor she'd ever studied under.

Just then, Pender swept in, her helmet under her arm and her sweater half unbuttoned. She was breathing heavily and looked like she'd run a marathon to get there.

"I'm late, girls," she said breathlessly. "Matty stayed home sick and I had to scramble last minute to find him a sitter. Lunch is on me for anyone who helps me get ready for my lesson on time."

Thinking of the painfully healthy lunch Marion had packed for me that morning, I brightened instantly. "For real food? We'll do anything."

Liza kept cleaning stalls while Pender got changed, and Hilary and I ran to bring Rabbit in out of the field. He was a dark brown horse with giant ears, a tiny white star on his forehead and a mischievous glint in his eye.

"Oh, this could be fun," Hilary said with a sigh. "He's a retired race horse, his racing name was Run Rabbit Run and he likes to live up to it. He came from the track with a lot of bad habits. Hopefully, he's in a good mood."

Rabbit saw us coming from halfway across the field. His head shot up, long ears swivelling around like satellites. He snorted and trotted a few steps in the opposite direction; looking over his shoulder as if he wanted us to chase him.

"Come on, Rabby," Hilary coaxed, waving a carrot in the air. "I have your favourite."

Apparently, Rabbit *was* in a good mood. After circling us a few times, shaking his head like he was telling us off, he turned and trotted up to collect his carrot. He calmly let Hilary slip the leather halter over his head. As soon as he'd finished his snack, he snatched the end of the lead rope between his big, white teeth and tossed his head up and down, waving the rope around like it was a prize. He continued to hold it firmly clamped between his jaws while we walked him back to the barn. He was covered in sand, even his face was plastered with dirt, and it took both of us ten minutes of hard brushing to make him clean. Hilary carefully wrapped his lower legs with the long strips of stretchy fabric called 'polo wraps', telling me they were there to support his legs and keep him from getting injured. She had me brush out his mane and tail so every strand lay smooth and orderly.

Pender, now dressed in black breeches and a vest, and with hair brushed smooth, made it back in time to put his saddle and bridle on while I polished his feet with oil as a finishing touch. He gleamed like he'd just stepped off the showroom floor.

"Thanks so much, girls," Pender hugged us gratefully as she stuffed a cookie in Rabbit's mouth and led him away, toward the indoor arena. I could see Claudia waiting for them inside, tapping her booted foot impatiently. But she had a smile on her face and I somehow didn't think she'd be too hard on Pender for not doing all the grooming herself this one time.

One by one, the boarders showed up, groomed, had their lessons, and dumped their dirty equipment in the tack room. Claudia had to work both Marcus and Ferdinand while Liza rode Quarry and Hilary rode Jerry.

As soon as anyone hung up their tack on the cleaning racks, I washed the metal bits that were all covered in horse slobber then cleaned the bridles and saddles with the sweet scented orange soap and a soft cloth. I threw their sweaty, dirty leg wraps in a wicker basket in the corner and tossed their used saddle pads in another basket.

The walls were lined with bridle hooks, each with a horse's name hung on a little plaque above it. The bridles all had little gold dog tags on them engraved with the horse's names so it was easy to hang each horse's bridle carefully on the corresponding hook and the matching saddle right beside it.

When the horses were done working, they were either put back in their stalls or out in the pasture, depending on the schedule of the day. Between rides, I would awkwardly sweep the aisles of sand and horse hair with one arm and wait for the next rider to be finished. It was steady work, but not too hard, and I was able to keep up reasonably well.

After the morning lessons were done, Pender went and picked us up boxes of delicious Thai food as promised and stayed to help us eat it. She even brought us a box from the bakery full of treats. She was really my favorite of the boarders so far.

After lunch, the outside riders showed up for their lessons, but they took care of cleaning their own tack; I just had to sweep the aisle after they were gone. I looked for Rob and Artimax, but they didn't have lessons that day.

* * * * *

Day after day, I worked at the barn; my arm slowly improved and the humiliation from that disastrous night at the Ling's lake house began to fade. I fell naturally into the barn routine and stopped noticing the pungent smell of horse whenever I arrived to work. I was stronger and every day I could do a little bit more with my arm.

"Astrid," Claudia called one afternoon, about a week later, as she paused on her way to the indoor arena to start Hilary and Liza's lesson. "You come sit by me and watch these two girls ride. We have to work on your education."

A twinge of fear shot through my belly, but I walked

obediently to meet her, my steps dragging. I liked and admired Claudia, but she was a little intimidating. She hadn't said much after I'd dropped my homework off to her last week, but then she hadn't looked very well that day, either. She'd just wordlessly handed me a couple more pages of questions without looking up.

She smiled as I slowly approached and threw an arm gently over my shoulder. "I've been watching you, Astrid. I can't tell you how much I appreciate your hard work and attention to detail. I think you're going to be an excellent addition to our team. Thank you for helping Pender last week; that meant a lot to her."

I looked up in surprise and she sent me a wink. "Pender has a lot of things on her plate and many limitations that other riders here do not have. Rabbit, too, has some limitations and yet, she shows up every day and works as hard as she can to be a partner to him. In the end, it's her hard work and dedication that will pay off in spades. We could all learn a lot from her."

I thought about Miranda and how hard she worked every day at her archery. Was she, one day, going to be better than I was? I kicked the arena dirt with my shoe and scowled. Of course she was going to be better than me now. She had my spot at training camp and maybe even my bow. She was probably going to end up at the Olympics with my dad as her sponsor while I was sent far away to military school.

I shook my head to clear it and followed Claudia to the bottom step of the bleachers.

Although Jerry and Quarry were both greys, the similarities stopped there. Jerry was tall with long, gangly legs and a head that looked a little too big for his body. His coat was a dark silver colour, speckled with lighter blotches of whitish grey. Quarry looked dainty next to Jerry, and his coat was so white it practically glowed, but he moved with a grace and confidence that the younger horse was missing.

Liza sat on Quarry's back much like Claudia did—stone-still, like she had melded into him. I never saw her pull on the reins once or tell him what to do and yet, there he was, prancing around like she was communicating with him telepathically.

Hilary was less polished; I could see slight movements of her hands and legs when she asked Jerry to do things, and sometimes he ignored her requests and she'd have to ask again. But she was patient and kind with him, even when she asked him to canter and he kicked out excitedly with his hind legs, tail swishing madly. I was beginning to see that horses didn't always do what they were told. They certainly had their own opinions.

"I have to confess, Astrid," Claudia said thoughtfully, "you have arrived at the barn at a very strange time. I have had some health challenges lately and I'm finding that I have to make some difficult decisions about the future. My doctor tells me that I have to step back and rest. Of course, I won't listen to him completely. But, it means that right now Liza will be taking over riding Marcus for me so I can focus on young Ferdinand's training until he is sold. It's very important to me that he gets a good home. And Liza is also going to be working with that awful mare Cole sent back from Germany. I don't know quite what he was thinking, but I don't really feel up to that sort of challenge just now. Liza will also be taking over many of my training rides for our clients. That means you'd be able to start working with Quarry once your arm has healed enough."

Even though horses still intimidated the heck out of me, a surge of excitement blossomed across my body. I'd been watching the riders for over a week now and a tiny part of me had begun to feel left out of all the fun. Besides, Quarry wasn't like all these other opinionated animals. I had the feeling he was the type of guy who would take care of his rider. He'd take care of *me*.

"He's a very kind schoolmaster," Claudia said, echoing my thoughts. "I have a strict policy that a rider must have an independent seat before they are ever allowed to pick up the reins. Some schools keep their riders on the lunge for six to eight months before they're allowed to move on. But we shall see how you progress. We will start on the lead line, move to the lunge line and then proceed from there. Yes?"

"Okay," I said, before I could change my mind. "Thank you."

"I have a good feeling about you, Astrid," Claudia smiled down at me. "And I'm hardly ever wrong."

* * * * *

Hilary's mom came to pick her up early to take her to dance practice, so I went for a walk down the rows of paddocks while I waited for Marion. Liza had said it was too nice an afternoon to bring the horses in so early so most of them were still out in the sunshine.

I ducked past Folly's paddock quickly just in case she decided to charge the fence again and then ambled slowly down the grassy laneway that ran between the pastures, inhaling the fresh smell of spring grass.

It was beautiful out; the sun shone gently down on me,

warming my hair and the bridge of my nose until I felt all snuggly and cared for. I didn't believe in a god like Hilary did; I didn't really believe in anything, actually, but on days like this I could almost believe that there was something up there looking down on me and smiling and saying, "Hey, Astrid, I know your life kind of sucks right now, so here's a beautiful day to cheer you up."

Marcus and Ferdinand were sharing a grassy paddock together and must have smelled the carrots in my pockets from over fifty feet away. They came trotting over and followed me down the fence line, making that low *huh huh huh* sound that meant they were interested in something. I could guess they were saying something like, "Here, girl, over here. We like carrots."

I stopped and leaned over the fence to touch their soft noses and then broke a carrot in half and tossed the pieces to the grass at their feet. They dropped their heads immediately, searching the ground like bloodhounds after prey, bumping their noses together and getting in each other's way, making me laugh.

When I reached the end of the laneway, I turned and made my way slowly back up to the barn, watching the horses graze and listening to the hundreds of birds announcing that it was Spring and that they were happy to be alive.

My thoughts, as they always did when I was alone, drifted to archery. Now that the early rains had stopped, the club would have opened up the outdoor range so people could practice on the 3-D targets. There were miles of trails through the woods with shooting stations set up along the way. Some of the targets were the size and shape of live animals like bears and moose, and they even had a section for shooting lifelike zombie targets. Even though I'd never dream of shooting a real animal, it was fun to practice shooting something three dimensional rather than a flat target.

I was so caught up in my thoughts I didn't realize I was almost back to the barn and had come up beside Folly's paddock. Not until there was a flash of bronze right beside me. I froze in place. There she was, right by the fence, ears flattened to her head and wild eyes glaring right at me. It was like those stories you hear about people getting trapped by a rattlesnake. If you tried to run away then you risked it chasing you down, but if you stayed still then it might strike anyway. Except Folly wasn't going to bite my ankle, she was inches away from my *face* with her huge, horrible teeth. I could just imagine those jaws closing on my throat; even if she didn't kill me, I would be disfigured forever and would have to wear one of those veils to keep from scaring the public.

I closed my eyes tightly, bracing for impact.

For a second, I felt a puff of hot grass-scented horse breath on my cheek. Teeth clacked next to my ear and then she was gone. Hooves thudded across the ground, moving away from me in the opposite direction.

I opened my eyes and exhaled all the breath I'd been holding; amazed I was alive and undamaged.

Folly stomped across her paddock to the furthest corner where she dropped her head and began to eat. But even from this far distance I thought I could see one ear rotated toward me and one beady eye watching me balefully.

* * * * *

That night, after dinner when we were putting dishes away, I asked Marion about the riding lessons. "Do you think Dad would be okay with it? I mean, the whole idea of me working at the stable was to punish me. I don't think he'd be happy to know I was enjoying myself."

"Oh Astrid, for heaven's sake, of course your father wants you to be happy."

I raised my eyebrows at her and she shook her head.

"Seriously, Astrid, the problem is that the two of you are too much alike. You both stew over problems without actually coming out and facing them."

"No, the problem is that he hates me and thinks I'm a loser like my mom." I clapped my hand over my mouth, but the words had already come out.

Marion stared at me open-mouthed. "What? Astrid, your mom was sick; addiction is an illness. She wasn't a loser and neither are you. Your father does not hate you. I don't know how to convince you that's the truth."

I shrugged and looked at the sofa. The unspoken rule in our house had always been to avoid the subject of my mom's addictions or my dad's temper at all costs.

Marion sighed. "All right, honey. We'll talk about this later. Enjoy your lessons."

I escaped to my room as fast as I could. With shaking hands, I pulled down my old wooden bow and just sat there holding it in my lap. I ran my fingers over the smooth, golden wood grain and thought about everything I'd lost.

Chapter Ten

The next day, Hilary's mom drove us to a tack shop after work. It was a place that sold brushes, saddles, bridles, and equipment for horses but also sold all sorts of boots and tight pants and fancy show clothes for people. It smelled great; like leather and sweet soap and lemon polish.

Even though I wasn't even close to being able to ride yet; Marion had said I should get outfitted so that I'd be ready when the time came. I could keep my riding things and a pair of grubby work clothes at the barn so that I didn't get my good clothes dirty. She'd also picked up a new sling for me from the pharmacy to wear when I was at home. She didn't mention that she didn't want our condo, or her car, smelling like a barnyard, but I could tell that was what she was thinking.

"Hey, Stacy," Hilary called out to the black-haired girl with glasses who was seated behind the counter. The girl blinked and looked up from the pile of books she had spread open in front of her. "Hi, Hilary, you brought a friend?"

"This is Astrid; she's just started working at Claudia's with me. She's going to start taking lessons soon so she needs a complete wardrobe."

"Lucky," Stacy said, raising her eyebrows and quickly scanning me up and down appraisingly. She looked friendly but then, that was her job; I wondered if she was thinking I was too fat to fit anything in the store. "I'd love to ride at Mud Lark, Claudia's the best. I'm too broke and busy with school, though. Sorry about all the mess, I'm taking some summer classes so I can keep up." She started to gather up her books, but Hilary stopped her.

"No, don't worry about us. We'll just start shopping and you can help us fit Astrid with a helmet when we're done. Okay?"

"Awesome, thanks, Hilary." Stacy was already sinking back into her text book, elbows on the counter and chin resting in her hands.

"I made a list," Hilary said briskly, suddenly all business-like. "We'll start from the bottom up. You need boots and long socks, then two pairs of breeches, gloves, and a helmet. There are some nice polo shirts here, too.

I sighed and followed Hilary's retreating back. I didn't usually enjoy shopping. It was boring for one thing, and it was always way too stressful trying things on. It was hard to find things that looked good in my size, and I was always paranoid that people were laughing at me behind my back. I'd learned to stick with a basic wardrobe and ordered most of my clothes online.

Marion had given me her credit card and told me to get whatever I needed, but I couldn't help feeling guilty when I saw how expensive everything was. That was one thing I'd learned growing up with my budget-obsessed dad—never take anything for granted and watch every penny. He hadn't become so rich by throwing his money around frivolously.

"Hilary, these gloves are sixty dollars," I said, trying on the pair of butter-soft leather gloves she'd handed me. They fit perfectly; like they'd been made just for me. "Claudia told me I didn't need anything fancy. Just basic safety gear."

"Yes, but these will last you forever if you take care of them," Hilary said. "If you buy quality stuff, it costs more in the short term but saves more in the long-run. Come on, Marion won't mind."

"Yeah, but my dad will mind when he goes to pay his credit card bill," I muttered to Hilary's retreating back. She wasn't listening to me anyway. She made me try on sets of tall leather boots until we found a pair that fit and didn't make me hyperventilate at the cost.

"Now, socks," she said leading me over to a rack of brightly-colored thin socks in all sorts of crazy patterns.

"Seriously?" I laughed. "This is what all these perfectly dressed, stick-thin, horse-people are wearing under their fancy boots?"

"Yes," she giggled. "You have to have some fun, right?"

"Right." I leafed through the different patterns, pushing aside the flowers, the dogs, the bright zig-zags and the pin-up girls until suddenly my hand stopped over a pair of brown and camouflage socks with arrows printed all over them. "Bingo," I said. "These are mine."

"Perfect!" Hilary squealed. "Now, follow me."

She headed over to a circular rack of breeches and was eagerly flicking through them one by one. "No, no, no; too boring, too flashy, too…oh wait, try these on, Astrid!" She triumphantly held up a minuscule pair of brown plaid breeches with a patch of brown leather on the butt. There was no way I was squeezing myself in to those.

"Too small, Hilary," I mumbled, glancing over my shoulder to make sure Stacy wasn't listening. She wasn't; she had her head in her hands and was staring down intently at the book in front of her. She obviously had forgotten we were here at all. Still, my cheeks burned.

"We need to go up a few more sizes," I said in a whisper.

"No problem," Hilary was not deterred. "Okay, let's see if we can find the same colours in a different size, then." She flicked expertly through the rack and fished up two more breeches; one in the same brown plaid and the other in a lighter plain cream colour. "Here, try these on, then."

"Can't I just wear my jeans?" I begged. "I don't need to look fancy, do I? I'm just pretending to be a rider, Hilary. We both know I'm not going to be any good at it."

"Oh, for heck's sake, Astrid. You can't wear jeans because they'll wreck Claudia's fancy leather saddle, okay. And just give them a try before you get so negative. We'll find a pair that you look great in. I promise."

"Okay," I sighed, reluctantly taking the ridiculous tight pants from her. I made sure the door of the changing room was tightly closed and started to get undressed, turning my back on the mirror so I didn't have to look at myself. *Just put them on to humour her,* I told myself. *Then you can prove to her that it will never work and get out of here.*

But surprisingly, the breeches slid on easily and when I

turned to face myself in the mirror they actually looked okay on me; they compressed my curves into a nice shape and were even comfortable to wear.

"Let me see, Astrid!" Hilary called from right outside the change room door.

I opened the door a crack and quickly pulled her inside. Even though I looked okay, I wasn't ready to put myself under the scrutiny of the sales girl or any customers who happened to walk in.

"Wow, you look great," Hilary said, nudging me in the shoulder. "See, I told you."

"I know," I said, smiling incredulously. "It's a miracle."

Hilary frowned. "No, it isn't, Astrid. You have to stop selling yourself short. People aren't judging you nearly as hard as you're judging yourself. There are girls out there who would kill for your figure."

I gaped at her in the mirror. Was she crazy?

"Don't look at me like that. I'm flat as a pancake, at least you have curves."

"Yeah," I snorted. "I have lots of those."

"So"—she nudged me again—"you're perfect exactly as you are, Astrid, and everyone can see that except you."

"Hilary," I began, and then stopped. She wasn't just making this stuff up to make me feel better. She actually believed what she was saying. Maybe it was her religion that made her overlook my deficiencies or maybe she was just too darn nice to see what everyone else saw. Whatever it was, I couldn't hurt her feelings by saying what I really thought, that besides her perfect, golden willowy self, I was a hulking shadow with messy hair, bulging thighs, and a stomach that wouldn't stay tucked away no matter how hard I tried. I hated almost everything about my body. I was practically a mutant.

"Maybe you're right," I lied, smiling for her sake. "And you *are* right about the breeches. They do fit really well."

"Of course I'm right. You should listen to me more often."

Hilary made me get a handful of polo shirts to go with the breeches and a thin leather belt. When we were done with the clothing, Stacy left her studies to help me find a helmet that fit comfortably.

"It was nice to meet you, Astrid," she said as we were leaving. "Have fun at your lessons. We'll see you next time."

I left the store exhausted but happy, clutching boxes and bags of gear plus a huge tub of chewy molasses treats for Quarry. It was one of the first times shopping that I'd left a store feeling better than when I'd walked in. I actually felt like I'd almost belonged there.

When I got home, I ran up to show Marion all my stuff and she made me try everything on and model it for her. She waved away my apology about the ridiculously large shopping bill.

"Wow, you look wonderful, Astrid. I can't wait to see you ride."

I looked up in alarm. "Well, wait a little bit for that. I'm probably going to suck at it for quite a while. And can we please hold off telling Dad?"

She laughed and shook her head. "You're so hard on yourself, Astrid. It's okay not to be perfect when you first start something." She gave me a little hug. "But sure, I'll let you tell your dad yourself."

That night before bed, I impulsively called Miranda. I felt

like I hadn't spoken to her in ages. She picked up on the third ring.

"Hello?" she said sharply as if she didn't have call display and knew it was me. She had never been a great conversationalist on the phone.

"Hey, Miranda," I said. "How was the fun match this weekend?"

There was a long pause. "Oh, hey, Astrid," she said weakly. "It was great. I mean, my scores were really good. Finally."

"What do you mean, finally? Your scores are always good."

"Yeah, compared to who?"

There was a dark note in her voice and I knew she was in one of her moods. Miranda had always been a little moody.

"Well, I'm glad you did well, anyway. I can't wait to get back to the range. My shoulder's actually healing pretty well."

"Oh, great," she said, thawing a little. "I mean, that's good news, Astrid. How's the horse poop job?"

"Good, the people are really nice there, and I'm going to start lessons and everything. I can't believe I'm actually going to ride a horse."

"Seriously? They're going to let you on a horse. Don't you have to be all skinny and perfect to be an equestrienne or something? You're not going to get all stuck up and snotty are you?"

I frowned, trying to be patient. Of course, Miranda didn't know how nice everyone was at Mud Lark; she'd probably never seen a horse up close in her life. "No, Miranda. Everyone is really nice, not stuck up at all. And this horse, Quarry, is special, he's really sweet...."

"Well, whatever," Miranda said. "At least you'll be getting

some exercise, finally. Even if it means you'll stink like horse poop. Oh and hey, thanks again for giving me your spot at archery camp. I know it's really going to give me an edge over the competition. I should go now, though, got to rest up for tomorrow. See you around. And don't break that horse in half."

She disconnected before I could say another word. I tossed my phone on the bed and then sat down beside it, not sure what to think. Had Miranda always sounded so mean? I wasn't *that* overweight and it wasn't like I'd *voluntarily* given up my spot at camp. But maybe she'd just forgotten that by now.

I sighed and stared down at my thighs critically. It was true, I'd gained a couple pounds since my winter visit to the "health spa." It happened every time I went; the effects of a macrobiotic diet and a prescribed workout schedule only lasted two weeks max once I came home. It wasn't like I pigged out on junk food all the time, either; not like most of the kids I knew. We didn't even have junk food in our house, but it was like I just had to look at food and get fat. And I hated the gym in our building. It was always full of old people and smelled like feet.

I was most definitely not stick-thin like most of the people who rode at the barn. Maybe Pender was heavier than me, but not by much. Even the pictures in the books Claudia had given me were all of rail-thin riders. What if I hurt Quarry when I sat on his back? He'd probably only known light, agile riders his whole life.

Don't be stupid, I told myself fiercely. *Claudia wouldn't have asked you to ride Quarry if she thought you'd damage him. She loves him and it's not like you've been begging her to ride, it was her idea in the first place.*

I looked over at my desk where I'd deposited the book on horse rider yoga without ever really looking at it again. It had never come up in my homework questions after that first day, and I'd been focused on just trying to keep up with my barn chores. I grabbed the book and flipped through, eyeing up the overly flexible women in the photos.

Some of these exercises, I can do, I thought, *Claudia asked me a long time ago to add them into my routine so I guess I should do it if I'm going to pretend to actually be a rider.*

I went through the book, sticking pieces of paper between the pages to mark where the easy exercises were so I could easily find them again.

I sat down on the floor and went carefully through a few movements and was surprised at how easy some of them were. I'd thought that yoga was only for perfect stick-people but apparently, it wasn't as difficult as it looked. I skipped the difficult ones and any that involved using my right arm, but there were still a whole bunch of the others I could do.

I worked for a half an hour and was amazed at how rested and happy I felt afterwards before I got into bed and fell into a peaceful sleep.

* * * * *

When I woke up the next morning, before the alarm, the world outside of our condo was shrouded in a thick white mist that blocked the view not only of the ocean and mountains, but even of the street below. It was cocooned inside a cool, moist cloud.

I took my coffee and my yoga book out on the balcony and peered over the edge of the railing, watching the nearly solid banks of fog float by. Every now and then, the mist parted and I could see the grey outline of buildings below. It was so thick I could reach out and scatter it into swirling fragments, I pulled my hand back and it was wet.

After a while, I sat down on the balcony floor and went through a few more of the exercises along with the physiotherapy exercises that I'd been given for my arm and shoulder.

"Wow, this fog is amazing," Marion said, joining me outside. She reached out tentatively to stir a passing cloud with one finger. "Oh, are you doing yoga, Astrid? Wait here; I have a present for you."

She disappeared and was back a moment later with a rolled up yoga mat under her arm. "It's brand new so you can have it. It's an extra one I bought. And you're always welcome to practice Tai Chi with me, too. My online practice group is really supportive."

"Thanks, Marion," I said shyly, too insecure to keep practicing in front of her. She stared dreamily out into the cloud bank with a far-off expression on her face.

"This is what we called Scotch Fog when I was growing up. You usually see it in the Fall and mainly in low lying areas. I've never seen it reach this high before."

I looked up with interest. Marion rarely spoke about her past and I wanted her to keep talking.

"Marion, when you were at the barn that time you said that Claudia's dog Caprice reminded you of a dog you used to have. Was that when you were a kid?"

"Oh yes, I got him for my tenth birthday. He was a poodle cross that looked quite a bit like Caprice. He was very smart and full of love."

"What happened to him?"

"Oh, well they never live as long as we'd like them to, do they? He was sixteen when he passed away. Taking him to the vet on his final day was one of the saddest things I ever had to do. It still haunts me."

We sat silently for a few minutes, watching the fog drift by.

"You could get a dog now," I said suddenly. "I've always wanted a pet and you liked Caprice."

She smiled over at me and took a sip of coffee. "Well, maybe someday. A condo isn't a nice place for a dog. They need a backyard. I don't think we have the right lifestyle for a dog."

"We could move," the words came out of my mouth before I'd thought about them, but once they were out I could totally see the logic. "We could leave the condo and move out of the city and get a house that has a yard for a dog."

"Oh, Astrid." Marion laughed. "Our home is beautiful. Now get dressed so we can get you to work on time."

Chapter Eleven

I'd almost thought Claudia had changed her mind about having me ride Quarry. It was weeks after buying my new riding things that she caught up with me sweeping the barn aisle after morning chores and pulled me aside. "I'm going to ride Quarry first, Astrid. Come into the ring when you're finished here and I'll get you up on him."

"Okay." I gulped. My hands went ice cold and the broom felt heavy, twisting clumsily between my fingers while I finished sweeping. I put the broom away and then woodenly climbed upstairs to the change room to get into my new breeches and boots. I stared at myself glumly in the mirror thinking of what a faker I was. I would never be mistaken for a real rider. Now, instead of fitting perfectly, the pants felt too tight and the thin socks slid around uncomfortably in my new boots.

Come on, get up, I told myself. *You only have to do this once. Then Claudia will see what a failure you are and she won't ask you to ride again.* The thought was strangely liberating, and suddenly I could breathe again.

I trudged down the steps and out into the arena where Claudia was cantering Quarry around in large, effortless circles.

"There you are, Astrid. Just in time, I have the big guy warmed up for you."

She hopped off and led Quarry up to the set up black steps in the middle of the ring. She slid off his bridle and replaced it with his leather halter and a lead rope. "Okay, up on the mounting block. I'll show you how to get on."

I climbed the mounting block steps slowly, feeling cold and awkward. From the top step, I could look down on Quarry's broad back. Even though I was only standing a few feet up, the arena footing looked very far away. I reached out a hand and tentatively scratched Quarry's neck. He turned around to look at me and *whuffled* low under his breath.

"Perfect. Left foot in the stirrup, hold the front of the saddle with this hand and swing your leg gently over. See, you're on a horse. No big deal."

It *was* a big deal, though. As soon as my butt met Quarry's saddle, my fear evaporated and this feeling of inexplicable peace settled over me. It was like that first time I'd held a bow and the whole world had seemed to stop. There was something sacred about the moment, as if I was stepping out on an epic adventure and there was no turning back.

"Okay, big guy, you're going to take care of me out there, right?" I leaned down and shakily ran my fingers through his silky mane.

"Of course he will." Claudia laughed. "And so will I. You're perfectly safe up there, Astrid. Today, we're just going to walk and let you get a feel for him. We're not going to worry about the reins at this point. I want you to focus on absorbing the motion of the horse. How does it feel up there?"

"Good," I said, smiling nervously and clutching the front of the saddle, "but it's a long way to the ground."

"And Quarry is just a medium-sized horse." Claudia smiled. "Imagine how I feel every time I get on a giant like Marcus."

"Are you *scared*?" I asked incredulously. "But you're a professional."

She laughed and patted my knee. "I'd say it's more exhilarating than scary. Although, when he's feeling fresh, Marcus is like a wild, young giraffe with his head way up in the clouds. I'll admit to being a little intimidated at those times."

She reached up and pulled the stirrup off the saddle and then went around and did the same thing with the other side so my legs dangled in the air. "We won't need these again until you've developed an independent seat. Stirrups and reins can act as a crutch. A real rider doesn't need either."

I laughed and felt my muscles relax into the soft leather of the saddle. It was a comfortable feeling; Quarry's ribs moved in and out gently as he breathed, pushing softly against my legs. He turned his head to look expectantly at Claudia and I could feel his spine and muscles rippling under me. It was a strange sensation.

"So, Astrid," Claudia said with a smile. "Here you are, on a horse at last. Before we start moving, we must help you find the right way to sit."

I stared down at her expectantly, wondering what she was talking about.

"Your horse is not a couch or a motorcycle, Astrid. They are incredibly complex, sensitive beings, able to feel the tiniest move that you make. They can feel the slightest flex of your muscles;

they can feel when you hold your breath, or if you tilt your head, or curl your toes. Riding such a sensitive creature is a huge responsibility. You cannot hope to influence or control them if you do not first have control of yourself, both in mind and body, understand?"

"Okay," I said in a small voice. Most of the time, it felt like I had zero control over my body; Quarry was going to hate being ridden by someone as clumsy as me.

Claudia patted my leg sympathetically. "Horses are also very forgiving," she said. "Just always try your best; be kind to them and always put their needs first. You'll come along just fine. Now close your eyes."

I held tightly to the front of the saddle and reluctantly closed my eyes.

"Good. Now, the first thing I want you to do is to focus on just your breathing. In through your nose and out through your mouth. Let your belly gently expand with each breath. Go on, try it."

I felt a little silly inhaling and exhaling in front of Claudia. I couldn't stop thinking about what I must look like to her sitting there like a lump and breathing great, raspy breaths through my open mouth. And I certainly didn't want to think about my belly "expanding." But despite myself, I began to feel better. My breath flowed through me easily and my body relaxed. Quarry's warm sides expanded gently against my legs as he breathed with me.

"That's it. Now let your weight sink down through your body and out the bottom of your boots. Just imagine that above your body is a waterfall and that the water flows *through* you, from the top your head and out through your heels. If you tilted too far forward, then the waterfall would push you over and if you tilted too far back the waterfall would push you backwards. But if you sit just as you are, calm and centered, then the waterfall flows right through you, anchoring you to the saddle. The weight doesn't rest on your seat, mind you, you don't want to sit like a lump in the saddle; it flows down through you and out your feet."

I cracked open an eye to see if Claudia was kidding me, but her expression was completely serious. I quickly closed my eyes again and focused on my breathing and my waterfall.

"Now, just keep that feeling and I'm going to walk him forward a few steps. Okay?"

I nodded and clutched the front of the saddle more tightly. Quarry swayed underneath me and I shifted to the side, momentarily disoriented. My eyes popped open.

"That's okay," Claudia said, bringing him quietly to a halt. "You just lost your balance. Riding a horse means coordinating two balances, two minds, and two hearts. It's not for the faint of heart. Did you remember to keep breathing?"

I exhaled the breath I didn't know I'd been holding and shook my head.

"Okay, so, now we try again. This time, your job is to merely breathe in and out like I showed you and focus on your waterfall. Got it?"

This time, I was ready for the alien feeling of Quarry lurching along beneath me. I determinedly focused on my breathing first, and gradually my body relaxed and my weight sank downward until I felt rooted deep in the saddle.

"Wonderful," Claudia said."Now you're moving with him instead of against him. Are you ready to add one more thing?"

"Sure," I said dreamily, not opening my eyes and still breathing with my whole body.

"So, a horse's hoof beats are like music, Astrid, and each gait, and by that I mean walk, trot, and canter, has a different tempo. The walk is a four beat tempo, the trot has two beats and the canter has three. In order to have any influence over, or be able to improve, a horse's gaits you must first be able to isolate the individual footfalls. So, at the walk, you can feel when each of his feet are moving. Keep your eyes closed and I'll let you know which ones are moving so you can get a feel for it. But keep your breathing active as well."

I nodded and smiled. This lesson wasn't anything like I'd expected. It was really fun.

"Right, so we'll start with the back feet. Now, here is his right hind foot lifting and moving forward; you feel his hips shift and his hindquarter muscles contract through the movement. Just concentrate on that one leg for now. Step, step, step. Feel it?"

"Um, maybe? I'm not sure."

"That's okay, try again. Feel your right hip and seat bone slide forward. Step, step, step."

"Oh, yes, now I can totally feel it."

"Good, so focus on the left hind now."

I let my concentration shift to my left side and gradually I felt what she was talking about.

"Good. These are the steps that propel you fluidly forward. So, it's right, left, right, left. See? Now you count them out loud for me."

It was simple for me to feel with my eyes closed, the movement of his hind legs pushed each of my hip bones forward in a rhythm, so, once I knew what to look for, it was pretty easy to tell which one was moving. "Right, left, right, left," I said in time with his steps, keeping my eyes closed.

"Okay, great, now the walk is a four-beat gait, so in between those steps the front feet are also moving. So when his right hind leg moves forward you know that the right front leg will be just about to move forward after it. Right hind, right front, left hind, left front; like that. See if you can feel what I'm talking about. Don't lose your breathing."

I hadn't realized that I held my breath when I was concentrating. I inhaled freely again and tried to feel all four legs.

"Ack," I said. "They're going too quickly. I'm getting them messed up now."

"Not as easy, is it? But you'll get there. We have all summer to practice. Another easy way to think of it is that when a front leg stretches forward, that shoulder has to come backward. See if you can feel when Quarry's shoulder slides back under the saddle; that means his front leg is extended. Forget the hind end for a moment while you get a feel for the front end."

I was quiet for a few moments while I concentrated but finally, I laughed in relief. "Yes, I found it. Now and now, right?"

"Good girl. Now switch to the hind end again. Now and now and now."

"Yes, that one is easy," I said.

"And back to the front. Call the beats when you feel them."

It was slower to get the feel again, but soon I had it. "Now and now," I repeated as I felt each of Quarry's front legs stretch forward. We circled the arena, switching back and forth until I could easily separate and identify Quarry's footfalls. When we finally stopped at the mounting block, I was grinning from ear-to-ear and, despite not moving above a walk, I was exhausted.

"That was an excellent beginning, Astrid. You are very in tune with him. That is a skill some riders are *never* taught, even those who have been riding for years. You're doing great."

I slid down from Quarry's back the way Claudia showed me, wrapped my arms around his neck, and gave him a big kiss. "I never knew riding involved so much *thinking*," I said. "It's more like archery or chess. I thought I'd be bouncing around on him until I fell off."

Claudia laughed and shook her head. "Not at my barn, you wouldn't. You will have two short lessons every day, Astrid; Quarry will enjoy the variety. Now make sure he gets a nice bath and then turn him out on pasture."

I thanked Claudia like ten times and led Quarry back down the aisle to the wash stall and was surprised to see Liza in the one next to us, brushing a sulky-looking Folly. The big horse pinned her ears at us and shook her head menacingly, but didn't move.

"Good lesson, Astrid?" Liza said with a smile, ignoring Folly.

"Oh, it was wonderful," I said. "I mean, it was nothing like what *you* do when you ride. We just walked and I learned to feel his legs moving." I stopped suddenly, realizing how childish I sounded. "Um, well, that probably sounds silly to you, but it was really fun."

"That doesn't sound silly at all, Astrid. You're starting to build the foundation for being a rider. You have no idea how lucky you are starting out with someone like Claudia and a horse like Quarry. I've been riding for years, and I still feel like a beginner sometimes. Horses are wonderful teachers that way; there's always something more you can learn."

"Yeah." Keeping a close eye on Folly in case she decided to make a lunge at me, I clipped Quarry into the cross-ties and undid his girth, pulling off his saddle and saddle pad. His leg-wraps came off next and I deposited everything in the tack room to be cleaned later.

I bathed him carefully, the way Hilary had showed me, letting a light stream of warm water trickle from the hose, first on his legs, then his shoulders and then up his neck and over his back. He stretched his neck out and closed his eyes in satisfaction, clearly ready to enjoy his warm shower and massage.

Folly grunted under her breath and shot us another dirty look, flattening her ears tight against her head until they practically disappeared. I stuck my tongue out at her before I could stop myself and Liza caught me. "Stop it, you two," she said with a laugh.

"She started it," I joked back. "Why is she so cranky all the time anyway?"

Liza sighed. "Part of it's her strong temperament, but part of it comes from being pushed way too hard too young. She's only seven, but because she's so talented, she was heavily campaigned overseas. And because she's so difficult, she wasn't always treated very nicely. She's angry with the whole world right now. Cole should have never bought her; she was borderline dangerous, and that's why she was cheap to buy. But it comes with a price. Hopefully, we can get through to her here and give her a meaningful job."

"Oh," I said, mulling it over as I carefully scraped the excess water off Quarry's side. I pulled a clean towel off the hook and rubbed it in brisk circles down his neck, fluffing up his hair in whorls. "That's awful that people were mean to her."

"It's a rough world out there for horses sometimes. They don't get to choose their careers or owners. At least, not most of the time; they're at the mercy of people, unfortunately."

I looked over at Folly who seemed to be listening to the conversation, her red ears flicking back and forth, and her eyes were tense with worry.

"It's okay, Folly," Liza soothed, "you're safe now. See, Astrid likes you, too."

I raised my eyebrows. "I do?"

"Sure you do, you just don't know it yet. All horses deserve love and respect, Astrid. Folly can't help who she is or what she's been through. We have to help her sort out her anger and figure out how to support her. She'll come around eventually."

"If you say so." I laughed. "But I think I'll stick to Quarry for now."

Chapter Twelve

The bruises on my right side had faded to a pale lemony yellow and my arm was well on its way to being back to normal. Every day, I practiced my physiotherapy exercises and my yoga, and slowly I began to heal. Each lesson with Claudia was just as interesting as the last. By the end of the week, I was able to pick out each of Quarry's footfalls at the walk, both with my eyes opened and closed. After the first day, I'd felt confident enough to let go of the strap and let my arms hang loosely by my sides so I was perfectly in balance.

And when Claudia moved us up to the trot, a two-beat gait this time, it was easy to adjust to the rhythm of his footfalls and let his powerful hind legs propel us forward. One-two, one-two; just like dancing.

Every night, at least those nights when my dad wasn't home, I took my old, unstrung bow out onto the porch and practiced shooting the horizon with imaginary arrows.

At first, my shoulder had screamed with protest each time I drew back my invisible bow string, but now I could get through the whole range of motion with only a light twinge now and then. When I was practicing, I sort of disappeared into a different world.

It was at the end of my first week of riding Quarry that my dad came home unexpectedly and caught me practicing with my bow out on the patio. I hadn't even heard him come up behind me until it was too late to hide. He stood in the doorway and watched me with a strange expression on his face.

I dropped the bow to my side and stared at him, a mixture of emotions swirling through me. Fear was the most prevalent one, but after that came shame at being caught and anger that he was probably going to try and take this away from me, too.

Just try it, I thought defiantly, *go ahead and take this bow away, too. I'll find another one, or I'll practice with an invisible one. No matter what you do, you can't stop me.*

He didn't yell at me or say anything mean, for once; he just stared at me curiously. After a long moment, he shook his head and turned, without saying a word, back inside.

I sagged with relief and wiped my sweaty palms on my t-shirt. That had been close.

Practice was over for the night. I slipped inside and padded quietly to my room, hanging the bow carefully up on its hook above the door. With any luck, he'd forget all about seeing me with it. I really didn't want to have it taken away, too.

I crept into the kitchen to find Marion busily chopping vegetables for what looked like stir fry. I slid up silently beside her and moved the cutting board over in front of me. I was not a cook, but I did know how to chop carrots.

"Why didn't you warn me he was coming?" I whispered, taking the knife she handed me.

"He wasn't supposed to come back this early," she said softly, flicking her eyes up to the doorway to make sure we were alone. "It was a surprise. He must have missed us."

I snorted under my breath. "Missed *you*, maybe."

"Give him a chance, Astrid. He's been away a long time; he's probably had time to think. Why don't you go on into the living room and ask how his trip went."

I shook my head, but she ignored me and pushed me slowly toward the doorway.

"For heaven's sake, Astrid," she said, "he won't bite."

She stopped pushing and turned to the fridge to take out a bottle of mineral water, and then pulled a glass from the cupboard. She filled it with ice, poured in the drink, and handed it to me. "Here, you can go bearing gifts, then."

She gave me another push, and this time I moved toward the living room without protest.

"Dad," I said hesitantly. He grunted but didn't look up from where he was seated in his arm chair. His WorldCor brief case was open beside him, papers falling out onto the floor. He had his tablet in his hands and was looking at it as though he meant to snap it in half. I groaned internally; I knew it had been a mistake to disturb him.

"Um, sorry, to uh, bother you, but Marion thought you might like a drink."

"Drink!" he bellowed, loud enough to startle me. "What makes you think I want a drink?"

My arm jerked backward, splashing liquid over the side of the glass onto the floor. I looked down at the mess in dismay, my face burning.

"Pay attention!" he snapped, lunging forward to take the glass from me and slamming it down on a coaster. "Go get a cloth and clean this up."

I didn't look at Marion as I stumbled back into the kitchen, but she intercepted me smoothly and took the cloth from my hand.

"Thank you for trying," she said quietly. "I'll clean this up if you'll steam the broccoli for me. I know how good you are at that."

I nodded but kept my eyes trained on the floor, wishing she'd left me alone and not pushed me in there in the first place; I knew it had been a mistake. I had no idea what had gone wrong this time. Why did every single thing I did around that man put him into a rage?

I could hear his and Marion's murmured voices in the living room.

"Astrid!" he yelled suddenly, making me jump again. "Come back in here...please."

I felt sick knots twisting in my stomach, like I would throw up any second. Why couldn't he leave me alone? Why had he bothered to come home at all?

I moved slowly to the doorway, my hands twisting nervously behind my back. "Yes, Dad?" I asked, my voice coming out in a tiny squeak.

"I apologize for my outburst," he said gruffly. "It's just this damned business, it has me on edge. These bloody politicians and environmentalists keep sticking their nose in everybody's business. I'm doing my best to pull us through. Thank you for bringing me a drink; that was very thoughtful."

I stared at him incredulously, not really sure what he was talking about. Was there something wrong at WorldCor that I didn't know about? I inched back toward the safety of the kitchen.

His eyes flickered to mine briefly and then moved to the window. He cleared his throat nervously. "Your stepmother tells me that you're doing very well at this horse ranch where you work. That's good to hear. And your shoulder is coming along?"

"Yes, Dad." I stopped my retreat and stared at him apprehensively, almost weak with the colossal effort of having a conversation with him.

"That's good." He smiled and it was a real, genuine smile; he looked like a different person. It reminded me of the photos I'd seen in the album of when he and my mom had first had me. I had the inexplicable urge to tell him all about riding Quarry and how wonderful it felt to be riding. I opened my mouth, but before I could speak, a shadow passed over his face. He frowned and rubbed a hand over his eyes in exhaustion, shoulders slumping.

"Good, good," he said vaguely, picking up his tablet and gazing tiredly at the screen. I knew my chance to bond with him was gone. I faded back into the safety of the kitchen without another word.

Marion tried again to make conversation once we were eating together at the table. "So, how was your trip, Bruce? You're home early."

"The new site in Belize was fine. They had some good core samples and I think we'll make some money there," he said tiredly, "but there was a little...well, a bit of an issue at the Blind

River site. Some yahoos blaming us for contaminating their water supply or some nonsense; it's all complete garbage, of course. It caused a bit of trouble for our home office here. I'll have to go to Vancouver tomorrow and sort everything out. I won't bore you with the details now."

I looked up with interest, Susan and Thomas's dad was is in charge of the office in Vancouver and the smaller, satellite WorldCor office in Victoria while my dad was away. I wondered if they'd heard anything about this.

Marion said something vaguely sympathetic and we lapsed into silence again.

When we were finished, I rose to clear the dishes so I could escape to the kitchen when my dad cleared his throat again.

"Astrid, I want you to know I didn't give your bow away."

I looked up in surprise, almost dropping the plate in my hands. I caught it just in time to avoid another scene, my face flushing red in embarrassment.

"I'm sorry I gave you that impression. I've been under a lot of stress lately and I may have overreacted to your incident at the party. It's in our storage unit downtown, and I'll make sure we fetch it for you when you're ready to start competing again."

Despite my discomfort, my face broke into a smile. "Really, Dad? That's great. Thank you."

His answering smile was almost shy, but then his phone rang and his face drooped as he pulled it out and stared at the display. "I have to take this," he said abruptly, disappearing in the direction of his office.

Marion squeezed my shoulder gently and together we

finished clearing the table and loading the dish washer.

I went to bed that night feeling lighter than I'd been in a long time.

Chapter Thirteen

My dad left for Vancouver the next afternoon, and later, he called to say he had to fly out to the WorldCor office in Texas right away and that he wouldn't be home to say goodbye. I found myself not quite so relieved that he was gone this time. I didn't exactly miss him, but it was close. He'd been decent the whole time he'd been home; he'd had breakfast with us and even talked about visiting the stable with me when he got back.

Marion sighed when she hung up the phone with him and went right into her office. "Syun," she said anxiously, "it's Marion. Do you know what's going on?" That's all I heard before the door shut.

I tiptoed down the hall and stood outside the office for a moment trying to eavesdrop, but the door was too thick for me to hear anything useful. Part of me wanted to barge in there and make her tell me what was going on; if they filled me in then maybe I could even help. But in the end, I went back to my room. Sometimes there were times when I chose to skip being an adult.

By the next week, my arm was so much better that I could

brush and saddle all the horses except for dangerous Folly. I still needed help with the leg wraps and some of the bridling, though. I was still wary of those big, white teeth, and I only felt fully comfortable around Quarry.

"Hey, Hilary, could you help me with Ferdinand, please? He doesn't want to put his bridle on."

No answer. She'd gone to one of the back pastures with Liza to fix a broken fence board and still hadn't returned. I sighed and looked up at the big horse who was staring at me innocently. "Come on, Ferdi, we've done this before. Just put your head down."

Ferdi tossed his nose up and down a few times and then lifted his head in the air, sticking it straight up, high above my head. There was no way I could hope to get the bridle on him like that.

"Um, do you need any help, Astrid?"

I spun around. I'd been so busy I hadn't even heard Rob and Artimax moving up behind me. Rob was staring at me with an amused expression on his face.

"No," I said, then I looked up at Ferdi and sighed. "Actually, yes, please. He does this sometimes and I can't get his nose down. Hilary usually does this part for me."

"No, problem. Hold Arti for me for a sec. I'll get the big guy suited up." We exchanged horses and Ferdinand, that traitor, dropped his nose instantly into Robert's palm and nuzzled him as if he were a long lost friend. Rob stroked his neck and then quickly slipped the bridle over his head. "Good boy, buddy."

"Oh, good, you're here, Rob," Claudia said. "Astrid, why don't you untack Artimax and put him in Ferdi's stall for a bit. I need to borrow Rob for an experiment I'm working on."

"Uh, sure," I said, confused. I got Arti settled and then ran upstairs to the viewing lounge to see what they were up to.

"What the heck?" It was Rob up on Ferdinand, not Claudia and he was trotting around the ring on a loose rein, headed toward a series of poles that had been propped up on some blocks. They weren't very high but when Ferdi caught sight of them his ears pricked and he broke into a canter. I didn't see Rob touch the reins, but he sat up a little straighter and the big horse slowed his stride just a hair before popping over the poles one after another. Rob laughed and reached down to pat the big horse enthusiastically on the neck.

Claudia strode over to them, her face stretched in a wide smile. I couldn't hear what she was saying, but it was obvious she was happy.

"Hey, Astrid?" Liza called out. "Can you come get the laundry, please?"

I headed back downstairs thoughtfully, wondering about what I'd seen.

The jumps were gone by the time my lesson came around and then I was too involved with my own riding to ask about them. I'd been getting more and more relaxed and balanced on Quarry over this last week. I wasn't just a passenger anymore; I had learned to move Quarry from a walk to a trot and back down again by just using subtle adjustments to my weight and breathing, and by tightening or loosening my abdominal muscles. To my delight, Quarry responded me to as if he could read my mind. It was pure magic.

"Well, my dear," Claudia asked me after I'd been trotting happily around in a circle, "do you fancy trying a canter today?"

"Sure," I said, a flash of excitement sizzling in my belly.

Claudia made a soft kissing sound under her breath and Quarry broke into a gentle rolling gate. It was so smooth that I barely moved in the saddle. I could feel his powerful hind legs propelling us forward across the ground, but I didn't get jostled at all. I knew I was grinning from ear to ear, it felt like flying. I closed my eyes and held my arms out to the side; I felt invincible.

"Good," Claudia called, "breathe deep and sink into your center of balance. Remember, you are like water, no tight muscles."

Inhaling deeply, I relaxed my legs and hips even more until I was following the rocking motion.

"Good job, Astrid!" Claudia called. "Now, stretch up and invite him down to the trot. Think of him rounding his back up like a stretching cat when he makes that downward transition."

"Ow," I said, bouncing a few awkward steps when he dropped down to a trot.

"Pretty good," Claudia said, beaming at me with her hundred-watt smile. "You want to think of him always stepping *up* into his transitions, not down. That jarring happens when there is a disconnect between his hind and front legs. As if you stalled a car. Take a break and we'll practice a few more transitions."

Once I had my breath back we got work. Cantering was like gliding on skates across an icy pond. It was so fast and beautiful I wanted to cry. I could imagine cantering with Quarry through green pastures or along the beach, his hooves cutting through the surf; it was magical. But each time I was brought back to earth by him suddenly breaking into a spine shattering trot. I pitched forward; body tensed at the jarring change in speed, and I clutched the front of the saddle with a squeak of fear.

"Just go back to basics, Astrid," Claudia said. "Breath-work first, center yourself, relax, and stretch down. Remember your visualizations. The trot and the canter are not two separate things; they are just two steps in the same dance."

"Right," I muttered, grimacing as I careened up and down on the rock-hard saddle. I was going to be one big bruise tomorrow. Gradually, it worked, though. I sank into the leather and found the familiar old rhythm again. Up into the wonderful canter and then to the bone-jolting trot until finally, without even understanding *how*, I got it; seamlessly, the canter flowed into the trot and back up again. Like water flowing gently over rocks in a stream bed.

"Oh," I said, struggling with the vague concepts that were swirling around in my head. "I think I understand."

"You'll find that riding is only about fifty percent physical work, Astrid; the rest is mental, philosophical, maybe even spiritual work. You're beginning to scratch the surface." Claudia smiled up at me.

I slid to the ground and gave Quarry a big hug around his neck. "You're a good boy," I told him, "Thanks for helping me learn this riding stuff. I'm sorry when I flop all over the place, I hope I'm not hurting your back."

Claudia smiled. "You're not hurting him one bit, Astrid. You're progressing along very fast. Besides, he loves teaching new riders, especially when they praise him and give him carrots. You can see why it's important for the horse to have new riders stay on the lunge line, though, right? If you had had reins when you lost your balance, you would have pulled sharply on his mouth instead. That's why it's important to establish a good seat position and become a tactful dance partner before we introduce the reins."

"I'm not much of a dancer," I said slowly. "But I don't feel as clumsy on him as I do on the ground."

Caprice bounced along beside me as I led Quarry back to the barn, and today I could appreciate her enthusiasm. I was practically skipping with joy, too. There were no words to explain how spending time with this horse made me feel.

With a sharp bark, Cappy blew past me and ran up ahead to greet someone.

I stopped in surprise to see two familiar figures standing awkwardly in the barn aisle. "Susan?" I asked, confused.

Thomas appeared behind her, looking slightly uncomfortable. "Hey, Astrid," he said, flashing me his usual charming smile. The one calculated to make any girl within a twenty-foot radius melt like butter. "Whoa, that's a big horse. Do you really ride here?"

"Yes," I said slowly, trying to figure out what was different about him. "I'm riding and working here for the summer. You know, until my arm heals and I can get back to the range."

Thomas looked at the ground and sighed. "I'm still really sorry about that, Astrid. It was an accident."

"I know." I shrugged. "And it was my fault, too. So, I haven't really heard from you guys this summer. What are you doing here?"

I turned Quarry into the wash stall and started to pull his tack off. He nudged me with his nose, reminding me that he still needed his carrot.

"Hold on, big guy." I laughed, scratching him behind his ears.

"Can I pet her?" Thomas asked hesitantly. He stood close behind me, so close I could feel the heat radiating off his perfect skin. I could almost reach out and....

I stepped back so I could breathe. Something about Thomas still drew me toward him like a magnet, but not seeing him every day in school had lessened my obsession somehow; it made standing next to him just a little more bearable.

"Sure," I said, ducking to the side to put a little distance between us. "He's a boy, actually, but he's really friendly."

Thomas reached out and ran just the tips of his fingers over Quarry's velvety nose. "Wow, he's soft."

I smiled shyly at him. "He is. So, what's up, you guys?"

"Well," Susan shifted from foot to foot, her forehead crinkled with worry. "Sorry to show up here, Astrid. We wanted to ask you something in person just so that there was, you know, no trace of our conversation."

"What?" I said in disbelief "Why? That sounds like a spy movie."

"I know, we're probably paranoid, but this is serious. We were hoping you might know what's happening with WorldCor. Our parents aren't telling us anything, but our dad has been sleeping at the office for the last few days and we know he's really worried."

"I was going to ask you guys the same thing," I said slowly. "All my dad said was that something went wrong in Belize. Sorry, that's all I know."

They looked at each other and then turned back to me. "Did

he talk about closing the Vancouver office?" Susan asked hesitantly. "Did he talk about firing anyone?"

"No," I said, "of course not. Anyway, your dad's worked at WorldCor for years. He wouldn't be fired for nothing."

They shot each other a look again, like they were speaking telepathically. "Well, the Belize incident is looking like it's going to be pretty big," Thomas said hesitantly. "A lawsuit would be really hard on the company right now, especially with the mining industry in such a slump."

"What slump, what lawsuit?" I asked, bewildered.

"See"—Susan nudged her brother—"I told you she wouldn't know anything. No offence, Astrid."

"*What* lawsuit?" I asked again, turning to Thomas. "Tell me."

"Oh, it's this whole rainforest thing," Thomas said, waving a hand dismissively. "Apparently, they were chasing a seam and a whole bunch of mercury and some other stuff got into the water supply. Some people got sick, and now they want to be paid off. It's been on the news and everything. You didn't hear about it?"

I shook my head. "No. Nobody told me anything. I can ask Marion about it tonight."

"Thanks, Astrid. Can you contact us if you find out anything? I mean, about any changes happening with the Vancouver office?"

"Sure," I said quietly. "No problem."

"Great, well," Thomas shifted his feet and looked at Susan. "I guess we're out of here, then. We should really do something together before summer's over, Astrid. You play professional badminton, right? My dad has a membership at this great club; you should come have a game with us and show us how it's done."

"Thanks, I have never played badminton in my life, unless you count in gym class. I'd be happy to meet you at the range for some archery, though."

Thomas stared at me blankly and then shook his head, laughing. "Right, archery, I knew it was something like that. Anyway, we'll see you around, Astrid. Don't be a stranger."

"Okay." I gave Quarry his carrot and got to work on getting him clean. Even though I wanted to, I didn't turn to watch them leave.

That night, I didn't ask Marion about the lawsuit. She'd been holed up in her office almost since dinner and every time I passed by the door she was deep in another phone conversation. I decided to leave it for another night.

Instead, I rifled through my drawers until I found an unused bow string lodged in the back; one my father had overlooked. Without hesitating I strung my old bow. I ran my finger along the string, that old feeling of familiar excitement thrumming through my veins. Eagerly, I took it out to the patio to practice.

This added a whole new element to my practice session; instead of pulling back an imaginary string, I pulled the real one back slowly, testing my shoulder against the weight, and then gently relaxed the string until it was level again. There was an initial sharp twinge right at the end of my collar bone, but after a moment, the pain faded and I tried again. I couldn't actually do a proper release without an arrow; I didn't want to risk hurting my only bow by dry-firing. So I inhaled and drew the string back carefully, held my breath, and then slowly moved the string back to its initial position on the exhale.

Then I did the whole thing over again in slow motion until I could hardly lift the bow. I smiled in satisfaction; my shoulder hurt, but it wasn't unbearable. If I did this every night, I would soon be strong enough to start practicing for real again.

Chapter Fourteen

I came in after my lesson the next day to find the barn ladies huddled around Pender in the tack room. She was sitting on one of the tack trunks, her face blotchy with tears.

"Don't let him push you around," Ally was saying. "You're entitled to have a life of your own, too."

"But he's sort of right," Pender replied and sniffed. "Horses are so expensive and we have three boys to put through college in a few years. He says we can't really justify me being so extravagant. Plus, time at the barn is time spent away from the kids."

"Oh, pshaw," Sadie said. "Maybe if he spent less time at the golf course...."

"I don't want to give up riding," Pender said. "I love it here and I love Rabbit. We didn't even get to go to our first show yet. I know Claudia says it's all about the artistic process, but I think it would be fun to get out at least once to see what it's like."

"Shhh"—Ally looked nervously over her shoulder toward the tack room door—"We don't talk about showing here, Pender. Claudia says—"

"Oh, for heaven's sake, Ally." Sadie put her hands on her hips. "Competition is not the devil's playground. I'm pretty sure we're not going to destroy our horses with one little event. It would be good for them to get out and do something interesting. Besides, Claudia used to show all the time before…well, you know."

"It might be my last hurrah." Pender sniffed. "Before I have to sell Rabbit…."

"Right, nobody blames you for wanting to show him just one time," Sadie added.

"Keep your voices down," Ally hissed. "You know Claudia isn't up to dragging us to a horse show. She'll think we're ungrateful."

"Who's talking about showing?" Claudia appeared in the doorway, her face white and pinched. She'd felt a little sick during the end of my lesson and had had to cut it short so she could go to her office to grab her medication. Now she looked positively deathly.

Ally stared at her, wide-eyed like a deer caught in headlights, and Sadie looked concerned. Pender just buried her face in her hands and sobbed even harder.

"What on earth is wrong with Pender?" Claudia said, moving over to her side and wrapping an arm around her heaving shoulders.

"It's Raaaaabit," was all Pender managed to get out.

"That waste of space husband of hers thinks she spends too much time and money at the barn," Sadie explained. "He wants her to spend more time at home with the kids."

"They're not even home most of the time." Pender hiccupped. "They have summer camps all day. He just doesn't want me to have anything of my own."

"It's on her "bucket list" to go to at least one horse show, Claudia. And honestly, I think we could all pitch in and make a day of it. You wouldn't need to do a thing."

"Oh, really?" Claudia asked wryly, looking around the faces in the tack room. Her gaze fell on me. "And what about you, Astrid, would you want to drag Quarry to a show and make him perform in front of other people?"

"Not if he didn't want to," I said slowly, looking around at the others for help. I glanced upward to the pictures decorating the tack room wall—almost all of them were of Quarry and Claudia showing all over the world. In every single picture, he looked like he had a big horsey smile on his face. "But, I love archery competitions and for me it's about having fun, not about winning. I just like shooting that much. I'll bet Quarry feels the same way."

"Oh well, you got me there." Claudia laughed. "Quarry did love showing, and I bet the old goat would enjoy getting back out there again. There is a lot of good to be had gaining show experience; it can enhance your partnership with your horse…or it can ruin it. It's your choice."

She got a far off look on her face, her mouth curved into a smile. "All right, ladies. If you really have your hearts set on it then we'll find a local schooling show for you to enter. You'll have to memorize your own tests, though, and help each other out. I want you all to act as a team and everyone takes turns calling for each other. Understand? And you always put those horses first. The second any of these horses isn't enjoying their job anymore, we come right home. Understand?"

"Yes." All three ladies were grinning like little kids.

Sadie's little fox-face was transformed by her smile. "Come on, ladies," she said. "Let's go find some suitable show dates." She grabbed Pender's arm, and she and Ally dragged her upstairs to the lounge to look at the laptop.

I stayed behind. "Claudia, did you mean for me to show Quarry, too? I haven't even used my reins or stirrups yet."

"You're actually further along than you think, Astrid," she said, rubbing her temples as if she had a headache. "If I have to hitch up the trailer and get up at 5:30 in the morning for a show then I may as well take everyone. It'll be a learning experience for you. Don't worry, we won't rush your training. If you're not ready to ride, then you can just help out the other riders."

Liza came into the tack room for her saddle, looking bewildered. "What are all the barn ladies squealing about, Claudia? It sounds like a party up there."

"We're going to a show," I blurted before Claudia could speak.

"What, who? Everyone?" Liza asked in astonishment. "Claudia, are you sure you feel up to it?"

"I'm not ready for the grave yet," Claudia said wryly. "You should take Folly." She fell silent at Liza's suddenly stony expression.

"She's not ready," Liza said firmly. "She's just beginning to trust humans, *just* beginning, Claudia. It's going to be a long time before she's ready to perform again. If ever."

Claudia and Liza locked eyes as if they were having a staring contest and finally, it was Claudia who looked away.

"She's your project, Liza," Claudia said with a shrug. "You do what's best for her. Take Marcus to the show then. It will be good for him to get out and gain some exposure."

"How about I just help out this time?" Liza said. "With this rowdy bunch showing, I think you're going to need some assistance on the ground."

I followed Liza into the aisle and was surprised to see that it was Folly she was tacking up, not Marcus. "Wow, you're going to ride *her*?" I asked skeptically. "Didn't you just tell Claudia that she didn't trust humans?"

"She doesn't," Liza said shortly. "Not completely, but she's trying hard. This is the next step in the plan. She's a well-trained horse, Astrid. She just has an attitude problem. But I think I'm getting through to her. Haven't you noticed a change?"

Come to think of it, I hadn't heard Folly banging on her stall door, or kicking things, or squealing in that irritated way in a long time. I could fill her grain bucket in her stall without losing an arm. Maybe she *was* improving.

"Are you becoming a nice girl, Folly?" I cooed to her like I would to Quarry.

Instantly, her head came up and she flattened her ears against her head, glaring at me with her upper lip curled back in a sneer.

"Easy, girl," Liza soothed, running a hand down her neck. Folly shot me one last look and then allowed her ears to come forward. She nuzzled Liza and made a low grunting noise under her breath as if she were talking.

Liza smiled and kissed the mare right between her eyes. "Good girl, Folly. Now let's hit the trail."

"You're not riding her in the ring?" I asked, envisioning Liza lying out in the woods trampled by this crazy horse. "Is that safe?"

"She hates the ring. My mission is to find all the things she enjoys and give them to her, see if she changes her mind about humans being bad and life being not worth living. And, right now, I think it's working."

Liza put on her helmet and walked Folly out the big front doors. She swung up easily into the saddle and trotted off down the road without looking back.

* * * * *

I waited until after dinner to ask Marion about riding in the show. "Everyone's going to pitch in and help out," I said as convincingly as I could, "so it would be letting down my team if I didn't go and support them."

Marion laughed tiredly and shook her head. "Of course you can go, Astrid. I mean, I should probably ask your father if it's okay, but he's pretty focused on everything going on at work right now, so I think we can just tell him when he gets back. I don't think he'd mind anyway. He'd be proud of you."

"Maybe," I said quickly, "but I'm just a real beginner. He wouldn't want to see me show until I'm a little more polished. And, at the rate I'm going, that might be never."

Marion frowned. "Astrid, he's not that obsessed with winning." She stopped and frowned. Maybe she was remembering all the tournaments where he'd paced anxiously on the sidelines or yelled at my opponents. "Anyway, if you don't mind an audience, I would love to come. I could even help."

"Thanks, Marion!" I said, leaning over to give her a hug. "That would be great."

"Oh, I almost forgot to tell you, I have an early meeting

tomorrow down in Victoria, so I won't be able to drive you to work in the morning. Hilary's family will pick you up first thing and then drop you off tomorrow night."

"Sure, no problem. I'll make us dinner when I get home."

"Thanks, Astrid," she said. "I know I can always count on you."

* * * * *

When I woke up the next morning, Marion was already gone and I had the whole luxurious condo to myself. I managed to find a freezer-burned package of bagels buried deep under the frozen fruit and made myself an illegal breakfast of carbs topped with a thick layer of natural peanut butter. I made coffee and then padded out to the deck in my pajamas, curling up on one of the softer patio chairs and slowly listening to the sounds of the city waking up underneath me.

Finally, it was time for me to get dressed and meet Hilary downstairs.

"Morning, Dom," I said to my favourite doorman. He'd been working security in the lobby for as far back as I could remember, and his once black hair was now snowy white. I used to see him every day when I'd take the bus to the range and had to leave through the front doors. Lately, we'd been just bypassing the lobby by riding the elevator down to the garage.

"Morning, Sunshine," he said. "Almost healed up from your accident?"

"Almost. I'm taking a break from archery and working at a stable right now. I never thought I'd like horses, but I really do."

"Horses, huh? Sounds fancy. My granddaughter asked for

riding lessons for her birthday. She's completely horse crazy; she has posters of them all over her room. The family's thinking of chipping in to get her a session at horse camp. We're just worried she'll become hooked and want her own pony."

"I can see that happening." I laughed. "They're addictive."

Hilary's car pulled up front and I hurried out to meet her. "Bye, Dom, and good luck with your granddaughter."

"Good morning," Hilary's mom said over her shoulder as I slid in the backseat beside Hilary. "We stopped at Tim Hortons to get breakfast, so I hope you're hungry. There's a coffee there for you, too."

"Wow, thanks," I said, unwrapping my egg and bacon sandwich, and inhaling the rich sweet smell of carbs, meat, and melted cheese. It was better than Christmas. I took a big bite and then swilled some coffee to wash it down. Delicious.

"We bought maple pecan Danishes, too, for dessert," Hilary said around a mouthful of food.

Hilary's mom laughed. "I don't know if you're supposed to have dessert after breakfast, my daughter. How about you save those for lunch. You can share them with everyone at the barn."

"Fine," Hilary sighed, rolling her eyes at me. I figured she'd attack those Danishes the second her mom's car left the driveway.

The barn was strangely silent when we got there. Even though the horses knew it was feeding time, they didn't nicker and bang the walls with their hooves like they usually did.

"Oh, they have their hay already," Hilary said, peering into Jerry's stall. She looked over at me in confusion. "I wonder if Liza came early and got everything done."

"Good morning girls." Liza stepped out from the feed room pushing the wheelbarrow full of grain buckets. "No lessons today, I'm afraid. Claudia got called to the mainland for a doctor's appointment. She's been on the waitlist for this procedure a long time, so she had to cancel everything when they called her last night."

"Procedure?" Hilary said slowly. "Doctors?"

"She didn't say what it was exactly, Hilary, but she said it was no big deal and not to worry. Jerry needs a day off from riding anyway. I think that once our chores are done, we should pack some snacks and take them for a hike. Folly loves to get out in the woods."

"You mean a trail ride, not a hike." Hilary laughed.

"No, I mean a real hike where you do the work instead of making them carry you. Give them a real day off."

Hilary raised her eyebrows. "Sounds like a lot of extra work to me," she said, laughing, "but fine, I'll give it a shot."

I thought it sounded fun, actually, and it was the perfect day for it. The morning air was still cool and the early sunlight filtered through the trees in the most beautiful way. Mist rose off the bottom fields and it looked like something out of a painting.

We turned all the horses out except Folly, Quarry, and Jerry, and finished cleaning the stalls and prepping the feed for dinner time. Liza had packed sandwiches and bottles of water, and we grabbed apples and carrots that we could share with the horses. Hilary added her bag of Danishes, and I had a few sesame snacks to throw in as well. Liza threw everything into her backpack.

We brushed the horses until they shone, but just as we were about to leave, a truck came rumbling up the driveway. "Oh no,"

Liza said. "I totally forgot to call Robert about his lesson. I thought I'd remembered everyone. Shoot."

She went out to the driveway to meet them and we could hear laughter, and then Rob came into the aisle leading Artimax by the halter. Behind him, his horse trailer was unhooked and the truck drove away.

"Hey, ladies," he said with a smile. "Do you mind some company on your hike? My dad had to take the truck to town for a few hours. Looks like you're stuck with me."

"Of course not," Hilary said. "It will be fun."

I just smiled at him shyly, suddenly not sure of what to say.

We finished grooming then clipped lead ropes to their halters and headed out the big barn door and down the laneway past the rows of grazing horses. Quarry followed me as gently as a lamb, and Artimax looked around at the world with a cheerful expression on his face. But Folly didn't know what to think of this strange new adventure; she had her ears pinned as if Liza was dragging her off to do something unpleasant and kept sending dirty looks to all the other horses.

Jerry bounced along on his toes beside Hilary, his eyes wide with excitement, swiveling his head around to look at everything.

"Back up, you big moose," Hilary said, pushing him out of her space, as he shoulder-checked her into a bush. "Stop crowding." She had to back him up a few times to get him to pay attention to her, but after that, he walked beside her excitedly, head bobbing and mane bouncing on his neck to the rhythm of his animated walk.

"Wow, this is *such* fun, Liza," Hilary said sarcastically. "Much better than riding."

"Give him a minute to settle down," Liza said with a laugh. "You'll see."

And he did settle down. His walk slowed to a normal pace, and Folly's face gradually lost that pinched, suspicious look; her ears came forward and she watched the world with guarded interest.

Liza knew where she was going; we headed past the rolling fields of grass, stopping now and then to let the horses graze on particularly tasty clumps of greenery, and followed a wide trail into the woods. At first, it was an open forest with young alders and poplars growing neatly on either side of the path, leaves fluttering in the light spring breeze. The ground was soft under our feet and sunlight filtered in, dappling the woods with flecks of yellow. I inhaled deeply; grateful to be spending the day out here. Quarry nudged my shoulder as if he was agreeing with me.

Gradually, the trees surrounding us grew taller and wider; the smaller poplars and alders gave way to stately cedar trees. As we moved deeper into the forest, they became progressively more ancient, trunks becoming wider and gnarled into twisting shapes. The temperature dropped and the woods became silent and dark; less sunlight made it through the thick canopy overhead and the little birds preferred the open, lighter forest over this dark, ancient one.

A shiver ran down my spine; I wasn't afraid exactly, but there was something powerful about this forest as if it were watching us silently as we passed. The ground was spongy and the horse's hooves left prints where they had sunk in the forest floor.

"Wow," Hilary whispered, tilting her head back and looking up at the gigantic trees. "This is real, old growth forest. I didn't even know there was any left around here."

"Yeah, it's Claudia's little secret. When she bought this farm, it came with a land covenant stating that the woods could never be cut down. Some of these trees are thousands of years old. Even if she sells the farm, they'll still be protected."

"Good," Robert said, "we need to protect land like this. All these big businesses only care about making money no matter how much of the planet they destroy. We have to stand together."

I gulped, wondering if he knew about the WorldCor lawsuit. What would he say if he knew my dad was involved in some sort of environmental disaster?

We walked in silence for a while, staring in wonder at the rich canopy of green overhead. Strands of lime-coloured moss hung on the ancient trees, and vines had wound around many of the trunks. It felt like we were the first people to hike these trails in centuries. Even the horses seemed to walk more softly, as if they knew this was a special place.

Up ahead, we heard running water and soon, we broke into a sunny glade full of grass. A tiny waterfall trickled down from the rocks and fell into a meandering stream that wandered out of the clearing into the thick woods opposite us. There were a few old pieces of brick lying at one edge of the clearing and the remains of an old chimney lay on the grass.

"This was the original homestead," Liza told us, giving Folly a pat on the neck and allowing her to drop her head and graze. She sat down on a foundation stone and unzipped her backpack. "Time to have lunch and let these ponies take a break."

I sat down in relief; my feet were tired and my calves ached from all the hiking. Still, I was having fun. Holding lightly onto the end of Quarry's lead rope, I let him stretch down to tear at the lush grass. I caught the apple Liza tossed me and bit into it eagerly. I was so hungry I ate it in just a few bites and then dropped the core under Quarry's nose. His ears flicked forward as he found his apple and he bobbed his head up and down as he crunched, eyes half-closed in a satisfied expression.

Robert came and sat down opposite me, letting Quarry and Artimax sniff noses to say hello first. "Hey, how's your arm doing?" he asked quietly. "You're not in your sling anymore."

"No, it's so much better," I said around a bite of the sandwich Liza had handed me. "I've started to take lessons with Claudia, too."

"Great," he said with a smile. "That's really good news. Claudia is the best; you couldn't start your career with a better trainer. I wish I could take more lessons with her, but my dad wants me to focus on the jumping."

"Oh, you jump?" I said with interest, looking over at the well-muscled Artimax.

"Yeah, I do Eventing. That includes cross-country, stadium jumping and dressage; you know, the ultimate test of horse and rider. I actually like dressage best, but don't tell my dad." He shot me a grin and bit into his sandwich.

"Aren't you mad that you don't get to focus on the sport you really like?" I asked slowly.

He shrugged good naturedly. "I get to have my own horse and I don't have to pay for my own lessons…yet. I don't mind eventing; we have lots of fun. I just know that when I'm older, when I'm on my own, I'll probably focus on dressage. It's no big deal. My dad's great, just a little opinionated."

"Are all Mexican dads really strict?"

I regretted the words as soon as they left my mouth. It hadn't sounded so stupid in my head, but hanging there in the air between us, it sounded awful. As if I expected him to know what every Mexican dad was like. I wasn't sure if I sounded racist or just dumb. Heat prickled up my neck.

Rob choked on his food, coughing and spluttering so hard that he fell off the stone he sat on. He grabbed at his water bottle, tears running down his cheeks. "Mexican!" He wheezed, and I was a little relieved to see that he was doubled over with laughter, not choking to death. "Is that what you thought, Astrid?"

My cheeks burned with mortification. Liza and Hilary had turned to stare at us in astonishment, and I buried my face in my hands, tears springing to my eyes. I hadn't meant to sound insensitive, but apparently, that's what I'd done.

"I'm Coast Salish, Astrid." Robert snickered. "Specifically, Snuneymuxw, and I guess that means you're on my land."

I didn't look up and he bumped my shoulder. "Come on, Astrid. I'm kidding. We're all good. You just took me by surprise, that's all. Why on earth did you think I was from Mexico? Not that there's anything wrong with that. Mexico's great."

"I don't know," I said miserably. "Miranda said something about it at that stupid party. I guess it just stuck in my head."

"Oh, yeah, that girl you used to hang around with. Isn't she the one who was caught shoplifting? She's hardcore."

I looked up in surprise; I hadn't heard anything like that about Miranda, but before I could ask, he'd turned away to say something to Hilary.

Liza and Hilary started reminiscing with Robert about all the shows they'd been to while I finished my food quietly and just listened to them. Gradually my cheeks stopped burning and I was able to breathe again. I shot some side looks at Rob, but if he was mad at me he sure wasn't showing it.

As soon as I was done I stood up and led Quarry down to the stream so he could have a drink. He slurped the water up thoughtfully and then flicked his head up and down, splashing water in all directions. He finished by dribbling water through his teeth and sticking out his tongue, making me laugh.

"All right, you guys," Liza said, standing up to bring Folly to the stream. "Time for us to head out. We still have some chores to finish up.

She drew Folly over to a large chunk of foundation and sprang nimbly up on her bare back.

"Hey, no fair," Hilary said. "I thought we were supposed to be hiking…and what about your helmet?"

"Right, we won't tell Claudia about the helmet thing." Liza laughed. "It's just through the woods. I'll hop off when we get closer to home."

Hilary glowered and marched back toward the trail muttering something about safety. I waited until Liza moved Folly in behind Jerry before I quietly led Quarry over to the rocks.

"Good boy," I whispered. I had to jump a little to get up on him and then shimmy myself into place but, like the nice guy he was, he stood like a rock until I was in position. "Okay, Quarry," I said quietly, "walk on."

I laughed at the feeling of his plump back swaying underneath me without the barrier of a saddle. He was like riding a comfortable old couch. We caught up to Liza quickly. She shot a look over her shoulder and grinned, giving me a thumbs up sign. Hooves trotted up behind me and I turned to see Robert astride Artimax, his legs swinging loosely at the horse's side. He winked at me as he caught up. "I know, pretty ironic that the Native kid buys an appaloosa, right? Doesn't get much more stereotypical than that."

"Huh?" I said, wondering if he was making fun of me again.

"You know, the Nez Pierce were the ones who developed the whole Appaloosa breed. Don't you know your horse history yet, Astrid? What kind of horse-crazy girl are you?"

His eyes were smiling so I knew he was teasing.

"Not a very good one," I confessed, laughing despite myself. "I really know nothing except from my lessons and what I've studied in Claudia's books. I hadn't really even touched a horse before this summer."

"Oh," he said, "well, I never would have guessed. You must be a natural."

We sank into companionable silence after that and I gradually relaxed against Quarry's warm back. The sun filtered through the trees and I tilted my head back to take in the natural beauty surrounding me. It was my first trail ride, I marvelled, and I was doing it without a bridle or saddle, trusting Quarry to take care of me no matter what happened. He marched solidly along, chaperoning me through the woods. I stared up at the ancient canopy, inhaling the deep, rich smell rising up from the forest floor, feeling like I'd been transported back in time.

We came out of the old growth forest and into the poplar grove we'd passed through earlier. Soon Liza swung her leg over Folly's back and slid noiselessly to the ground and I did the same thing, landing with a soft thud on the earth. My heart was singing with joy; it had been one of the best things I'd ever experienced.

The horses seemed to feel the same way; when we got back, their ears flopped lazily to the side and they snorted happily when we turned them out into their pastures. Even Folly looked happy, all the tension drained out of her. She shook her head and gave me a companionable little bump on the arm with her nose as Liza led her past me.

"That's weird." Liza checked her phone messages and then frowned, forehead crinkled in worry as she listened. Finally, she sighed and stuffed the phone back in her pocket. "You're free agents tomorrow, girls. Claudia says she's cancelling lessons again tomorrow and she's not feeling well enough to socialize. She just wants to spend a quiet day at home with the horses, alone. I'll help her feed and clean out."

Hilary and I looked at each other in confusion and then back at Liza. "You have to clean the whole barn by yourself, though. That's a lot of work if Claudia's not feeling well."

"It's totally fine." Liza smiled. "Claudia just doesn't want to be around a lot of people when she's feeling so bad. I'll just go slow. These lucky horses won't know what to do with two days off in a row."

I smiled back at her, but couldn't help feeling uneasy. There was something lurking behind Liza's smile. She was worried and wasn't telling us.

We put the horses away with flakes of hay to munch on, and Rob brought a hay-net from his trailer so Artimax could snack while they waited for their ride home.

I slipped into Quarry's stall and ran my hands down his neck, practicing the techniques I'd learned from my Horse Massage book. After a few moments, he stretched his neck far out and gave a low snort of appreciation, closing his eyes in bliss as I hit a good spot.

"Is that something you learned from one of Claudia's books?" Robert was leaning in the open doorway, watching me curiously.

"Um, yeah, actually it is. I've been studying a horse massage book and practicing on some of the horses here. They love it."

"I can see that. I'd like to read it when you're done. If Claudia says it's okay, I mean. Artimax gets really tight just above his hips sometimes if he jumps too much. I'd like to find a way to help him."

"Sure," I said, "actually, I could teach you an easy technique right now if you like. I was showing it to Hilary on Jerry the other day. It's pretty simple."

"Thanks, that would be great." He moved aside so I could slip out of Quarry's stall and led me back to where his horse was standing.

I patted the big, spotted horse gently and then ran my hands over his back and hips. He didn't flinch when I used a little more pressure so he couldn't be suffering too badly. Still, he sighed deeply when I began to work his gluteal muscles, stretching out his neck and sticking his head up in the air.

"Yep, that looks like the spot." Rob laughed. He watched me for a few more minutes and then said, "Okay, let me try so I know what I'm doing when I get home."

I stood back and shook out my arm painfully; massaging horses was hard work. Robert stepped up and took over where I had left off. He was a good student and I only had to give him a few pointers before Artimax was again getting the massage of his life. Robert broke off laughing and gave the horse a good natured slap on the rump.

"Thanks, Astrid. I think that's really going to help him. Maybe you could show me more when I come for the next lesson."

"Sure," I said, suddenly feeling shy again. "Um, it looks like your ride is here. Guess I'll see you later."

He started to lead Artimax down the aisle and then paused, looking at me curiously. "Hey, if you give me your number I could text you when I know when my next lesson will be. Just so we make sure to meet up. Do you have your phone on you?"

"Ah, okay." I pulled my phone out of my back pocket and handed it to him so he could add his number. Then I told him mine, only stuttering a little. This was the first time a boy had ever asked for my number. I didn't know what to think.

He's just being friendly, you idiot, I told myself fiercely. *Didn't you learn anything by trailing around after Thomas like a lost puppy? Boys don't look at you that way.*

Still, it was nice to have made a new friend. I was definitely moving up in the world.

* * * * *

When I got home that night, Marion hadn't returned. I'd already decided to make us some spaghetti for dinner, so after grabbing a shower and a quick snack I started chopping the vegetables so I'd have everything prepped to throw in the frying pan when she walked in the door.

When she still wasn't home, I started to get nervous. It wasn't like her not to call if she was going to be late. I checked my cell and was surprised to see that I had five messages from Marion.

Oh, no, I forgot I turned off the ringer when I went riding. I quickly listened to the messages and was relieved to hear that she hadn't been in an accident or hospitalized or anything.

"Astrid," the first message said, "our board meeting is running late and they want to meet tomorrow as well. Would you be okay if I stayed down here one night and came back the next day? Maybe Hilary's parents could pick you up again."

The next few messages sounded more urgent, as if she was imagining my lying in a ditch somewhere unable to get to my phone. I quickly dialed her number

"Thank goodness you called, Astrid. I was just about to head home to make sure you were okay. Where on earth were you?"

"Sorry," I said, wincing at the worry in her voice. "I had my ringer off. Sure I'll be fine by myself for the night. I can catch up on my reading."

"Okay, sweetie, I'll be back by dinnertime tomorrow. Could you call Hilary and see if the Ahlbergs could give you a ride to work tomorrow?"

"Oh I don't have to…." I stopped before I could tell her that my work day had already been cancelled. An idea bloomed to life in my head. A whole day on my own stretched out in front of me. The possibilities were endless. "I mean, of course they'll drive me. I'll ask them as soon as I hang up."

"Thank you for understanding, darling. I'll make sure I bring you back a nice present from town."

"Oh, you don't need to do that, Marion," I said quickly. "See you tomorrow." I hung up, feeling guilty. There she was thinking about buying me presents when I was about to go behind her back and do something awful…or at least something she probably wouldn't approve of.

My next call wasn't to Hilary; it was to Miranda.

"Astrid?" Miranda's voice sounded distant on the phone, like a stranger's voice, "Wow, it's been a while. How are you?"

"Great," I said, getting to the point, "Miranda, I need to meet you at the range with your key. If I don't practice soon, I'm seriously going to go nuts."

Miranda was silent for a moment. "Is your shoulder better already?" she asked slowly. "That healed really quickly. Did you get your bow back?"

"I'm using my old one," I said impatiently. "It's not pretty, but it works. I'm going to have the whole day free tomorrow, but I don't have my key. Could you meet me there? It would be just like old times."

Another long silence. "Great. Just like old times." She sighed. "Um, sure. I guess so."

"Thanks so much, Miranda. Let's meet first thing tomorrow morning then. I don't work and Marion has to go to a meeting. I'll have a few hours. I just want to shoot a couple of arrows to see if I've lost my touch."

Miranda did not sound very excited at the thought of seeing me. Maybe she was picturing what my father would do if he caught us. There was no chance of that, though; he was safely in another country.

"Okay," she said finally. "I'll meet you at the gate at 8:00 then."

"Great," I answered. "It will be just like the old days."

Miranda didn't say anything else before she hung up. I stared at the phone in my hand for a long time before putting it back in my pocket.

Chapter Fifteen

The next morning, I leapt out of bed as soon as the alarm went off. I threw on some jeans and a t-shirt, and brushed my hair with lightning fast speed. I had to make every second count. I packed up my bow, my old string, arm guard and glove, and headed as fast as I could out the door. I didn't have my own arrows anymore, my dad had seen to that, but I was sure Miranda would let me use hers.

The elevator seemed to take forever going down, but finally, I reached the front lobby. It was paved with a pattern of dark and light slate tiles, and I was so excited I hopped to the door using only the dark tiles like I had when I was a kid.

The bus stop was only a couple of blocks away, and I almost danced through the sweet spring air with wings on my feet. I flashed the driver my bus pass and hopped on board, amazed that everything was going so smoothly. If it was this easy to sneak around why hadn't I done it before?

The bus ride to the outdoor range was about twenty minutes long, but the stop was right in front of the gates. I could already see Miranda waiting there, her arms crossed tightly over her chest and her red hair braided back from her face. She looked nervous and I wondered if she was afraid of being caught or was afraid to face me again after taking my spot at the training camp.

"Hey, Miranda," I said brightly, determined to be mend the rift that had opened up between us. "Thanks for meeting me here. I'm really missing shooting."

She bobbed her head a little and squinted at me, her mouth pulled back in a tight smile. "Sure thing, Astrid, I guess I kind of owe you for taking your place in camp."

"Not really," I said with a sigh. "I couldn't have taken the spot anyway; I'm glad you got it."

She bit her lip unhappily. "I guess so, but I still feel bad. Your dad was really scary when he told me to take it. I just sort of went for it."

"Yeah, he can be like that. But it's all good. Can we go shoot now? I don't have that much time."

"Right, of course." She fumbled with her key in the lock while I waited impatiently.

We walked in silence along the treed pathway that I'd known so well only months ago and I inhaled deeply, feeling the same peace settle in my bones that I had found when I was at the barn. It was funny that there were some places in the world that could make you feel more alive and some, like my condo sometimes, that could make you feel dead.

We came across the first set of targets. Plain circles mounted on wooden frames set side by side in a wooded clearing. I strapped on my arm-guard, fingers fumbling with the straps, and slipped on the glove that would protect my fingers from the bow string.

This is it, I thought, stringing my bow carefully. *I'm finally back where I belong.*

"Okay if I borrow a couple of arrows?" I asked. "My dad has mine stashed somewhere."

"Yeah, I guess so." Miranda took her time stringing her own bow, and I fairly danced in impatience waiting for her to hurry up. Didn't she know how important this was? Didn't she care?

When she finally held it out, I snatched the first arrow from her hand impatiently, feeling the cool carbon fibre length of it resting in my hand. For a second, I closed my eyes, my body going through the long familiar pattern of its own accord in one swift motion. Lift bow, nock arrow, inhale, sight, hold breath, exhale, release. I didn't have time to second guess myself. I stayed motionless as the arrow launched into space, drilling through the air until it plunged into the center of the target, burying itself into the red.

"You have got to be kidding," Miranda said incredulously beside me. "Seriously?"

"What?" I glanced over at her target to where her own arrow was sitting a few inches from the center.

"When did you last practice?" She demanded, grabbing my arm in a pincer-like grip. Her hand was shaking and her eyes had a wild look to them.

"Ow," I said, breaking her hold and rubbing the sore spot where her fingers had dug in. "What do you mean?"

Her chin jutted out in a hard line and tears sprang to her eyes. "Just answer the question, Astrid. When did you last freaking practice?"

I stepped away from her, alarmed by her fierce expression. "I don't know; it's been a couple months, Miranda, but I do exercises with the bow every night. And I do yoga now. Maybe that helped?"

She balled her fists together at her sides. "Maybe it *helped*," she mimicked angrily, "well, it didn't bloody hurt, did it? Is there nothing that can stop you, Astrid? You don't practice, you don't go to the gym, you eat like a whale, and you get everything you want handed to you on a silver platter. You're spoiled rotten and you don't even have a clue how good you've got it. It's not fair. It's not fair at all!"

She gripped the lower limb of her bow in both hands, knuckles white, glaring at me like she was about to start swinging. "You know what, Astrid. I *hate* you!" Her face twisted in rage and she swung the bow back over her shoulder.

I ducked instinctively, but instead of clobbering me, she let out a guttural scream and launched it as far as she could, not even flinching when it ricocheted off the ground, bouncing wildly end over end until it landed on the pathway with a clatter.

"Miranda." I stared at her in horror. Bows like that were crazy expensive, and Miranda's parents had had to scrimp and save to get it for her. It had been drilled into all our team members from the beginning to always respect our equipment. Always. She'd lost her mind.

"Oh, shut up, Astrid. What does it matter anyway, now? Don't you see, I'm no good? I can practice and practice until I'm blue in the face, but I will never, ever be half the archer you are. Don't you understand how much that kills me? How terrible it is to be friends with you? Astrid, this is the only thing I've ever wanted in my life. I just don't see how you can take this from me."

I stared at her open mouthed, trying to take in what she was saying. For some reason, my thoughts turned to Pender and how Claudia had said she wasn't really a naturally gifted rider, but she still showed up at the barn every single day, even though she and Rabbit had to work hard for everything. There were lots of other riders who had more money, talent, and fancier horses, but Claudia had said that in the end it would be Pender who succeeded because of all the hard work she put into her riding.

I wanted to tell Miranda that a Silver medal at the BC Games was hardly failing, and that her career was just starting, and that if she wanted it bad enough she would make it happen, but as soon as I opened my mouth to speak, she held up a shaking hand. "Don't, just don't. Astrid, there's nothing you can say."

She turned on her heel and marched away, her back stiff and her hands clenched at her sides. She didn't look back when I called her name.

Sighing, I walked over and pulled her discarded bow out of the shrub it had become lodged in and brushed it off carefully. There were some scratches on the upper limb, but other than that it looked undamaged. I set it gently on one of the wooden benches that lined the pathway. I looked down at her abandoned quiver and felt my lower lip began to tremble. It would be hard to erase the memory of the look of hatred on her face; only my dad had ever looked at me that way. I'd thought Miranda was my friend.

I reached down into her discarded quiver and slowly drew out another arrow, running my fingers over the soft feathered fletching at the end until I'd calmed down. I stood up and nocked my arrow into my old bow, and carefully aimed at the plain target in front of me. The arrow sung through the air, burying itself in the middle of the target with a satisfying *thunk.* I drew out another arrow, and then another and another. I kept shooting until my shoulder throbbed, and I knew I'd probably pushed it too far. Slowly I walked down to the target and pulled my arrows one by one, feeling calmer.

"Astrid?"

"Earl!" I spun around and was across the grass and into his open bear hug before the word was even had even left my lips. Earl had been like a father to me for the last three years, and I'd had no idea how much I'd missed him.

"Good to see you, girl," he said, grinning down at me as he ruffled my hair and gave my shoulder a good-natured slap. "Does your father know you're here?"

"Nope." I shook my head and grinned back at him. "I snuck down here with Miranda, but my time's almost up. I have to be back before noon just in case Marion comes home early. Oh, I'm so glad to see you, Earl. I've missed this place so much, you have no idea."

Earl's smile faded and he put a hand on my shoulder. "You've had it rough, kid. Any idea if you'll be back this fall?"

"I really hope so," I said. "My dad's been a bit nicer lately, and he told me that my bow is in storage; he didn't give it away, after all. I've been practicing every night off my balcony, too."

"What?" Earl's face paled. "Astrid, you could kill someone...."

"Not with real arrows, Earl." I rolled my eyes. "I'm not a complete idiot. I've just been going through the motions. I think it's helping me keep my edge."

Earl visibly relaxed. "Yep, that's what a lot of sports

psychologists say; visualization is just as important as physically practicing. Your brain can't tell the difference from when you pretend to shoot and when you really shoot. That's why it's important to always be positive in what you visualize. I have a book I can lend you on the science behind it if you like."

"That would be great, Earl, thanks. I think Miranda should read it, too. She was real scary earlier, Earl. She sort of went crazy and threw her bow. She said she hates me and that she thinks it's my fault she's not winning."

Earl shook his head and stooped down to pick up Miranda's abandoned gear from the bench. "She's been nursing that grudge for a long time, Astrid. She's always been jealous of you, but I'd hoped she'd outgrow it as her own talent developed. One day, I hope she figures out that it's her own anger and insecurity getting in the way of her success. She has talent, but has not developed the mental fortitude that it takes to be on top. But, enough about the heavy stuff, what have you been up to?"

As we walked to the gate, I filled him in on my grounding and my work at the barn and the lessons. I told him all about Quarry and Claudia, and how I'd started practicing yoga twice a day. There was so much to say and so little time that my words kept tripping over themselves in my effort to get it all out.

When we reached the bus stop, Earl laid a hand on my shoulder gently. "Good to see you back here, Astrid. Next time, don't be so much of a stranger. You are welcome here anytime and there is always a place for you."

Tears welled up in my eyes and I brushed them away impatiently. "I'll be back," I assured him, "this place is home to me."

I waved to him from the bus window and then sank back into

my seat, suddenly aware of the burning in my shoulder and arm. I would have to ice it tonight or it was going to hurt at the barn tomorrow. I looked down at my watch and frowned. It was much later that I'd expected, and there was a chance that Marion would be home by the time I got there. I would have to figure out a way to explain it to her.

I walked the last couple of blocks to our building and pushed slowly through the doors to the lobby. "Hey, Astrid!" I looked up to see Dom standing by the concierge desk. He eyed my bow and whistled under his breath. "You all healed up now, kiddo? Back to training?"

"Um, not exactly," I whispered, looking around furtively to make sure we were the only ones in the lobby. "I'm still technically grounded from the range."

He raised an eyebrow and then sent me a wink. "Gotcha, okay, my lips are sealed." He made an exaggerated motion of sealing his lips and throwing away the key and waved me to the elevator. I climbed on board and pushed the button for the twelfth floor about a hundred times to make the thing move faster. It slid upwards smoothly and I hastened to my front door and slid inside.

I was lucky. Marion wasn't home and in fact, she didn't get home until just before dinner and she was too tired to pay much attention to me other than to thank me for making supper and to give me my present—a silver necklace with a little blue topaz horse pendant.

"Oh, Marion, I love it," I said, burning with guilt that I'd lied to her. "You really, really didn't have to get me anything. But, thank you so much."

I snuck a bag of peas from the freezer when she wasn't looking and snuck off to bed as soon as I could. I popped the last pill in my pain-med supply and fell into an uneasy sleep, the bag of peas slowly numbing the pain in my throbbing shoulder.

Chapter Sixteen

The next morning, I had to down another couple ibuprofen to make the pain in my arm subside to a dull throbbing ache. If Marion noticed me dragging myself around she didn't say anything. She was unusually quiet until we'd reached the car.

"Astrid," she said softly, "I received a phone call from Miranda yesterday."

I froze, icy fear clawing at my belly and tears stinging my eyes. Why did Miranda hate me so much?

I cleared my throat about a dozen times before I could trust myself to speak. "What did she say?" I asked in a small voice.

"She was looking for your father; she thought it was his number. She said she wanted to thank him again for giving her the spot at training camp, and for letting you come out and shoot with her at the range yesterday."

I shook my head in disbelief, unable to believe Miranda would stoop so low, if it had been my father's cell he would have killed me, he would have driven over my bow with his car and then literally killed me.

"Did you go to the range yesterday, Astrid?"

I nodded miserably.

"Is that why you're in so much pain today? Did you overdo it?"

I nodded again, tears pressing at the backs of my eyes.

"We'll give it a few days to rest, and if it's not better by the middle of the week, we'll have to make an appointment to have it looked at. There's a reason you're supposed to rest."

"I know," I whimpered, staring down at my hands. "I'm sorry."

"Are you sorry for sneaking out?"

I was about to say yes, to say anything necessary to get out of trouble, but the words wouldn't leave my mouth. I wasn't sorry, even with the pain I was glad I'd gone. The range was home to me and seeing it again, even once, had filled me with hope and courage. I turned to look at Marion and slowly shook my head.

"I'm sorry if you're disappointed in me, and I'm sorry I didn't tell you I was going, but I'm not sorry I went there."

"I see." She nodded and didn't say anything else until we reached the barn. Instead of leaving me at the barn entrance, she parked the car carefully and turned off the ignition.

"Let's see this horse of yours," she said, turning to look at me. Before I could react she'd opened her car door just as Caprice appeared out of nowhere and leapt onto Marion's legs, barking and prancing.

"Caprice, down!" I said, throwing open my car door and moving to Marion's rescue. I rushed around the car to pick the little dog up but, to my surprise, Marion didn't look upset.

"It's okay, I don't mind," she said, patting Caprice's head softly.

Caprice sprang away and stood on her hind legs and pirouetted in a small circle, showing off and barking her high-pitched bark.

"You're such a pretty, smart dog," Marion crooned to her, "yes, you are." The dog barked again and pounced on Marion with her front paws like a cat.

I stared at them in amazement. Marion, who normally hated contact with any hint of dirt or germs, practically had her face buried in Caprice's fur and she was actually laughing.

"Oh, Astrid, she's such a lovely little dog." Marion followed me down the aisle with Caprice trotting at her heels. There was no sign of Claudia, so why was her dog here?

The horses nickered excitedly as we passed, pushing their noses against the bars of their stalls. "Soon guys," I told them, "I'm right here." But where was Claudia?

I found her in the hay stall, struggling with the hay nets. Her face looked pale and strained.

"Claudia, what are you doing here? Where's Liza?"

"Oh, Astrid, thank goodness you're here. I told Liza she could sleep in today and Hilary is at her soccer game, but really, I underestimated how sick I'd feel after treatment. Would you be comfortable feeding and putting the horses out yourself?"

"Of course," I said, trying not to think of all those hay nets needing to be filled and the hungry horses waiting to be fed. It was going to take me forever to do by myself.

"Can I help?" Marion asked from the door to the hay room. She was holding Caprice cradled upside down in her arms like a baby and the little dog was looking up into her face adoringly. I couldn't believe she was actually holding an animal. She was morphing into a completely different person.

I shook my head doubtfully. "It's pretty dusty in here, and your clothes will get all messy."

Marion looked around carefully and then set Caprice gently on the ground. "I think I can handle it, Astrid. Show me what you need me to do."

Between the two of us we got the horses fed, watered, and the buckets scrubbed. Claudia found gloves and a dust-mask for Marion to wear so she wouldn't have to breathe in too much hay and get her manicure completely destroyed with dirt. I was so thankful that she'd been there to help me.

I decided to wait for Liza to arrive before I started on stalls. Claudia reappeared from her office when we were done, looking a little less pale. "I've cancelled lessons for today, but I think I have just enough in me for one. Tack up Quarry, Astrid, and we'll show Marion what you've been working so hard on."

"Really?" She didn't have to tell me twice. I brushed and tacked up Quarry quickly; hands trembling with excitement. This was the first time anyone was going to see me ride and I wanted to be perfect.

I climbed onto Quarry from the mounting block, and settled myself quickly in the saddle as Claudia clipped the lunge line to Quarry's halter.

Quarry moved into a choppy walk that was much different than his usual marching gait. I frowned, wondering why things didn't feel quite right. He felt changed somehow, stiff and clumsy, which was not like him at all.

"Remember to breathe, Astrid. Start with your breathing and

then visualize yourself riding loose and free. Can you feel how stiff you are?"

I looked at her in surprise. "Me? It's Quarry who's stiff."

She shook her head. "A horse is a reflection of his rider, Astrid. Let's see what happens when you're relaxed and supple."

I took in deep breathes, stretching my legs and shoulders and arms, letting the tension drain away. I felt myself sink deeper into the saddle and suddenly Quarry felt like his old self again. His hind legs propelled me forward smoothly and we moved together as a cohesive unit, like a centaur. A smile lit my face, and I heard Claudia laugh.

"Told you," she said lightly. "Now move gracefully into the trot."

We spent the next half an hour working on upward and downward transitions and then Claudia asked us to halt. "So, today we're going to build on the seat aides we'd touched upon last week. Ask Quarry to move forward into a trot and then you're going to ask him to gently spiral in toward me as if I were the center of a curved seashell. Does that make sense?"

"I think so," I said. "I'm just going to make the circle gradually smaller until I reach you, right?"

"Exactly. Keep him moving forward on the circle, and gradually move him toward me. Use your eyes to find a smaller circle and take it slow."

I waited until I'd relaxed into Quarry's trot rhythm before adjusting my gaze slightly to move onto a smaller circle. Without hesitation, Quarry's body moved in that direction. I trotted one full lap before looking in again for an even smaller circle. This time Quarry's butt swung out so he was partly facing Claudia but, even moving sideways, he somehow managed to keep trotting.

Claudia laughed. "That was a little too much. Adjust your position and invite him back out to the circle. Remember that his hind legs will follow your hip position and his shoulders will follow your shoulders so direct your hips where you want to go."

Right. I nodded and sent Quarry smoothly back out. This time I was more careful about how I asked him and gradually we spiralled in toward Claudia. By the time we reached her, we were in such a tight circle that Quarry was practically trotting in place. He sank down on his hind quarters, his powerful hind legs taking his weight and his front end danced lightly, rhythmically, in the air. With a thrill of excitement, I realized that we were actually doing a piaffe; we were one step away from him rising up into a levade, one of the first upper level movements of the Spanish Riding School. I was really riding.

Claudia stood right beside us with a big smile on her face and shook her head. "Okay, you big show-off," she said to Quarry. "I suppose you're proud of yourself."

Quarry's trot steps broke to a walk and then he drifted into a halt, dipping his head and snorting through his nose with pleasure. His eyes were shining.

"Wow, Claudia that was amazing!" I said, beaming with all my might. "Thank you so much."

"Thank him." Claudia shrugged. "That was his idea. It was his favourite move back in his time. Now let's try that exercise again, you two, but this time no piaffe."

We practiced the spiral exercise a few more times until Quarry and I could increase and decrease our circle easily.

Marion clapped when we were finished, and came over to the middle of the ring to stroke Quarry's neck wonderingly. "That was wonderful, Astrid. You looked like a professional out there."

I blushed, knowing it wasn't true. I was still a beginner, not even off the lunge line; there was a long way to go before I could ride like Liza or Claudia, but I knew Marion couldn't see that. She smiled up at me with pride shining in her eyes.

Hilary showed up to help with the rest of the chores and Marion sat up in the viewing lounge to have coffee with Claudia and Caprice while we worked.

We left after lunch, and as soon as in we were in the car, I turned to Marion excitedly. "Marion, you need a dog."

She startled and looked at me in surprise. "We don't have a lifestyle for a dog, Astrid, your father travels so much for work."

"Yes, but *you* don't," I insisted. "You stay home all day to work and you hate to travel. It would be the perfect home for a dog."

She was silent for a long time, but I could see her thinking.

I tried again. "You do know poodles are hypoallergenic, right? And Claudia says they don't shed hair at all."

She tapped her fingers on the steering wheel and sent me a grin. "Okay, I'll think about it. But, what about you not telling me that you're such an accomplished rider? When were you going to let us know?"

She was teasing, but I felt that same glow of pride again.

* * * * *

The next day, Claudia seemed back to her old self again, although still a little drawn and pale looking. Lessons were back on track and the barn was once again bustling with activity.

In my morning lesson, we went over all the things I'd learned so far; we practiced upward and downward transitions from walk, trot to canter, and then moved on to the lateral work we'd touched on yesterday, channeling his forward energy into sideways movements like on the spiral. Quarry was fresh after his days off, and it felt like there were springs on his feet.

"All right, Astrid, bring him over here to me. We're going to add a new element."

"Really?" I squealed in excitement, looking at the bridle in her hands. "I'm ready?"

"You're ready." Claudia laughed. "Your seat is solid, and you are light and in balance. You are in control of your breathing. I don't have to worry about you hurting his sensitive mouth. Do I?"

"Um, well, I'll do my best," I said, a little apprehensively. "I don't want to make any mistakes."

Claudia slipped the bit between Quarry's teeth and carefully fixed on his bridle, smoothing his mane under the crown piece so everything lay perfectly flat. "Now," she said, turning abruptly toward me, "shoulders back and core engaged, just like we've practiced; seat bones even, upper arms dropped loosely to your sides without tension. You hold the reins just like this, see. Firmly, but lightly, as if you were holding two delicate baby birds between your fingers. You don't want to crush them, but you don't want to drop them, either. Reins are a method of communication, never about control, always about connection. Understand?"

I nodded, a little alarmed by the thought of crushing baby birds between my fingers.

"Now, we will start on the lunge line just like we have been doing so you can acclimatize to this new point of contact. If we have done our job right then adding the reins should change *nothing* in the way you ride, or at least very little. Everything comes from the seat first; it is your connection to his entire body. Your reins are just there to collect some of the forward energy you are creating and recycle it backwards when needed. But for now, you will just *feel*."

At first, it was awkward; my attention wanted to go to the reins because they were new and unfamiliar, but Claudia's voice drew me back time and again to my breath, my weight, my core, until I was again rooted firmly in the saddle. I could feel Quarry lightly mouthing the bit, not leaning on it, but holding it softly, small vibrations ran up the reins into my hands making me aware that he was there, listening to me.

We practiced both directions at the walk, trot, and canter, but by now it felt familiar and not strange at all. Finally, Claudia unclipped the lead and said in a quiet voice, "Change nothing, look where you want to go, and trot around the outside of the arena, please."

I stifled the thrill of excitement that rippled through me and breathed deep, relaxing into my saddle. Quarry's ears swivelled back toward me and he seemed to be saying, "finally, we're doing something more interesting than going around in circles."

I trotted out along the arena wall, feeling like I'd won the lottery; the sense of power and freedom was nearly overwhelming. When we'd circled twice, Claudia said, "bring him to a walk, please."

I breathed into the downward transition and Quarry drifted from trot to walk as lightly as a snowflake. When Claudia came over, there were tears in her eyes. “I’m sorry, Astrid.” She smiled. “It just makes me so happy to see the old guy bringing yet another young, aspiring student along. He really is a fantastic teacher. And you are a fantastic student; I’m proud of you.”

“Really?” I said, grinning down at her. “Thank you so much for teaching me, Claudia. I never thought riding was anything like this. It’s magic.”

She laughed and patted my knee. “Sometimes, it sure feels like it. All right, that’s enough for now. We’ll practice more this afternoon. I think our plan will be lunge work in the mornings and ridden work in the afternoons. How does that sound?”

“Great,” I said, beaming.

The weeks flew by in a blur of summer happiness. I was getting fitter every day, and my ability to ride Quarry effectively improved by leaps and bounds. He was a generous teacher and soon, Claudia allowed me to add stirrups to my saddle during my lunging lessons. At first, I hated them. I’d become used to letting my legs stretch down unhindered and often, I felt the stirrups got in the way.

“It’s up to you Astrid. Personally, I’m glad that you prefer not using them. Too many people see them as a crutch. But if you want to show you’ll have to get used to them.”

I reluctantly agreed and, after a while, I forgot they were even there, and by the time the date for our schooling show came around, I felt confident enough at the walk, trot, and canter, that Claudia okayed me riding Quarry in a Training level test.

“Don’t be upset if you don’t get the highest score, though, Astrid. You’ve only been riding a few months. We’re just doing this for fun and to get you some experience, right?”

"Right," I agreed. I honestly did not have any expectations. Even with archery, I wasn't *really* competitive, even though it was nice to win and get a few medals. Mainly, I just enjoyed shooting for its own sake; and that's the same way I felt about riding.

Pender, Sadie, Ally, and Hilary had been drilling for weeks; their horses had their whiskers and ear hair clipped, and all the horses except Riverdance had their manes pulled so they lay flat and even and ready for the tiny, even braids that was the mark of a show horse. Riverdance's foot-long mane would be braided into a French braid, called a 'running braid' that ran down his neck and was tied off at the bottom.

I'd gone over my test, first at home in the living room, and then in the arena on Quarry. It was a short test and not too hard to remember, especially when I knew Hilary would be reading it out loud for me on the actual show day.

Everyone but me had decided to ride two tests each to make the most of their show experience, but I was happy just doing one. I knew Claudia was going to have her hands busy watching over everyone, especially since Rob and a couple of the other outside riders had decided to show as well, and that she was going to need me to help Liza on the ground.

Chapter Seventeen

The morning of the horse show my alarm went off at 4:30, and I leapt out of bed, already wide awake with excitement.

It's no big deal, I told myself, shivering with anticipation as I got dressed; *it's just a schooling show.*

My training level test was practically the easiest test possible, and I'd been in so many archery competitions over the years that I wasn't afraid of crowds, but still, I didn't want to let Claudia or Quarry down.

Marion insisted I eat a bowl of granola and fruit to keep up my strength, but I only managed a few bites before I leapt up to check my gear for the millionth time. It was just a schooling show, so technically we didn't have to dress up, but Claudia insisted that if we were going to show at all then we were going to do it properly. I had zipped my new show shirt, stock tie, jacket, and cream breaches into a garment bag. My helmet was packed away and I'd cleaned my black boots until they shone. I was as ready as I was ever going to be.

I danced around impatiently while Marion packed nutritious lunches for us both and carefully made sure we had everything before we left the condo.

“Let’s go, let’s go. We’re going to be late,” I said in irritation, sudden onset of nerves making my voice harsher than it should have been. I sounded like my dad did whenever we were going anywhere. The thought made me calm down quickly.

“Sorry,” I told Marion, hastily. “Thanks for taking me to the show. You didn’t have to drive me.”

She smiled serenely at me, ignoring my rudeness like she did my father’s, which was a sobering thought. “You’re going to do just fine; just learn lots and have fun.”

She was quoting Earl. It was what he said to us before every single tournament. He never cared if we won or lost, he always told us to pick one goal for a tournament and work toward that. Claudia had said much the same thing, and I’d decided that being relaxed and riding an accurate test would be my only goals for my first show, and to have fun, of course.

Hilary met me in the barn doorway, hopping up and down, her face aglow with happiness. The aisle was full of horses and riders in various states of chaos. Caprice blew past us, yapping and spinning in wild circles as she ran up to Marion.

“Hey, little one.” Marion knelt down to stroke her head and instantly Caprice calmed down, her eyes closed blissfully as she leaned into Marion’s hand.

“Oh, Marion,” Claudia said in exasperation. “Could you please take her with you? She’s driving everyone crazy today.”

Marion’s hand stilled and her face sort of shut down like she was trying hard to think of something she’d forgotten. Caprice’s poodle coat had grown long again, and the curls were stuck with bits of hay, shavings and heavens knew what else. I knew Marion was thinking of what a smelly, dirty dog would do the interior of her car.

Finally, she sighed and stood up. "Sure, I could do that, Claudia. Let me just get a blanket." She moved to her car and opened the trunk, pulling an unused wool blanket out of the emergency kit. She carefully spread it out on the front seat so it covered every visible bit of leather and then allowed Caprice to jump inside.

"Thank you so much, Marion. Her leash is around here somewhere…I think."

"Don't worry about it, Claudia," Marion said quickly. "I'll meet you at the show. Astrid, text me if you need me to pick up anything." She gave me a big hug and then drove away with Cappy standing on the front seat. The barking started before she'd even left the driveway.

"Well, that's one thing out of the way." Claudia laughed. "Come on, girls, let's get the rest of these horses ready."

Rabbit stood planted in cross ties nearest the door, leaning backward and wrinkling his nose in distaste while Pender tried, in vain, to strap on the rest of his shipping boots. He lifted his front foot in the air and stared down suspiciously at the green and gold boot that covered his left leg from hoof to knee.

"Come on, Rabbit," Pender wailed. "You lived on the race track, for heaven's sake; you've had shipping boots on a thousand times before." He wasn't listening to her; he snorted and backed away from her, leaning his weight on the cross ties, the whites of his eyes showing.

"Wait, Pender, he's about to lose it." Liza appeared at Rabbit's side just before he exploded. "Stand up, you big baby," she said moving him forward and unclipping him so he didn't break the cross-ties. She patted his neck and stuffed a carrot in his face while Pender finished getting him dressed.

"I've lost my hair net," Ally moaned running down from the viewing room. "I can't go until I find it. I'll look awful."

"Ally, you could wear a paper bag over your head and still look amazing," Sadie said, laughing. "I'm pretty sure you packed your hair net already. It's in the car with the rest of our stuff."

Claudia stood in the midst of the chaos, a small smile curling at the edge of her mouth. "Oh, ladies, I am certainly glad my days of show nerves are over. Everyone needs to take a moment for some deep breathing; we all need to think calming thoughts. You need to be peaceful leaders in order to support your horses, especially those getting their first taste of showing; they need to have a good experience or they won't want to do it again."

"Yeah." Liza shook Pender's shoulder gently. "This is supposed to fun. Otherwise, why would you put yourself through it?"

"To show my rotten husband up?" Pender laughed and then everyone else did, too. The nervous atmosphere dissolved just like that. Even the horses seemed to deflate a little.

Quarry was in his stall munching hay, his mane braided, and a clean green and gold wool sheet wrapped snugly around him.

"Wow, Liza, he looks great."

"Well, he has to look his best," she said with a wink. "Since he's going out in public again after all this time. He's a little fatter than he was last time he showed."

"He's not fat," I said defensively, slipping a carrot between his teeth, "he's perfect. Aren't you, boy?"

He crunched the carrot happily, bobbing his head up in down in satisfaction.

"See? He agrees with me."

"Okay, I'll put his boots and bumper cap on if you go help Ally get Severus dressed. Remember to stay calm, though; the horses can pick up on whatever you're feeling."

I nodded and moved down the aisle, practicing being tranquil and serene. Ally had found her hair net and was adjusting the beautiful green show sheet so it fit her horse perfectly. His black coat glistened and stood regally, like a prince, while we put on his boots.

Soon, all the horses were wrapped snugly in their jackets and travelling boots. Their leather halters were topped with little leather hats that fit over their ears so they didn't accidently bump their heads on the trailer.

We'd already packed the trailer the night before with everything we needed, but Hilary and I grabbed the checklist and went inside to go over it again, just in case. Luckily, the show was nearby; if we did forget anything, it would be easy to run home to get it.

"All right, we'll load Quarry first so he can set a good example for the others. Severus can go next, then Jerry, then Rabbit, and then Riverdance; we'll stick the two scaredy-cats in the middle so they stay quiet."

Rabbit was the only one who hesitated to load, but with a few kind words and a carrot from Liza, he finally stepped in. Soon, all the horses were locked in tight, Claudia started the big trailer up with a rumble, and were ready to go.

Hilary, Liza, and I squished into the back seat of Claudia's white truck while Pender rode in the passenger seat up front. Sadie and Ally followed closely behind in Ally's little gold Tesla.

I hadn't known what to expect from my first horse show but, despite my excitement, the show grounds turned out to be really casual and low key. Our tires crunched up a long gravel driveway, and at the end of that were a group of long, low barns and a scattering of various-sized arenas. A few horse trailers were parked in front of the barns, and here and there people led blanketed horses around, but it wasn't as packed as I'd thought it would be.

"Where is everyone?" I said, looking at the rows of empty temporary stalls set up alongside one of the barns.

"It's early," Hilary yawned, "and this is a schooling show, not a recognized event. Most people just arrive, warm up, ride their tests and then leave. Only barns with a bunch of horses and riders at different levels will be here all day. Like us."

"The lower level tests will ride first," Liza added, "and those ones will be the busiest, with the most entries. Usually, there are fewer and fewer riders as the tests get more difficult. At a local show, like this, there are often only a few entries in the Prix St. Georges, and sometimes nobody rides the big Grand Prix tests."

Because we were going to be there all day, Claudia had gotten stalls for all the horses plus a tack room for us where we keep all of our equipment. It was also a place where we could change into our show clothes.

The Introductory, walk-trot tests would ride first, followed by our Training level tests. That meant Rob and I would be riding first out of all of Claudia's students. I was glad to get my own test out of the way first so I could enjoy the rest of the day. Hilary and Pender were riding at First level, Ally was riding at Second, and Sadie was doing a Prix. St. Georges test with

Riverdance. Claudia had also agreed to ride Severus in Prix St. Georges for Ally, since he was actually trained to a higher level than his rider was.

Hilary and I unpacked the wheelbarrow and pitch forks we'd brought and headed to the big, covered pile of shavings at the end of our barn. Each stall took two full wheelbarrows so it took forever to get all six horses set up. We hung up their water buckets and hay nets, and set up the tack room so it looked reasonably organized.

While we worked, Claudia trekked up to the office to get our entry packets and our numbers.

Finally, it was time to get the horses unloaded. Riverdance sauntered off the trailer and gave a big yawn, barely bothering to look around before he led Sadie toward his stall. He'd been competing and showing in breed shows in Brazil since he was a foal so not much fazed him.

Rabbit, on the other hand, came off on his hind legs, prancing and jigging with excitement, his big ears whirling in all directions. Pender's face was white with apprehension as she clutched his lead rope in both hands, digging in her heels to slow him down.

"Put him away for a few minutes while we get everyone unloaded," Liza said, "then we'll take him for a walk. He'll settle down in a few minutes. He probably thinks he's back at the race track."

"That's what I 'm afraid of," Pender said grimly, pulling a reluctant Rabbit toward the barn and using both hands to pry him into his stall. She left his halter on just in case he decided to break out. He latched on to his hay net, tore a huge mouthful off and wheeled to his stall door so he could peer out anxiously.

Jerry, too, was upset with the change in his routine. He took one look at the unfamiliar landscape show waiting outside his trailer and planted his feet, snorting dramatically.

"Come on, pony," Hilary said, tugging at his lead rope.

"Don't rush him," Liza warned. "Give him a chance to take in his surroundings."

"Oh, he's just being silly," Hilary said, distractedly tugging on his lead. In her haste, she pulled too hard and the brass snap attached to the halter flipped upward, hitting him on the chin with a sharp crack. Jerry tossed his head in alarm, half-reared, and then leapt forward out of the trailer, knocking Hilary's shoulder and sending her flying. He clattered down the ramp on his own and made a beeline toward Riverdance's stall, his sides heaving with excitement.

Riverdance stared at him indifferently before sighing and nudging his hay-net a little closer so Jerry could reach over to have a bite.

Liza walked over to pick up the dragging lead rope and gave Jerry a soothing pat on the shoulder before calmly leading him away from his friend and settling him in his own stall.

"Are you okay?" I asked, kneeling down beside Hilary. She was half-sitting, holding her elbow in one hand, face flushed and creased with pain.

"Yeah," she said shakily, "but poor Jerry. I didn't mean for the snap to hit him like that. I feel awful. He's just a baby and I rushed him. What if he hates trailering now, or showing; maybe I've ruined him."

"He doesn't look too ruined," Claudia said, appearing behind us with an armful of entry packets. "Are you hurt, Hilary?"

"No, just a little bruised," Hilary said, rubbing her elbow and straightening out her arm experimentally. "I'll be okay."

I helped her up and dusted the grass off her side. She squeezed my hand in thanks and then disappeared into the tack room.

Severus was unsettled after all the drama Jerry had caused but, after a few suspicious snorts, he went quietly to his stall.

Quarry, of course, came off like the old pro he was, craning his head around to check out his surroundings.

"He's looking for his adoring fans," Claudia said and laughed. "Of course, he assumes everyone is here to see *him*. Now, if you don't mind, kids, I'm going to make the rounds. I haven't seen some of these people in a long time. Back soon."

Liza and Pender unpacked the folding table, and we set up chairs and a coffee machine and the boxes of pastries Sadie and Ally had picked up for us. Then, when everything looked organized, Liza went to park the trailer, and the rest of us sat on folding chairs to snack on pastries and study the ride times.

"This is so much fun," Sadie said, munching on a cinnamon bun. "I've missed this; I'm glad we came."

We all nodded in agreement. Hopefully, the riding part was as much fun as the setting up and eating pastry part.

"Look what I found in the parking lot," Liza said, appearing with Rob and Artimax in tow. The big spotted horse strode along wearing a fancy red and black cooler, looking cool and collected. "We have his stall all set up for him, Rob; it's the one on the end there. Get him settled then help yourself to breakfast. We'll help you move your gear over afterward."

"So, this is the order," Liza said, once we were all settled, pouring herself another cup of coffee. "Astrid's riding first, and Hilary is calling for both her and for Rob, who rides about twenty minutes later. Rob, your second test will come pretty quickly after the first one, but you'll have enough time to go back to the warm-up ring and keep him moving. We don't want Artimax standing around too long.

"You two will need to be tacked up and in the warm-up ring about a half-hour before your rides. Quarry will just need a small warm-up to loosen him up, but Artimax will need a bit longer. As soon as you two are done, you need to get your horses cleaned up and put away so you can help Pender and Hilary get their horses ready. Rabbit and Jerry will need a lot of time to settle, so I expect you all to be on hand to help out. I'll be calling their tests, but I need you all to act as a team to support them.

"After that, we'll have a bit of a break until after lunch when Ally rides her second level test. She's decided not to have a caller, but stay on hand to step in just in case she changes her mind."

"I won't," Ally interrupted blithely. "I know that test inside-out. I won't forget it."

"Okay, well, Sadie will do her Prix. St. Georges test at around three o'clock, if everything is running on time, and Claudia is scheduled to ride just after her with Severus. There aren't that many upper level entries, so I think we'll just keep Severus out and give him another warm-up after your test, Ally, so that he stays loosened up for Claudia. And that will wrap up our day. It's going to be a long one, but there will be plenty of time for fun, too. Make sure you all get enough to eat and stay hydrated. After we finish our breakfast, we'll take these horses for a walk around the grounds to get them used to everything."

After breakfast, we slipped the horses halters on and headed out to get them acclimatized. Quarry bounced along beside me, his eyes bright and his ears pricked happily. He reached over and gave Artimax a gentle nip on the shoulder as if he were saying, *look at all this, Artimax, isn't it fun?*

Jerry couldn't stop dancing and fussing beside Hilary, and Rabbit tried to bolt from Pender twice before Liza took over and marched him firmly through the show grounds.

We took them up to the food truck which was busy selling breakfast sandwiches and coffee to the early morning crowd, the smell of bacon and fried onions making my mouth water. Once Jerry got close to the food truck, he didn't want to leave it again. He stared in through the little service window with his ears pricked watching the cook frying bacon as if it was the most interesting thing he'd ever seen. His nostrils flickered and he made little nickering sounds under his breath.

"Come on, goofball," Hilary said, laughing. "I promise I'll buy you a veggie-burger later, extra cheese."

She patted his neck and waited until he'd had his fill and was ready to move on. I was sure she didn't want a repeat of their earlier incident. She was still rubbing her sore elbow every so often.

We walked the horses around the outside of the empty warm-up ring so they could take a look, and then headed out toward a large grassy area. We let them graze peacefully for fifteen minutes so they could watch the action from a distance and relax, watching the people and horses come and go.

The riders who'd already put on their show clothes looked so polished and professional; suddenly, I felt a stab of uneasiness.

Did I really belong here with all these elegant looking people? They'd all probably been riding much longer than me. I glanced at Quarry who was busily ripping up tufts of fresh grass without a care in the world—he looked beautiful and so elegant in his row of neat braids.

"You're the best horse here," I whispered to him. "It doesn't matter whether I belong here or not because you do and you'll take care of me."

He snorted contentedly and then bumped my knee with his nose as if to say, "don't worry, I've got this covered."

When we tugged on their ropes to lead them back to their stalls, they were much more relaxed, tails swaying gently back and forth. Even Rabbit's pointy ears were flopping to the side and he snorted rhythmically under his breath with every step. Pender suddenly looked white, though and, once Rabbit was put away, she quickly disappeared to find the restrooms.

"All right, Astrid," Claudia said briskly, arriving suddenly and clapping her hands together. "Go get dressed, and the girls will get Quarry tacked up and spotless for you and make sure all his braids are perfect. We'll give him a light warm up and then you'll be all set for your test. I know you've memorized it, but we'll have Hilary call it for you since it's your first time out. Are you nervous?"

"Not anymore," I said truthfully. "I'm having fun."

"Good girl," Claudia said, "that's the right answer."

"Well, maybe you can give Pender a pep talk to share some of your bravery," Ally said, coming up behind me. "I think she's throwing up in the bathroom right now."

"I most certainly am *not*," Pender said indignantly, appearing behind her. "I may have taken a little something for my nerves, but don't count me out just yet."

"I wouldn't do that," Ally said quickly. "We're all in this together, Pender. You're going to be great."

I retreated to the change room and pulled on my clothes. I hadn't worn the cream coloured breeches very often since buying them; I preferred the comfortable plaid ones that I wore all the time, and I was surprised to find that they were a little big on me. I had to cinch my belt up two extra holes to make them fit. I slid into my tall boots and then put on my show shirt, jacket, and gloves, and attached my stock tie.

When I emerged from the change room, Marion was there, along with Hilary's parents. "Oh, Astrid," she said, clasping her hands together. "You look so grown up. I need to get lots of pictures of you."

"What happened to Caprice?" I asked, staring down at the now perfectly groomed dog, wearing a new plaid leather leash and collar set.

"Oh, the groomer had a cancellation and Claudia said it was okay. They had these adorable collars and leashes on sale, too, so I went ahead and splurged."

She tied Cappy to the table leg and then lined everyone up together and took about a million photos. Then she had to take some of just me and Quarry. "Oh, that's beautiful. We'll have to frame that one. Oh, I almost forgot your present."

She pulled a small blue box out of her pocket and handed it over, eyes shining.

I opened the lid and gasped in surprise. "Oh, Marion, I love it. Thank you." I pulled the delicate silver earrings out of the velvet box. They were each fashioned into matching centaurs, each holding a bow, drawn to fire.

"I thought of you the second I saw them," Marion said in excitement.

"Thanks, Marion," I said with delight. I fixed them on right away and moved over to where Liza was running a sheep skin mitt over Quarry's spotless coat. He looked amazing. Artimax was tied beside him, and Hilary was just polishing a bit of dust off his saddle. His brightly-spotted coat glistened in the sunshine.

Rob appeared out of the change room and did a twirl to make us laugh. "Do I look like a dressage-king, ladies?" he said, wiggling his eyebrows.

"You look good," I said honestly, and then blushed when Hilary snickered and poked me in the side. "What, he *does* look good," I protested, not sure what was so funny.

"Helmets on and then up you get, you two," Claudia said with a smile. "It's show time."

Rob and I swung onto our horses and walked side by side to the ring, the rest of our crew trailing behind. The horses left back at the barn neighed in chorus when they saw Quarry and Artimax leaving them behind. Quarry didn't so much as glance back at them; his ears were pricked toward the ring as if he knew it was time to perform. There was a slight prance to his step and he arched his neck gently. I reached down and ran my gloved fingers down his neck full of love and pride. I was so lucky to be riding this beautiful horse.

"Rob, let Artimax walk on a loose rein for the first five minutes. Set your watch. Then move him into the trot and we'll get to work. Astrid, you come over here for a moment."

She smiled up at me when I reached her side. "Quarry doesn't need too much of a warm-up. So we're going to start with the same routine we do at home. Drop your stirrups and let your legs stretch down. Focus on making your seat bones even. Your hips align with his hips. Do a few circles around me at the walk and when you're ready, move into a slow trot."

It was easier for me to concentrate without stirrups for some reason. My legs lengthened down, muscles relaxing, and my chest opened up. Soon, Quarry and I were moving harmoniously together, even though there was noise and crowds and a crackling loud-speaker. Claudia kept us down to one end at first, but gradually she had us use the whole ring and, whenever there was space free of other horses we practiced a few steps of leg yield and some shallow serpentines.

"Nice," Claudia called. "You two look great, Astrid. I think you're ready to go in."

Hilary ran a cloth over my dusty boots while Liza cleaned the slobber off Quarry's bit so he looked clean and tidy. The rider ahead of me was still in the ring. Quarry and I rode into the narrow channel that surrounded the ring and walked calmly around until the bell rang, which meant we had forty-five seconds to enter the ring. Quarry picked up a trot before I'd even asked and carried me into the ring. We halted at X, in the middle of the ring, and I offered my salute. And then we were off.

Hilary called out my test from ringside in her clear, strong voice, but I hardly heard her; Quarry and I had practised this test so many times I could have done it asleep. It was easy; we were just doing the same movements I did at home with him every day. Quarry could have probably done the whole thing without me.

We did our final halt and salute, and I heard the people from our barn clapping and whistling behind me. The judge smiled at me and beckoned me to ride over to her. It was a real schooling show, so we were supposed to go up and get feedback after every ride.

"That is a lovely horse," the judge said, leaning down from her stand. "How long have you been riding with Claudia?"

"Just a couple months," I said, blushing.

"Well, you are doing remarkably well. You have a very light, effective seat. Claudia's students always did so well, though. We've missed seeing her at the shows these last few years. You say hello for me. And good ride."

"Thank you," I said, patting Quarry's neck. We rode out of the ring and were instantly surrounded by the group from the barn.

"Nice, Astrid." Liza patted my leg. "Very quiet and accurate ride."

"Great job, Astrid," Claudia said, "how did your first taste of showing feel?"

"Wonderful," I said, "thank you so much for bringing me, Claudia, and letting me ride Quarry."

"You're welcome. Now, get him cooled down and leave him in his stall with some hay. We'll take his braids out once Rob's done. I need you back here so you can watch his ride, and then we'll need to start getting Hilary and Pender ready."

Marion met me as I walked Quarry back to the barn. "Wonderful job, Astrid. I videoed the whole thing, and I sent your dad a ton of pictures. He's so proud of you, sweetie."

"You sent them to Dad?" I asked, a sick feeling clawing at my stomach. "He's not mad?"

"Of course not, silly, he thinks it's wonderful. Get down, Caprice." She pulled the little dog back to her side and waited for a horse to pass by. "Now, *sit.*" Caprice sat obediently and stared up adoringly into Marion's face. I'd hardly seen the dog listen to anyone before, she usually ran wild and did whatever she liked.

Back at the barn, I pulled off Quarry's tack and gave him a quick brush down before settling him in his stall for a snack. He hadn't even broken a sweat during our test, but I sure had. I hung my jacket up and pulled off my damp helmet. I decided to stay in my breeches and shirt, though; they made me feel like I fit in, like I was a real rider.

Marion headed toward the bleachers so she could keep Caprice from leaping on anyone, and I trotted back to the ring. Claudia was finishing Rob's warm-up, and I stood by the rail watching the pair move flawlessly around in a working trot. Artimax stretched forward into a ground-covering gait, and then moved into an effortless canter. They were beautiful to watch.

"All right, you're next in two, Rob. Bring him here and we'll polish you up."

Rob's face was motionless with concentration, and he didn't even look down when I wiped his boots clean. Artimax bobbed his head up and down excitedly and shifted from side to side as Liza cleaned his bit and rubbed a smudge that had appeared on his bridle.

Finally, he was in the ring, moving forward at a working trot.

Hilary called his test but, like me during my test, I wasn't sure if Rob actually heard her or was just going around on auto-pilot. Their ride was brilliant. Artimax's striped hooves flashed across the ground, his movement brilliant and expressive. He lightly mouthed the bit and stretched into Rob's light contact obediently. It was wonderful to watch, and when he finally left the ring after a long talk with the judge, we all burst into excited applause.

Claudia thumped him on the leg so hard I thought she'd injure him, but he just grinned down at her with his hundred-watt smile.

"That was brilliant, Rob," she said. "You've brought him a long way in such a short time. You should be really proud of yourself. We need to get you some more horses to ride."

"One horse is just plenty, thank you very much. Don't go giving him ideas, Claudia." Rob's dad appeared with a wry smile on his face. "Well, son, I guess that wasn't half bad." He patted Artimax on the neck and winked at his son. "Not as good as watching you jump, though. Now that's something."

"Daaad," Rob groaned, "you're cramping my style here. I have to keep him moving before the next test. Our work's not over yet."

"You're the boss," his dad said good-naturedly. "Nice job out there."

They stared at each other for a moment, grinning as if they were sharing a good secret, and then Rob steered Artimax to the warm-up with Claudia following closely behind them.

"You must be Astrid." Rob's dad turned, fixing me with a sharp expression. "I've heard good things about you."

"You…you have?" I squeaked, wondering what on earth Rob had told him.

He clapped me on the shoulder and his face broke into a smile. "I saw your ride out there. You did really well, especially for your first show. Did Rob ever tell you that he used to throw up before every single competition?"

"No." I laughed. "I would have never guessed he was nervous."

"Well, he's been riding since he was little, so at some point he got over it. I like to bring it up from time to time just to tease him, though." He winked at me and turned to watch a few of the other rider's ride their tests. His eyes narrowed in concentration and I imagined he was calculating how everyone stacked up against his son.

Finally, it was Rob's turn, and again he rode a flawless test. He sat so quietly, and Artimax moved with so much freedom and expression, that they seemed miles above everyone else.

We all walked back to the barn together, chattering excitedly.

Back at the barn, we discovered that Rabbit had rubbed half his braids out on the wall of his stall so they had to be redone, and Jerry had pooped in his shavings and then rolled in it, so he had a big stain on his butt that we had to scrub out, but eventually the two of them looked respectable.

Hilary and Pender disappeared into the tack room to get changed while the rest of us scarfed down granola bars and drank bottled water.

Since their tests were both so close, they were going to warm up together first, and then Claudia would somehow watch Hilary's test while simultaneously making sure Pender didn't have a meltdown.

At first, Jerry snorted at the horses in the warm up ring and spooked violently at the crackling loudspeaker, but after that he settled down and got to work. Rabbit, on the other hand, seemed to get more and more wound up; he kept his head high in the air and squealed at any horses who came near him, scooting sideways and almost unseating Pender.

"Pender, let him walk," Claudia called to her. "He needs time to calm down. Walk him around the ring and do some leg yields when you can, but don't let him kick anyone. As soon as he's calm we'll do some walk-trot transitions. Keep his mind busy. Liza, keep a close eye on them, please."

Pender narrowly stopped Rabbit from biting a delicate chestnut gelding as it passed by too closely. He was definitely reliving his days at the racetrack; he didn't want anyone to pass him.

While Pender gave Rabbit time to simmer down, Claudia focused on warming up Hilary and Jerry. I could tell Hilary was a little nervous; her face was pinched in concentration as she tried to pilot Jerry around the now-crowded warm-up ring. Jerry started out tense, but gradually he settled down to work and was able to relax. They did transitions and some lateral work, and then it was time for Hilary to go in. Liza was reading her test and I knew Hilary had been nervous about messing it up.

"You'll ace it, Hilary," I whispered, wiping her boots down with a towel to make sure they were free of dust. "You've got this."

"Thanks, Astrid," she whispered back and then she was off, Jerry's powerful hindquarters propelling her toward the ring at a brisk trot.

We needn't have worried. She was a wonderful rider and, despite her nerves, she put in an excellent test. Jerry was happy and forward and only spooked once; he tried hard to listen to everything she asked of him. Hilary accepted our congratulations, and then headed straight for the warm-up ring to where Liza was waiting.

Rabbit strode over to us looking more relaxed—his long neck arched more like a horse than upright like a giraffe. Pender had managed to let go of her grim grip on the reins and actually seemed to be enjoying herself a little.

Rabbit's big ears swirled around and he danced sideways a little when he entered the competition ring, but other than that, he was pretty good. He was stiffer and less relaxed than Jerry, but overall he was obedient and Pender made it through her first test without too many mistakes.

"Good job, Pender," we congratulated her, patting her knees and Rabbit's neck in praise.

"You did it, Pender," Claudia smiled. "See, all that worry over nothing. It's just like schooling at home."

Just then Rabbit popped his head up and neighed from deep in his chest—he'd seen another horse he didn't like across the show grounds and I was pretty sure he was yelling something bad at him.

"Yeah, just like home," Pender joked. "I like my old Rabbit better than the race horse version."

Claudia laughed. "Okay, don't let him lose focus. Let's get this guy back to work. Hilary's already over there."

Both horses had their heads in the game by the time they came back for their second tests. Jerry moved through the ring like a steam train, neck arched and strong legs plowing through the sand in a steady rhythm.

Rabbit, too, swung along smoothly, his large ears flopping softly to the side as he quietly listened to Pender's aides. Pender visibly relaxed and, by the end of her ride, joy lit up her face.

When she came out of the ring after talking to the judge, she was beaming. "She liked our test," she gasped. "She said we have potential."

"Of course you do," Claudia said firmly. "I've always told you *that*, Pender."

There were still a handful of First Level tests to go, and then we had an hour break for lunch so we had some time to rest.

We got Rabbit and Jerry brushed and put away in their stalls with food and then everyone but Claudia went to the food truck to load up on carbs.

"Did you want me to bring you something, Claudia?" Hilary asked.

Claudia shook her head and picked up the truck keys. "No, I'm just going to have a quick nap in the truck where it's quiet. I have a bit of a headache, but a power snooze should fix it. I'll set my alarm and be back in forty-five minutes. You girls keep an eye on things."

"Okay, no problem," Hilary said, but I saw her and Liza shoot a quick, worried look at each other.

I bought myself a double cheeseburger, a plate of fries, and a coke then looked down guiltily at the overflowing tray in front of me. Marion wasn't going to be happy if she caught me eating like this. She'd even packed me a healthy bagged lunch so I wouldn't pig out.

"Rob," I whispered fiercely. He was next in line, but he hadn't ordered yet. "Would you please split this with me? I ordered too much."

"What? That's hardly a full meal." He laughed. "You can get that down, easy."

I flushed beet red and felt the unexpected prickle of tears behind my eyes. I started to turn away, but he quickly put a hand on my arm to stop me. "I didn't mean anything rude, Astrid, honestly. I wouldn't do that. I'll order another drink and dessert for both of us and we'll split, okay?"

He looked full of concern and I nodded shakily. Otherwise, I was going to have to throw out at least half of this food. "Okay, thanks."

We made our way back to the barn and everyone crowded around the plastic table to eat. Hilary's parents chatted happily away with Marion, and Rob's dad. Marion nibbled away at her home-made lettuce wrap and drank her mineral water. She beamed at me happily and didn't seem to notice that I was sharing cheese, carbs, and sugar with Rob.

Ally was first up after our lunch, but since there weren't that many tests being held in the afternoon, Sadie got Riverdance ready, too, so we could all go up together. I watched in fascination as she braided the golden horse's long mane into a beautiful French braid that lay flat against his neck, weaving a yellow, silken cord into it that almost matched the color of his hair. She tied it off at the bottom in a neat loop and kissed him on the forehead.

"He's so beautiful," I said, stroking his neck gently. "He reminds me of Quarry a little."

"Well, Andalusians and Lusitano's are fairly closely related, and they have a similar build and way of moving, too. I wouldn't have anything else, that's for sure."

"Neither would I," I said and she flashed me a smile.

She slipped on his saddle, leaving his girth loose, and looked over to see if Ally was ready. Then she headed to the tack room to get changed, too.

Hilary and Liza had Severus all tacked up and looking perfect, his black coat glistening. Ally had touched up her makeup and looked like a model for riding clothes with her tailored jacket and breeches. Together, they were stunning.

"There you are, darling." A man in a suit, hair perfectly styled, and white teeth flashing in a blinding smile, walked straight up to Ally without stopping and lifted her right into the air, kissing her on the lips without even saying hello.

"Dale," she squealed breathlessly, "put me down, you've smeared my lipstick and I have to fix it now." She frowned at him, but her eyes were dancing, and the next moment she broke into a smile. "Seriously, I'm glad you made it. You're just in time to see us ride. Hold the big guy while I fix myself up."

She handed him Severus's reins and walked away without a backward glance. "Hello, ridiculously expensive horse," the man said as Severus eyed him suspiciously. "We meet again." He cracked a smile at the rest of us and shrugged good-naturedly. "Hello, ladies. I'm Ally's husband. Good show so far?"

"Yes, it's been great," Pender said, speaking up when nobody else did. "We've all done really well. Claudia prepared us perfectly. Severus and Ally ride next."

"That's why I'm here." Dale flashed his smile again and

gratefully relinquished the horse back to his wife. "I'll video your round from the bleachers, darling. Best of luck." He air-kissed her so as not to mess up her make up again and disappeared.

Ally was glowing with happiness. "I'm so glad he came. It's like pulling teeth to get him interested in Severus. I really want him to be a part of this world. At least in a small way."

"All right," Liza said, "mount up, ladies, you have horses to show."

Both Ally and Sadie had shown many times in the past and knew how to put their fears aside and get down to work. Even though there was no sign of Claudia when we reached the ring, both ladies started their warm-up. "Keep an eye on them," Liza hissed. "I'm going to find Claudia."

She was back in ten minutes with a bleary-eyed Claudia following slowly behind her. "I'm sorry, Liza," Claudia said. "My medication made me much sleepier than usual. This day has taken more out of me than I thought it would."

Liza was tight-lipped and white-faced. "I know, Claudia, you look awful. You should never have taken this on." Her eyes brimmed with tears and she suddenly gave Claudia a tight hug. "Okay, what can I do to help?"

Claudia heaved a large sigh and looked thoughtfully at Sadie and Ally. "I'll finish warming these two up. They barely need me anyway. But, Liza, you must ride Severus for me in his big test this afternoon. I just don't feel up to riding."

Liza crossed her arms over her chest. "No, no way, Claudia. I don't have anything to wear and Ally doesn't want some working student to ride him. She wants *you*."

"Nonsense." Claudia laughed. "You're just as good a rider

now as I am, Liza. You just need more miles under your belt. Ally wants Severus to be shown to his full potential and you can do that for him. You'll need to start developing your own clients at some point, and Ally would be a great asset to you once I'm, er, retired."

Liza's lower lip trembled and she wiped her eyes impatiently with the back of one hand.

"Just this one time, then, as a favour to me," Claudia cajoled. "Please, Liza?"

Finally, Liza sighed and blew out a deep breath. "I don't have anything to wear," she said half-heartedly.

"You'll fit into my clothes." Claudia visibly brightened. "They're in the tack room in a garment bag. I'll let Ally know about the change of plans."

Liza shook her head and trudged back toward the barn, and Claudia strode across the ring, smile in place, to help Ally and Sadie.

"Ally, he looks fabulous. And I think he knows it," Claudia called to her. "And you look beautiful, too, my dear. You make an amazing team."

I could see Ally's smile light up from across the ring. Severus' steps became lighter and loftier, as if he'd heard the compliment and was puffing himself up.

Their two tests went beautifully. There were only a few people riding at their level, so Ally rode her tests nearly back-to-back and kept a smile on her face the whole time.

"Darling, that was wonderful," Dale said, kissing her cheek while deftly avoiding Severus who was trying to rub his sweaty head on whoever got close to him.

"Was it?" Ally asked, grinning. "I didn't notice." She jumped down lightly from the saddle, patting Severus enthusiastically. "You were such a good boy, Sev, now you just have to do one more test and then you're done for the day."

"Are you really okay with me riding him, Ally?" Liza asked shyly, arriving fully dressed in Claudia's show clothes. They fit her like a glove. "I know you wanted Claudia to be the one to show him in his first Prix St. Georges test."

"Oh, Liza, don't worry. It's not like you haven't ridden him before. He likes you; now hop up and ride this animal. We'll be watching."

Liza let Ally give her a leg up and then walked Severus to the warm up ring. She wouldn't have much time to warm up, but then, Severus was already loose and supple from his tests. Claudia was coming from the ring walking slowly beside Sadie and Riverdance, one hand on the golden horse's shoulder as if using him for support.

"Are you okay Claudia?" Hilary asked anxiously.

"Of course, my dear. I am just a little tired, that's all. Let's all focus on Sadie's ride. She and Riverdance are ready to blow the judge away."

Sadie smiled down at her fondly, and then her eyes narrowed into a look of concentration. "I'm up," she said. "I'll be right back."

There weren't that many people watching the tests by the end of the day, and many of the riders had already left as well. But those who were left were utterly silenced as they watched Sadie pilot the little gold horse around the ring. He moved flawlessly, his powerful hind end propelling him forward, neck arched proudly, and golden tail flowing out behind him. He looked like something a queen would ride, like he was out of a fairy tale.

As soon as Sadie did her final salute, the judge stood up and beckoned her over. We saw her reach out and shake Sadie's hand, and then gently run her hand down Riverdance's neck. Sadie nodded happily, and then they were on their way toward us.

Sadie jumped down and kissed her horse on the neck. "Well, the judge sure loved him. She thanked me for bringing him here."

"Well, of course she did." Pender laughed. "He's fabulous."

Finally, there was just Liza left. Her face was pale as she headed to the ring, but she nodded to Ally and Claudia, and I knew she'd be okay. Her test turned out beautifully. She made a few small errors, but overall, Severus did Ally and Dale proud. They were both grinning when Liza and Severus came striding back toward them.

All in all, it had been a wonderful day. And despite not having any expectations besides just surviving my first show, I came away with a fifth-place ribbon. Sadie and Ally both had firsts, Liza had a second, Pender had a third, and Hilary and Rob had placed second in their tests. I looked down at the marked test sheet Liza handed me in confusion. There were a bunch of written notes and then a 65 scrawled across the top.

"We'll pull apart your test scores tomorrow, everyone," Claudia said tiredly. "Right now, I'm ready to get home."

I decided to save my questions for the next day.

When we finally pulled back into our own familiar barn driveway, exhausted but happy, I was surprised to see a large, gleaming black horse trailer pulling quickly out of the barnyard.

"Oh, it's Cole," Claudia said, sounding excited. "I didn't know he'd be back so soon. What a nice surprise."

"Yay," Liza said under her breath, just loud enough for me and Hilary to hear. Hilary looked less than impressed, too. Pender was silent in the back seat.

"All right ladies," Claudia said. "Let's get these guys unloaded and everything put away. We'll worry about laundry tomorrow."

The horses came off the trailer like lambs; they were tired after their big day and ready for bed. Even Rabbit had his big ears flopped to the side and his lower lip hanging. He went into his stall and straight to his hay net.

Quarry was last, and when I led him down the trailer ramp, Claudia was standing there with a tall, black-haired stranger who stared at me with raised eyebrows and a quirked smile.

"So you're the girl who convinced my mom to let you show the little white guy, hey? I'd like to know how you did it. I can't get her to do anything I say."

"Um...." I stared at him. "Actually, it wasn't my idea. It was Pender's idea to show. You'll have to ask her how she did it."

"I mostly cried," Pender said, passing by with an armload of dirty saddle pads. "And there was some begging. Nice to see you back, Cole."

"Hey, Pender, still trying to make your racehorse do dressage, are you? Any progress?"

He looked at Pender in a superior sort of way as if he were laughing at her, but she pretended not to notice.

"Yes, definite progress," she said with a tight smile.

"Cole, Pender is doing wonderfully with Rabbit. All the girls are coming along nicely. But I want to hear all about you, son. Any success?"

Just then Caprice ran up barking, she bounced excitedly off Coles leg, tiny claws scuffing his expensive looking boots. Cole scowled and pushed her roughly to the side with his foot. "Manners, dog." He growled. "I had some success, mom, but not as much as I'd like. The judges are so crooked over there; it's all political. If you don't know the right people, or if you're not from the *right* family, then you don't get the high scores. It's as simple as that."

"Cole," Claudia said, laying a hand on his arm. "You know that's not the case…."

"I'm tired," he said abruptly, shrugging her hand off and marching toward the barn. "Liza," he snapped, "when you're done unloading, I need you to poultice Montego's legs. He's stocking up; the trip home was hard on him."

Liza raised her eyebrows and stuck her tongue out at his retreating back.

"Sorry, Liza." Claudia laughed in embarrassment. "He must have jet-lag. He always gets rude when he hasn't had enough sleep."

"Huh," Liza said, "is *that* why he's rude?" But as soon as the trailer was unloaded, she went into the stall where Cole's horse was and gave the big animal a pat.

"Has he been overworking you, big guy?" she crooned. "He's an awful horseman, isn't he? Like hell you got these puffy legs from the trip home."

She looked up when I slipped in the stall beside her. "You didn't hear me say that," she said. "Here, I'll show you how to do this, just in case you ever have to do this on your own someday." She taught me how to carefully apply the clay poultice to his leg and wrap it. It was supposed to draw out any heat and inflammation from the legs. Even to my untrained eye, I could see that his lower legs were puffed up from the knee down.

"He looks just like Marcus," I said, studying the big horse. I patted him gently on the neck. "They could be brothers."

"Oh, they are." Liza laughed. "Full brothers. Claudia used to own their mother, but the mare passed away a couple years ago. Montego is one year older than Marcus. But Marcus had a better start being trained by Claudia so he's going to last a lot longer than Montego. Cole doesn't train his horses with their long-term health in mind."

"Oh," I said, not really understanding. Besides his puffy legs, Montego looked in perfect shape to me.

"Come on, I'll show you his other horse. You're going to love him. He's a big softy."

The horse in the next stall was chestnut like Folly, but he had a huge white blaze that took up half his face. At the top, it twisted sideways over one eye, and at the bottom, the blaze slid right off the side of his nose and curled around underneath his chin. He was beautiful, and when we approached he stuck his lips through the bars and flapped them at us as if he were talking.

"This is Dynamix…we call him Mixer. If Cole doesn't ruin him, he'll really be something special. He has the talent and the personality."

"He's beautiful," I said, looking at his intelligent, wide set eyes and silky coat. "Why do you think Cole will ruin him?"

Liza bit her lip. "I really need to learn to shut my mouth

sometimes. He just frustrates me; I mean, he was raised by Claudia so it's not like he doesn't know how to train horses properly. But, a real trainer is smart enough to take the time to let horses develop both physically and emotionally before pushing them further. Cole has no patience and he'll take any short cut available if he thinks it'll bring him closer to his goal. He only wants to win and doesn't care anything about their long-term health and soundness."

"And Liza here is such a superior horse-person that she's able to judge us mere mortals," a deep voice said from behind us.

I spun around, feeling guilty even though I hadn't said anything wrong. Liza turned more slowly and fixed Cole with a baleful stare. Apparently, he'd been lurking around the barn rather than going to the house to sleep.

"I've known you since you were fifteen, Cole. I've had enough time to develop an accurate opinion of your horse skills."

"You're just mad because I dumped you."

"Don't flatter yourself," Liza spat. "I was crazy to go out with you in the first place. You're egotistical, mean, arrogant and...and—"

"Children," Claudia said calmly, coming up and laying a hand on Cole's shoulder. "I thought you'd have this all out of your systems after all these years. Please act like professionals when you are in my barn."

Liza looked down, blushing, and Cole almost managed to hold back his smirk.

I backed out of there as fast as I could. I hoped the barn wasn't going to be that tense from now on. Cole and Liza were like oil and water, and they obviously had some sort of bad blood between them. Maybe Cole was only home for a short time and he would take off showing again. Hilary had said that he'd mostly been away for the last few years.

"Are you ready to go, Astrid?" Marion said, coming down from the viewing room with Caprice in tow. She yawned and stuffed a novel into her purse. I jumped guiltily. I'd totally forgotten she was waiting for me upstairs.

"Yes, sorry, Marion. Thanks for waiting."

I grabbed my garment bag with my show clothes in it, and my ribbon, and we headed for the car.

That night, Marion and I ordered sushi to celebrate my first successful show experience and ate it out on the balcony with fizzy fake champagne to toast with. I was still grinning from ear to ear from my wonderful day. Even archery hadn't made me feel this good.

"Oh, I forgot to tell you," Marion said. "I texted a video of your ride today to your Aunt. I thought she'd like to see it. I hope you don't mind."

"Oh." I sat up straighter with interest. "No, I don't mind. Did she see it already?"

"She did." Marion nodded. "She was very impressed. She was hoping you'd come and visit her for a week over winter break. She has lots of horses you can ride and you can get to know her again."

"Yeah," I said, "that would be fun. Tell her I'd love to come. I hope I can still ride when school starts. I mean, if I can fit it in with archery."

Marion smiled at me and started to clear away the empty food cartons. "I'm sure we can figure something out."

Chapter Eighteen

The next day, Marion dropped Hilary and me off a bit early so she could do a skype conference with her office from home.

To our surprise, the horses already had hay and the lights in the indoor arena were blazing.

"Come on," Hilary whispered, pulling me upstairs. We didn't turn the lights on in the viewing lounge. We sat in the dark and watched quietly as Liza cantered Folly beneath us. Folly was transformed. Gone were the pinned ears and stilted, angry movements. Instead, she was cantering in great, joyous leaps, her expression brave and interested. She looked like the high-class dressage horse she was. Liza leaned slightly forward in the saddle, urging Folly onward. It was beautiful to watch.

When they dropped to a trot, Liza bent forward and patted Folly's neck enthusiastically, her expression rapt. I suddenly felt like I was witnessing a private moment that wasn't meant to be shared. Hilary and I walked slowly downstairs without saying a word.

"I hope Cole never sees her doing that," Hilary said finally. "He'll want Folly back for sure if he knows she's that talented."

"I guess that's why Liza's riding her so early in the morning," I said slowly. "Is Cole really that bad?"

Hilary shrugged. "Not always. He can be really funny sometimes in a sarcastic sort of way. He's just competitive, I guess, and he's not always very nice to the horses. He has a temper."

She twisted her face into a frown and I could see her struggling not to say anything too harsh about Cole. She really tried to always see the good in people.

When Liza finally brought Folly out of the arena, we were already starting to turn some of the horses out on pasture.

"She looks happy, Liza." I smiled, noticing the horse's tired but content expression. I reached out and stroked a hand down Folly's sweat-soaked neck as I passed. She didn't even bother to pin her ears at me, just snorted under her breath and shook her head.

"Oh, she's getting there," Liza said, giving Folly an affectionate slap on the rump. "Aren't you, old girl? Ladies, would you mind getting Marcus ready for me while I get this princess her bath and turn her out in the pasture? I didn't realize I'd been in there so long."

"Of course," I said and went to pull the giant out of his stall.

Claudia was late coming to the barn that morning. She was pale and had dark circles under her eyes. She winced when Caprice barked her usual greeting to us.

"Girls, would you mind terribly if Liza gave you your lessons today? I'm not feeling quite like myself this morning. Or I could ask Cole if he'd teach you, too. He's giving Sadie her lesson this afternoon."

"Oh, we'll take Liza," Hilary said quickly. "Is there anything we can get for you, Claudia? Did you want a coffee?"

"Oh, that would be lovely." Claudia smiled. "I'll be in my office doing some paperwork. The trailer is coming for Ferdinand today."

"Oh," I said, my stomach knotted. "I didn't know he'd actually been sold."

"It was a last-minute sale," Claudia said, smiling. "I ran into an interested buyer at the show. It's okay, I found him a great home."

Liza came in to take over Marcus, and Hilary and I went upstairs to brew three coffees in the Keurig and have a snack. Caprice followed us up and led me to the cupboard where her cookies were stored. Hilary ran Claudia's coffee downstairs while I sipped mine on the couch with Caprice curled up tightly beside me, her paws wrapped around a bone she'd pulled out from between the cushions.

Down below, Liza had brought Marcus into the ring and was letting him walk around on a loose rein. Claudia came in and went over to sit on the mounting block in the middle of the ring. We could see her and Liza talking quietly together.

Suddenly, the big arena door opened with a bang, and Cole strode in leading Montego. Claudia greeted him with a smile, but Liza looked away, pretending not to notice him.

Cole swung up expertly from the ground like a cat, and after walking for only half the length of the arena, he drove Montego forward into a ground-eating trot.

"Wow, those horses look so much alike." Hilary said, appearing beside me.

I nodded, but privately thought that Marcus was much more handsome. Montego was beautiful, but he had a nervous, tense way about him. His tail swished anxiously with every other step, and he gnawed the bit between his teeth as if he'd bite right through it. Suddenly, he plunged forward, yanked his head down between his knees, and let out a massive buck that would have sent me flying into the wall. Cole sat like a rock on the horse's back—his body barely moved, and he calmly gathered the reins and sent the horse forward into a rocking canter. The horse bucked a few more times, but his heart wasn't in it. He settled down and submitted into obedience.

Still, you could tell that he wasn't a willing partner to Cole. He was beautiful and powerful, and he was doing all the same movements as Marcus, but lacked the brilliance and joy that Marcus displayed.

Hilary pursed her lips and shook her head. "I'm surprised Claudia doesn't give him heck for riding him so tight like that. If it were anyone else, she would have kicked him off her property. She has a blind spot where that son of hers is concerned."

Watching Claudia study the two riders in front of her, though, I wasn't so sure. She had a sad, thoughtful expression on her face, and hardly said a word for nearly the whole time they rode. When she did finally move into the center of the ring, she ignored Cole and worked just with Liza.

We made sure Ferdinand was extra shiny before the trailer showed up to get him at noon. He lipped at my hair and pushed me playfully with his head whenever I had to pass in front of him to get a new brush from the grooming tote.

"Stop that, you big baby," I said and laughed, tapping the end of his nose. "You'd better behave for your new owner."

A truck started up the driveway, trailer bouncing along behind it. I peered out eagerly to get a look. "Oh, it's just Rob," I said, "he must have a lesson with Liza, too."

Claudia appeared at the door of the arena and bounced toward us, her face looking better than it had in months. She stopped beside Ferdinand and gave him a quick, affectionate hug.

Ferdinand's ears perked up when he saw the horse trailer. He lifted his big front foot and pawed the ground impatiently, pulling on his cross-ties.

"Hello, Rob, Lanny," Claudia called out as Rob and his dad approached. "The big guy is all ready for you."

"He's big, all right," Rob's father said, crossing his arms over his chest and staring at Ferdinand skeptically. "What do you think, son? Is he half the horse she said?"

"Dad." Rob flushed beet red. "I've known Ferdinand forever. He's exactly what Claudia says he is."

Lanny winked and held out his hand for Claudia to shake. "I know it. Sorry, Claudia, just teasing. Your word is good with me."

Claudia didn't look offended; she was beaming at them both. "Thank you for doing this, Lanny. It means a lot to have my furry kids placed in good homes."

To my surprise, Rob's dad turned away abruptly to clear his throat. "Load him up, Rob," he said, his voice shaking. "I'll meet you at the truck. Claudia, I'll call you later and discuss those other…er, arrangements."

Claudia's smile only dimmed a little bit. She rested her hand gently on Rob's shoulder. "He's yours now, Rob. You take good care of him, understand? He's a sweet, sensitive boy who needs a kind hand. Give him time to grow up and he'll turn into an amazing horse for you."

"Thanks, thanks so much, Claudia," Rob said, his voice trembling a little, too. "I promise I'll take good care of him."

"I know you will, and I'll see you next week for those lessons. Girls, help him load up, please. I need to get back to the arena before Cole and Liza kill each other. You really can't leave them alone for long without a fight breaking out."

She winked at us and headed back toward the indoor without a backward glance.

"Oh my gosh, Rob," Hilary squealed. "How did this happen?"

"I have no idea," Rob said, looking a little bewildered. "She approached my dad yesterday and made some sort of deal. He wouldn't share many of the details with me, but he said she insisted that I *had* to have this horse, and that she wasn't going to take no for an answer. It's pretty amazing because it would have been hard for us to afford a horse like Ferdinand. She's even doing those first few months of lessons free."

We all stared at each other silently. It was a wonderful thing Claudia had done for Rob, but why had it all happened so quickly. Was she sicker than we thought?

"Well, I'd better get this big guy home," Rob said, clipping on Ferdinand's lead rope. "His stall is all set up for him and Artimax will be happy to have some company."

"See you next week," I said. He waved his hand in the air, but didn't look back; his gaze was already fixed adoringly on Ferdinand.

"Well, I'm really glad Rob has him," Hilary said. "Ferdinand is so sweet and sensitive. I know Claudia was worried about selling him to just the right home."

The arena door slid open with a sharp bang, making us both jump.

Cole strode out, his face like a thundercloud. He stalked down the aisle toward the wash stall pulling an unhappy Montego along behind him. Claudia trailed in his wake, looking anxious but determined.

"Some mother you are," Cole spat. "You sold a fantastic prospect right out from under your own son. I didn't even get a chance to find out how much potential he had before you pawned him off on some Mexican groom."

"Oh, Cole," Claudia said with a sigh. "Ferdinand wasn't your type of horse at all. Rob, who is a good, paying client by the way, was the perfect match for him. Besides, you have two perfectly good horses already, and that's where your focus needs to be right now. Montego's legs still aren't right; you are drilling him too hard. He's going to break down if you keep going down this path."

"I'm not into babying horses," Cole said haughtily. "I'll leave that up to you girls to do. Excuse me, I need to get out of here."

Leaving Montego still fully tacked in the wash stall covered in sweat, he pushed past us roughly and strode from the barn. We heard the engine of his little black Cayman roar to life, and then he peeled out of the driveway in a spray of gravel.

"Sorry you had to see that, girls. I love Cole dearly, but we disagree on a few things. Like all parents and children, I suppose. Now, Liza will give you your lessons today and, with any luck, I'll be feeling better tomorrow."

But the next day, she wasn't feeling better. In fact, she was worse. She still made it down to the barn, but she just crept to her office with her coffee and said she didn't want to be bothered.

Liza gave us our lessons, and when I was leading Quarry back down the aisle I heard Caprice's high-pitched bark coming from inside the office.

"Claudia?" I asked, peering inside. She didn't answer; she just sat frozen, staring blankly out the window. "Claudia, are you okay?" Caprice barked again, this time more frantically, pawing at Claudia's leg to get her attention.

Finally, Claudia shook her head and turned to look at me with a dazed expression on her face. "Sorry, what was that Astrid?" she asked, her voice slurred. She blinked as if she were coming out of a deep trance.

"What's wrong?" Liza appeared in the doorway behind me, her face lined with concern.

"I just need to lie down," Claudia said tiredly and suddenly, her eyes rolled back in her head and she collapsed on the table in a heap.

"Go put Quarry away," Liza ordered. "I'm calling the ambulance right now. Claudia, can you hear me?"

I untacked Quarry with shaking hands. He didn't seem to know there was anything wrong; he just stared at me calmly with his wise eyes and let me brush him and turn him out into the pasture. Hilary and Liza were both sitting with Claudia when I got back. Claudia was awake but still looked dazed.

"It will all be okay," Liza said, although she didn't look as though she believed her own words. "The ambulance will be here any minute and Cole is on his way, too."

The ambulance came quickly, and the attendants wasted no time in putting Claudia on a stretcher and lifting her inside. Liza went with her and just as they were leaving, Cole screeched up and leapt out of car, face pale with anxiety. After a quick conversation with the EMTs, he followed behind them in his car.

Hilary and I looked at each other, still in shock over what had happened. "That was awful," Hilary said and then suddenly burst into tears. That was all it took to get me going, too, and we hugged and cried until we felt a little better. The sound of Caprice's anguished howls brought us back to earth—she'd been locked in the office and we'd forgotten all about her.

The little dog bolted down the aisle as soon as I opened the office door, whimpering and sniffing in all directions, looking for Claudia. She was inconsolable and nothing we tried—not treats or cuddling—seemed to calm her down.

We made sure the barn was spotless and the horses taken care of, but nobody had returned by the time Marion came to pick us up that night. She gave us a careful hug as we tearfully told her what had happened.

"Oh, that's horrible," she said, picking up Caprice, who'd come to cry miserably at her feet. "Poor Claudia. Did you try and call Liza?"

"We were too scared to call her," Hilary said. "You know, just in case it was bad news."

"Well, I'll call her for you, then," Marion said and dialed Liza's number.

We listened in as Marion said a few words to Liza and then listened intently, her face troubled. "Yes, I see. Oh, I see. Oh. Yes, of course. We'll take care of everything."

She hung up and sighed. "Claudia had a bad reaction to her medication. It caused her to have a series of mini-strokes. She'll need to stay in the hospital for observation for now. Hilary, would your parents let Caprice stay with you? Liza isn't allowed to have pets at her apartment and she doesn't think Cole will be a very good dog sitter."

"He doesn't like dogs at all," Hilary said with a frown. "My parents wouldn't mind, except I have my choir trip coming up. We're going to Banff for a few days. I don't think they'd let dogs in the hotel."

"Oh." Marion sighed. "Well, I suppose Cole...."

"Wait, why can't we take care of Caprice? I know our building technically doesn't allow dogs, but there are like three dogs living there right now, Marion. Plus, that guy has the pet pig. Nobody would say anything, especially if it's only for a few days."

"Well, I suppose it wouldn't hurt," Marion said thoughtfully. "If it's just for a few days. I need to have the carpets cleaned anyway next week, so it would be good timing."

I went to the office and rifled through the cupboard where I knew Claudia kept extra food and cookies for Caprice. The bag was half empty, but it should be enough to last a small dog a few days. Caprice didn't want to leave the farm. She howled and tried to hide when it was time to leave. We had to carry her to the car, and then I kept her on my lap the whole way home to keep her from jumping all over the place. Even cuddled up against me, she whined softly under her breath. It sounded like she was crying.

We didn't have a dog bed or anything for her, so Marion

found some old towels in the linen closet and lined a cardboard box with them to make a nice cushy place for sleeping. At first, Marion set it up in the kitchen but as soon as we were done with dinner, and we went to our separate rooms like we always did, Caprice had a melt-down. She tore around the condo, first running to my room to howl, and then to Marion's office, barking and carrying on. Luckily, our condo didn't share any walls with anyone because keeping her presence a secret would have been impossible.

"Oh dear," Marion said with a sigh, emerging from her office. "She's probably feeling really lonely right now. How about we set her up in the living room and I can do my paperwork out there."

"Or we could watch a movie," I suggested suddenly. "We haven't done that in...uh, forever."

Marion stared at me as if she'd never heard of such a thing. She glanced between me and the big screen T.V. that had barely ever been used in its life. My dad watched sports occasionally when he was home, but that was about it.

"We could make popcorn," I said hopefully. "Without any butter, of course," I added quickly.

"Okay." Marion brightened. "Let's settle for popcorn and a movie then. Nothing violent please."

While Marion made popcorn, I set Caprice's bed beside the couch and picked out a romantic comedy I thought we would all enjoy. It turned out to be really funny and even Marion laughed at all the right parts. Caprice curled up in her bed and fell fast asleep as soon as the movie started, her little legs twitching as if she were running.

When the first movie was over, Marion amazingly agreed to watch another. It was the best time I ever remembered having with her. When the credits for the second movie rolled up I looked over and saw that Marion, too, was curled up in a ball at the opposite end of the couch. I draped a blanket over her and tiptoed to my room.

In the morning, I slept in until it was almost eight. When I finally woke up and stumbled to the living room, the blanket was neatly folded on the back of the couch and Caprice's dog-bed was nowhere to be found.

"Marion?" I said sleepily. "I'm late for work. We have to feed the horses." I stopped in the kitchen doorway in surprise. Marion was there fully dressed and making pancakes. Caprice sat at her feet staring up at her lovingly. I rubbed my eyes to make sure I wasn't seeing things and then stumbled to the coffee maker.

"Good morning," Marion chimed. "Liza called. She and Cole are feeding the horses this morning so you can go in a little later. Liza asked if you'd do night feed."

I yawned and nodded. "Of course. Did she say how Claudia is doing?"

"Much better." Marion smiled. "Apparently, she's eager to get back to the barn, but the hospital wants to keep her a little longer. I told Liza we'd keep Caprice for a few days until Claudia was back on her feet."

"Oh, that's great," I said. "Did she sleep in your room last night?"

"She was lonely," Marion said defensively. "She very quietly slept in her box beside the bed. I hope your father doesn't mind too much because he'll be home tonight. He called from the airport."

"Great," I said again, but this time with less enthusiasm.

I shook off my worry as I bit into Marion's delicious pancakes. They were light and fluffy and sort of melted in my mouth. "Wow," I said, "what did you put in here? They're amazing."

"They're banana pancakes," Marion said proudly. "No flour, I looked up the recipe online. They're healthy for you. Well, sort of. Maybe not the syrup part."

I stared at the pancake on my fork suspiciously, but then shrugged and took another bite. If Marion said this delicious pancake was somehow healthy for me then I wasn't going to argue.

We took Caprice with us back to the barn and she ran around barking excitedly looking for Claudia, ignoring our calls while we looked on helplessly. When she couldn't find her, she went up to the viewing room and curled up on the couch, sulking. "Just a few more days," Marion said, patting her head soothingly. "She'll be home soon."

I helped Hilary and Liza finish cleaning stalls, and then I brushed Quarry until he shone since Liza said he needed a day off from riding. Cole didn't show up again, and I wondered if he was still at the hospital with Claudia.

* * * * *

That night, my dad came home, and he was in a surprisingly good mood about Caprice being our houseguest. He even snuck the little dog some meat off his plate when he thought we weren't looking. Who knew my dad had a soft spot for animals? I certainly would not have guessed it.

"So, Astrid," he said over dinner. "Marion says you're doing well at this horse ranch of yours. Any chance of arranging a visit to see you ride?"

My fork stopped halfway to my mouth and I'm pretty sure my heart stopped beating.

"I've been telling your father all about your riding," Marion said to fill the silence. "Liza could give you a lesson on Quarry tomorrow, since Claudia is away."

I took a deep breath. What was the big deal? He was just going to watch me ride once and then fly back to whatever site he was working at and hopefully forget all about me. At least he wasn't yelling at me anymore.

"Sure," I said. "As long as Liza doesn't mind then it's fine with me."

"Good," my dad said, wiping his mouth and roughly pushing back his chair, the squeaking noise making Caprice yelp in surprise. "Looking forward to it."

Then he disappeared into the office and shut the door.

Chapter Nineteen

My hands shook as I slipped Quarry's soft leather halter on over his head. I wished that Hilary was here to joke around with me and calm my nerves, but she was preparing for her choir trip.

"Okay, boy, this is it. We can't be nervous. It's just an ordinary ride on an ordinary day, nothing special at all. We'll get you all cleaned up and then we'll have a nice lesson with Liza. No big deal."

Quarry pushed his face into my shoulder and closed his eyes with a sigh while I ran my hands through his silky mane. Was it just my imagination or did he suddenly look old today, as if the weight of the world had settled on his shoulders?

"Come on, buddy."

I took a deep breath and walked forward confidently, trying to convince myself I was going to ride brilliantly and wow my dad.

Quarry took a faltering step beside me, the toe of his right front foot stretched out and not quite touching the ground.

"Oh, no, Quarry, what did you do? You're hurt!"

There was nobody within calling distance and I'd left my cell phone in my backpack. I kept heading toward the barn, step by painful step, until we finally made it into the aisle.

"Liza!" I called. "Come quick, Quarry's hurt!"

She was at my side in an instant, running her hand down Quarry's leg and scrunching her face up in concern. "His leg is hot from the knee right to the coronet band. There must be a lot of inflammation in there. Let's put him in his stall so he can rest and I'll call the vet."

He sighed gratefully when he reached his stall and could stand on the soft bedding rather than the hard ground. He pushed his hay net around briefly but didn't eat.

Worry sank like a rock into my stomach. Quarry loved food. If he wasn't eating then he must really be in a lot of pain. I hoped the vet would hurry.

An hour later, the vet had Quarry standing in the aisle with a portable x ray machine lined up with the horses' front foot. Liza stood at his head, looking sick with worry, stroking his white neck softly. Quarry was everyone's favourite, but he was also Claudia's special horse. It would be awful if something happened to him while she was stuck in the hospital.

"Okay" the vet said finally. "Well, I found our culprit but you're not going to like it. I actually see two things going on here." She pointed to a dark spot on the x ray right near the toe of his foot. "First, he has a huge abscess brewing, and that's what is causing part of the acute pain. We'll lance it today to give him some relief."

She stared at us with a grim look on her face and pointed to the x-ray again. "That's the easy part to deal with. See this line running here? That's not supposed to be there It looks like a fracture in the navicular bone. Has he been painful before today?"

"No." Liza shook her head. "Never. He's always been sound. I don't know how we wouldn't notice an abscess."

The vet shrugged. "With horses anything can happen; he probably stepped on a stone and bruised his sole when he was galloping in the pasture. Sometimes these things take days, even weeks, to show up. Regardless, he's going to need stall rest and some special shoes. We'll nerve block him today to give him some relief. And we'll run some bloodwork just to get a baseline. He has a long, slow road ahead of him and, given his age, he might not fully recover." She sighed and stood up, stretching her back out. "The other option, of course, given his age, is to have him humanely euthanized."

I gasped and Liza stiffened, one hand sliding up to grasp his halter protectively. She glared at the doctor. "He's more than paid his dues as a horse, and if rest is what he needs then he'll get it here. As long as he's sound enough to be comfortable and pain-free then Claudia will be happy."

"Good." The vet smiled thinly. "I'm happy to hear it. Not all my clients would do the same."

"Well then, they don't deserve to have horses."

The vet first drew a large vial of blood from the jugular vein in Quarry's neck to test it back at the lab. Then she injected him with a sedative. Once he was sleepy, she lifted his foot and used a thin, sharp blade to cut into the sole of his hoof until she'd reached the pocket of infection. A squirt of thick, yellow fluid shot out, the rancid smell making me gag. There was so much goop in there, it must have been awfully painful for Quarry.

Once it stopped oozing, the vet scrubbed his hoof and then wrapped it in a bandage to keep it clean. She wiped the back of his injured leg with rubbing alcohol and then injected a small vial of liquid using a tiny needle. Then we led him slowly to his stall. He stood in the corner swaying back in forth under the effect of his sedation.

"You'll have to soak it twice a day and keep it wrapped in between times so it stays clean," the vet said as she was getting into her truck. "He'll be on stall rest for the next seven days. I'll come take a look at him next week and see how he's making out. Hopefully, you can start hand walking him then, too."

"I have to go tell Claudia," Liza said, looking upset. "I have to let her know that he's being looked after properly. Keep an eye on him, Astrid. He should wake up soon, but text me if you're worried. No hay or treats for at least an hour, though, okay, otherwise he could choke. I have to get to the hospital."

As soon as she was gone, I slipped over to Quarry's side, overwhelmingly grateful that he was going to live. But I couldn't help a few selfish tears from filling my eyes and rolling down my cheeks. As happy as I was that he just needed time to heal, I couldn't help realizing what his injury was going to mean to me. I loved riding Quarry, and now I didn't have a horse at all. I couldn't believe my riding career was over just like that.

"Astrid?" It was my father's voice behind me, sounding gentle and concerned. "What's happened? Are you hurt?"

Without thinking, I turned, not stopping until I was standing next to him, leaning my forehead against his shoulder as I let out a few, stifled sobs. Surprisingly, he patted my back a few times before pushing me gently away.

"Quarry's hurt." I sniffled. "He might never be ridden again."

"Oh." My father nodded sympathetically, looking at the bandage on Quarry's foot. "This is the white horse you were riding at the show, right? He certainly was beautiful to watch. He looks like he's being well taken care of here. Isn't there another horse you could ride in the meantime? I was looking forward to seeing what all the fuss was about."

I gritted my teeth, knowing there was no way to explain to him what Quarry meant to me. I wasn't sure if I even wanted to ride another horse, or if I'd be able to. Quarry felt like an extension of my own self, the rest were just, well, horses.

"Hi there." Cole appeared behind us like a shadow, flashing his hundred-watt smile at my dad. "Mr. Kendrick, I'm Cole, Claudia's son. I'm the head trainer here while my mom's away. If you're interested, I do have a horse Astrid could ride today, one of my up and coming prospects. It would just take me a minute to have one of the grooms tack her up."

I stared at him blankly for a moment, thinking hard, there weren't any extra horses for me to ride, unless, unless he meant....

"Liza!" Cole called out in his commanding tone. "Tack Folly up for Astrid, please; she'd like to try her out."

I stared at him with my mouth hanging open. He couldn't possibly mean for me to ride Folly. "No, Cole. Liza's at the hospital with *your* mother." I hadn't meant the words to sound hard, but I saw him wince.

"Anyway, I can't ride Folly. Claudia said she was Liza's project. And Folly doesn't trust anyone but Liza yet."

"Astrid," Cole said slowly as if he were talking to a two-year-old child. "Folly is actually *my* horse. I sent her back from Europe so we could develop her talent here. I've been overseeing Liza's work. She's gotten the basics down with Folly, but now it's time to develop the mare's potential. I think you would actually be a good match for her. And as for trust, horses will submit to whoever shows them who's boss. They don't have room in their pea brains for anything more complicated than that."

He and my dad laughed at his stupid joke, but I felt sick and confused. I knew what happened when I stood up to my father, and there was nobody around to back me up.

"Well, Astrid, get this horse ready and we'll see what you can do. I made a special trip out here to see you ride and don't have much time left. Let's get a move on."

"Give her a try, anyway," Cole said, reasonably. "If you don't like her then you can just let me know."

Both he and my dad were staring at me like I was a complete dolt, waiting for me to answer.

How bad could it be? I asked myself. *Cole will be right there.*

Well, for one, she could kill you, I answered in my head. *She's totally dangerous and unpredictable. She doesn't care about you like Quarry does.*

But she's been really good lately, I argued silently, *and your dad is waiting for an answer. He's been trying to be nicer these last few visits. You don't want to ruin it now, do you?*

But what about Liza, I argued, *she'd be so mad if she found out.*

Liza's not here. Just this one ride and then your dad will fly out to who-knows-where and you won't have to see him for another few months.

"Fine." I sighed. "I'll do it. But just this once."

"That's my girl," my dad said, clapping me awkwardly on the back. "I'm just going to my car to make a quick phone call, but I'll be back in time to see you ride."

I grabbed a carrot from the tack room and trudged out to the pasture to get Folly. She came to meet me at the gate and took her carrot eagerly. She had been getting much better lately. Now, anyone could turn her out or bring her in at night, and she didn't try to bite or make faces when we fed her. She'd come a long way under Liza's careful watch.

"Sorry, girl," I said, slipping on her halter. "If you can just avoid killing me for this one ride then I promise we'll never have to do it again."

She snorted and nudged my chest, wiping bits of carrot on my shirt.

"Okay, I'll take that as a yes."

She stayed in a good mood while I brushed her and tacked her up, and her ears only started to flatten when Cole appeared in the barn doorway, whistling under his breath.

"Well, hello, Folly," he said, sending her an unpleasant look. "Still as charming as ever, I see."

I noticed that he kept a good distance away from her.

"She's a fantastic horse," Cole suddenly said in a louder voice, making both me and Folly jump. "She's outside of your comfort zone, I understand. But that's where brilliance happens. And, Astrid, you and this horse together could be brilliant."

Cole turned and flashed smile at my dad, who was marching up behind us. "Ah, Mr. Kendrick. I didn't know you were back already. Astrid and I were just discussing Folly's potential."

"Okay, let's get this show on the road," my dad barked. "I

have to be at a meeting in an hour."

"Don't worry, Folly," I whispered, following my dad and Cole toward the ring. I wondered what on earth I'd gotten myself in for.

While Cole talked glowingly to my dad about Folly's bloodlines and stunning attributes, I led the increasingly sulky horse over to the mounting block, trying to control my breathing.

Imagine you're riding Quarry, I told myself. *This is just another lesson on a horse that you love. No big deal.*

Folly stood obediently, only swishing her tail once as I lowered myself slowly to the saddle. Sitting on her was much different than being on Quarry. She was huge, for one thing. It was like being perched on a high cliff over the ocean, peering down at the turbulent water below. Dangerous, possibly shark-infested, water.

I glanced over at Cole, but he had his back to me, still talking to my dad.

What would Claudia tell me if she was here? I thought desperately. *She'd say I'd have to relax my body and concentrate on my breathing first.*

"Eaaasy girl," I said softly, stroking her neck. I crossed my stirrups over the front of the saddle like I always did and asked her gently with my seat to walk forward. She tensed for a moment and then exhaled slowly and moved obediently into an uneasy walk.

"That's it," I crooned, "this is just an easy ride. Just you and me walking around the arena, nice and relaxed. I'm just going to pretend that I'm Liza and that Claudia's right here telling us what to do. We'll just stay on a loose rein until you're ready."

Folly heaved a deep sigh, and I could feel her mouthing the bit gently. She dropped her head and her back loosened the tiniest bit. It wasn't quite so much like riding a rocket anymore.

"Okay, Astrid!" Cole clapped his hands together sharply, startling us both. Folly pinned her ears flat against her head and kicked out viciously to the side. I yelped and grabbed the reins harder than I meant to, jabbing her in the mouth.

"That's right. Pick up a contact right away with this mare. Don't let her slop around like that."

Folly's whole body went rock hard as soon as I picked up the reins. I could feel her teeth grinding against the bit, even though I was barely touching her mouth. She rooted her nose outwards, tossing her head and pulling the reins through my fingers.

"Don't let her get away with that! Take a firm contact. No, more, more, more. You want ten pounds of pressure in each hand."

I shortened my reins a bit more and looked uncertainly to where Cole stood with my dad. I had no idea what he meant. When I rode Quarry, I only had the lightest of contact with his mouth. Claudia always said to imagine I was holding two delicate baby birds between my fingers.

Cole strode over to me and grabbed the reins when Folly tried to scoot away from him. "Astrid, this horse needs you to support her and contain her energy. To do that, you have to have a firm contact at all times. Here…." He pulled her reins short until her neck was arched in a tight curl and then slid the leather between my fingers, squeezing them in a bird-crushing grip. "Now hold on tight and ask her to move forward. When she resists your rein aids, you need to tighten your abs to stay rooted in the saddle and add lots of leg. Understand?"

"But, but I'm hurting her mouth," I said miserably. "She can't move forward if I have her all crammed in like this."

"No, Astrid, *she's* hurting her own mouth by resisting you. Once she submits to your pressure then she won't feel uncomfortable. She just needs to know you're boss first."

I nodded uncertainly and asked her to move forward again, hating how much I was pulling on her mouth. Just for a moment, she ducked her head and eased the pressure on the reins. *That's it, Folly,* I thought miserably, *just stop fighting.* She took two steps that felt almost light and collected, but the next moment, she'd plunged forward with an angry squeal and tried to scrape my leg against the arena wall.

"Forward! Kick her if you have to," Cole yelled. "Don't let her think on her own for a single second…drive her forward where you want to go."

I want to go home, but I didn't think that's what Cole meant. I managed to pilot Folly in a big, wobbly circle around the middle of the ring, my arms aching with the strain of holding on so tight. A bead of sweat trickled between my shoulder blades down my back.

"Better, now ask her to canter right from the walk. It's better to let her get out some of that energy."

Reluctantly, I shifted my seat bone back a hair and Folly rewarded me with a large buck and a leap to the right that nearly tore my arms from their sockets, before surging into a canter.

Even though it was terrifying and pretty much out of control, for a moment, I could feel why everyone thought Folly was a great horse. She propelled us forward across the area like a Pegasus, all power and wind and terrifying speed. If she hadn't also been trying to kill me, it would have been amazing.

Cole shouted some things I couldn't hear, and I just concentrated on staying upright and keeping Folly turning in smaller figure eight circles in the hopes that she'd eventually tire herself out and stop.

Every time we switched directions, she surged forward with her ears pinned into what was either a buck or a lead change, I couldn't quite tell. All I knew was that when she eventually slowed to a jarring trot of her own accord, we were both covered in sweat and exhausted. Folly's ears sagged to the sides and there were big strands of sweaty foam lathering her neck. I was like a limp noodle with barely enough strength to lift my arms.

"That was fabulous," Cole said, coming up to take her reins and give me a pat on the knee. He had a compact video camera on one hand. I hadn't even noticed him videoing us. Great, there would be evidence. "Just brilliant for your first ride. There is real, untapped potential there, Astrid."

I was too weak to argue, I just wanted off this crazy animal.

"Wow, Astrid." My dad strode over, his eyes gleaming with something close to pride. "I have to say I'm impressed. Cole here says you show real talent. That mare is perfect for your career, something to grow into and take you right to the top. There's a show at the end of the month you can try her out in."

I was still reeling from my ride, so I was sure I must have heard him wrong. Hadn't they noticed that Folly had almost killed me out there? I could barely stay on her back, let alone stop her. I was lucky to be alive.

"Show her?" I said in a wobbly voice. "There's no way I can—"

"It's a great idea," Cole interrupted. "We'll start small, of course. We won't do anything you're not ready to do, Astrid."

"But I don't want—"

"Wait, don't say anything else yet. I have to show you something. Get her cooled out and them come up to the viewing room."

I slid shakily to the ground as soon as they were gone, tears pooling in my eyes. "I am so, so sorry, Folly," I said, leading the sweat-drenched mare to the wash stall. She didn't look at me and she didn't nuzzle me for treats like Quarry would. She was too tired to resist as I hosed her down and carefully dried her off. I threw a sheet on her and led her back to the pasture. At least she could stay outside and enjoy the rest of her half-ruined day.

Slowly, I made my way upstairs to the viewing room.

"That took you long enough," my dad said grumpily.

"Sorry, we're a little short staffed today," Cole said smoothly. "Sit down and watch this, Astrid."

He fiddled with his phone and somehow an image of me and Folly popped up on the big screen T.V. that dominated one wall of the viewing lounge.

Suddenly, there I was, looking white-faced and grim on top of Folly's powerful body. But, wow, was that really me riding? It looked like Hilary or maybe even Liza up there. As Folly surged forward, I moved with her, riding the powerful wave of motion like a surfer on the sea. From the outside, it looked like I had everything *almost* in control, as if it were me directing Folly's movements and not the other way around.

When the short clip was over, Cole turned to me with a grin. "So, what do you think now?"

My dad and Cole were both staring at me intently, waiting for me to say something. "Uh, I still think she's way too much horse for me," I said slowly. "I'm not experienced enough...."

"The only way to gain experience is by *doing* the work, Astrid," my dad said testily, his face tensing with disappointment. "You can't expect to be handed things on a silver platter in this world. An opportunity has fallen into your lap. Are you going to stay weak for the rest of your life? Are you going to just lay down and give up? Or are you going to take the bull by the horns and take charge of your life?"

My face blazed with a mixture of mortification and panic. I looked back and forth between the two of them, heart thudding in my chest. They didn't care that Folly scared me. I need to explain somehow. "Dad, I tried—"

"There's no *try*, Astrid," my dad snarled, rising to his feet as his phone began to beep. "Trying is for people who are settling for second place. Do you want to be a second place loser for the rest of your life or do you want to win?"

I stared at him blankly, wondering if I'd somehow been switched at birth. How could someone as driven as he was have a daughter who didn't care one bit about winning? Who just wanted to get through life without being yelled at or called a stupid failure.

"You're spoiled, Astrid, that's the problem," my dad said, staring down at his phone, white-knuckled, as if he were about to crush it.

"I...I'm sorry." I wasn't sure what I was apologizing for, but it seemed the right thing to say.

"Don't apologize, just make it right. Are you going to ride that horse or not?"

"I…guess I could…."

"Fine." He waved his hand dismissively through the air. "Good decision. Make me proud. Lordon…what news do you have?"

He'd already jammed his phone against his ear and was marching down the stairs toward his car, any thoughts of a daughter long forgotten.

Cole and I sat staring at each other, speechless. "Wow, Astrid." Cole cleared his throat. "He's…quite intense, isn't he? Don't worry about Folly, though. It will get better with every ride. You'll see."

I didn't see at all. I especially didn't see how I'd landed myself in this predicament. I went downstairs in a fog and sat in Quarry's stall for a long time, watching him slowly wake up and take an interest in his surroundings. I brought him a hay net and was still sitting in the corner of his stall staring blankly when Rob poked his head over the door.

"Astrid?" he asked uncertainly. "Where is everyone? Liza was supposed to schedule a lesson with Ferdi, but she's not answering her phone. I came over to see what was up." He peered more closely at my face and then rolled the door open. "What happened?" he asked quietly, sitting down in the shavings next to me so close that our shoulders were touching. I leaned against him slightly, letting the warmth from his skin thaw me a little. He felt so alive compared to me. I felt like a stone statue that had been hollowed out on the inside.

"Astrid, you have to talk to me or I can't help. What happened to Quarry?"

"He...he had an abscess," I said hesitantly. "And the vet said something else, too, but I can't remember. A little bone in his foot is broken. It means he has to rest, though...no more riding."

"Okay," he said slowly, "but that's not why you're so upset."

"No, I...." My lower lip trembled and then the whole story poured out of me like an avalanche. I wanted to shut up, but I just couldn't stop talking. I even told him the part where my dad had called me a loser. "I know I'm stupid to care." I sniffled. "I should be used to it by now. I'm such a baby."

Rob sat silently beside me, and I knew he must be horrified at having me blubber at him. My face must be a blotchy, wet mess. I waited for him to get up to leave, but instead he reached over and took my hand, squeezing it tightly.

"You're not a baby," he said, his voice sounding angry. "And you're not stupid. You shouldn't have to get *used* to people treating you badly, Astrid. This situation is really messed up. Folly is not a safe horse for many people. Cole must be crazy to have you ride her."

"I think it's the money," I said. "Hilary said something about him being desperate for sponsors or something."

"Yeah, he probably couldn't even sell Folly right now," Rob said thoughtfully. "She's too unpredictable. So, what? He's planning on convincing your dad to buy her?"

"I'm not sure." I shrugged. "I guess if Cole was teaching me, he'd get the money for lessons instead of Claudia or Liza. I'm not sure if he really had a plan. He probably just saw an opportunity and went for it."

"He's an idiot," Rob growled. "Claudia will set him straight."

"Oh, you can't tell her," I said, clutching at his hand. "She's so sick. I don't want to worry her. I'll figure this out somehow. Hopefully, I can talk to my stepmom tonight and she'll sort my dad out."

"Okay," Rob said doubtfully. "Well, what about Liza?"

I dropped my head in my hands and groaned. "I know. She's going to kill me. I'm not sure how I'm going to explain it to her."

"Come on," Rob said, pulling me to my feet. "Let's get out of here. We'll figure it out over a pizza. My treat."

My heart lit up when he said that and then fell again. "I'd love to, but Marion's going to be here to pick me up any minute."

"Oh," he said, disappointed. "Okay, well maybe next time. I'll text you tonight."

Before I could react, he'd pulled me into a tight hug and then he was gone. I stared after him, missing the warmth of his hug, wishing more than anything that I'd accepted his invitation.

* * * * *

Rob's support had somehow infused me with the courage I needed. That night at dinner, I decided to give it another shot. Marion would have to back me up. She knew more about the barn than my dad did. It wasn't the greatest of timing—he had been holed up in his office all evening and he'd snapped at Caprice when she'd tried to climb into his lap at the table. But I needed to talk to him before I had to face Liza at the barn tomorrow.

"Dad," I said hesitantly, once he was halfway through dinner. "Can I talk to you about Folly?"

He looked up distractedly from his food and frowned as if

just realizing that there were two other people seated at the table with him. "Who? Oh, the horse. Yes."

"Dad, Folly is too much horse for me. She's meant for an upper level rider and I'm not there yet. I might be someday," I added quickly as he set his fork down on his plate. "Just not now. I need a horse like...well, like Quarry."

"I see," he said quietly. "And where are you expecting this magical horse to come from?"

"I...I'm not sure," I stuttered. "I hadn't really thought—"

"That's right, you didn't use your head, Astrid." He closed his eyes and took a deep breath before opening them again. "Astrid, I really don't have the energy to deal with this right now. Earlier this summer, you made a terrible mistake, and I can see you've worked hard, exceptionally hard, to remedy the situation. Your stepmother and I are proud of you."

"I, well, thanks, Dad," I said, not sure where this conversation was heading.

"Astrid, if there's one thing that I hate, it's a quitter, someone who backs down when the going gets tough. You were sailing along fine until Quarry got hurt, but one little rock in your path and you want to give up. I'll make a deal with you, Astrid. You move out of your comfort zone and put 100% into your riding career for the rest of the summer, and I'll get your bow back to you and you can head back to the archery range all you like. Cole says there's a show coming up the second week in September, just before school starts. Ride Folly in that and make me proud. After that, you can decide if you want to drop riding or not."

I stared at him in confusion, thoughts churning through my

head. Did that mean that if I *didn't* ride Folly that I couldn't go back to the range again?

"Astrid, this new horse, er, Folly, is going to make you step up your game. Give it a hundred and ten percent. She's going to need you to make a commitment to your sport, to your career. You understand? Folly is a horse who can take you right to the top. Most riders would give their right arm for an opportunity like this."

I could tell the words weren't his; he was quoting directly from Cole.

I turned to Marion, desperate to find a tactful way out of this.

She cleared her throat a few times and then set down her utensils carefully. "I don't know, Bruce," she said softly, "Astrid seems to be quite afraid of Folly. You don't want her to lose her confidence now when she's just started riding."

"Cole wouldn't put her on a horse who was actually dangerous, Marion. The animal is just more powerful than Astrid's used to. The horse is a real athlete who demands perfection. She was amazing, really. Quite the firecracker."

"Yes, but I don't think Astrid is experienced enough to handle a horse like that—"

"Nonsense," my dad slammed his fist down suddenly on the table, making me jump. I knew right then the conversation was over. "If she can get her head out of the clouds then she might actually make this work. I have to put my money somewhere, Marion, and pretty darn fast, too, or someone else is going to get it. It might be a good investment. Cole said we could get her cheap and sell her at a really decent price once she's had the kinks worked out of her."

What, I thought in horror. *He can't be talking about buying Folly now. He said it was just for the month. And why would he have to hide his money?*

"Oh, Bruce," Marion said in dismay, "surely it's not that bad, yet. The lawyers said it was looking promising."

"They have to say that. The wolves are snarling round the door, Marion. I'll be lucky if I don't end up in prison. If they can't shift the blame to Ling, then I'm sure that's what will happen."

"What do you mean?" Marion asked in alarm. "Richard works for you, why would he be blamed for anything?"

"He set up that site in Belize. Someone has to go down, Marion. Do you want to see me put behind bars?"

"Of course not!" Her eyes were wide with shock. "But, but, darling, if he didn't do anything wrong…then how could he go to prison?"

They stared at each other wide-eyed and then he stood up and offered her his outstretched hand. She hesitated and then took it, rising from the table without a backward glance. It was like I wasn't even there. They disappeared into the office, leaving me alone with a table full of half-eaten food.

"Fine," I said into the silence. "Don't worry about me. I don't even exist."

I reached over and snagged my dad's uneaten dinner roll off his plate. I was only ever allowed half a roll and always without butter, but *he* always managed to polish off two or three himself. I slathered it in butter and stuffed it in my mouth, closing my eyes in what should have been guilty pleasure. Tonight, the taste was bitter in my mouth. Marion's chicken sat on her plate and I reached over and grabbed that, too. I kept going until I finished everything on the table, even though it tasted like cardboard. I ate until I didn't feel so hollow anymore.

The food sat like a rock in my stomach that night as I tossed and turned. I hadn't texted Rob, and I didn't even look at my phone when it beeped. I didn't know how to tell him what I'd overheard at dinner. I wasn't sure I understood it myself. Was my dad some sort of criminal monster who was about to put Susan and Thomas's dad in jail for something he didn't do? Had I even heard it right?

I hadn't managed to fix anything about my Folly situation, either. How would I explain to Liza tomorrow that I'd ridden her beloved horse? No, not just ridden her, but practically *hauled* on her mouth until Folly had kicked out in anger. I had just about ruined all Liza's hard work in one ride. And I didn't ever want to get back on Folly; the thought terrified me. How was I going to get out of riding for a whole month?

I rubbed my aching shoulder and stared outside at the moon. *You could fall off on purpose,* a little voice inside of me said. *You could get hurt just enough so that you wouldn't have to ride for a long time. Everyone would feel sorry for you and take care of you.*

Yes, but then I couldn't do archery, I reasoned, *and I couldn't help out with barn chores. Liza's going to need everyone's help with Claudia being so sick. I couldn't bail on her now.*

* * * * *

The next day the answers were no clearer for me. I drove to the barn with Marion in silence, both of us lost in our own thoughts.

"Your father's flying out tonight," Marion said as I reached for my door handle. "He won't be back until next week. I'll…I'll talk to him about this horse when he gets back, sweetie. I know you're scared."

"Okay," I said, not looking her in the eye.

"Astrid, I don't want you to worry about what you heard last night. Everything is going to be okay."

"Nobody is going to jail?"

"Oh, sweetie. I honestly don't think it will come to that. Your father is just upset and overwhelmed. That's not your job to worry about, though. I want you to have fun the rest of this summer, okay? And, darling, do give this horse an honest try, make sure that you're not running away from a challenge." I looked up at the sad note in her voice. "Astrid, I've spent the last ten years of my life running away from things that scare me. It's painful for me to even leave the house sometimes. I don't want that for you. I want you to be fearless."

"Okay," I said quietly, easing out of the car. "I'll try, Marion."

I walked slowly to the barn, caught up in a tangle of my own thoughts. Was I really just being a baby avoiding Folly?

The barn lights were on and Liza was already handing out hay down the aisle. She smiled at me brightly; obviously, she didn't know about yesterday's ride yet.

"Morning, Astrid!" she sang out. "We have a tight schedule today so we have to get cracking."

"All right." I went into the feed room and started mixing grain, smiling a little at the excited *huh huh huh* noises coming from the horses. They knew exactly what time it was.

"As soon as we're done stalls I'm going to ride Folly then

Marcus, Jerry, then Severus. Astrid, I'll need you to help me tack up and put away after each ride, okay?"

"Sure," I said, wondering how Folly would react when I tried to tack her up.

"Ally's on a Mediterranean cruise this month, so I'll be riding the big guy. Then I'm going to give Sadie a quick lesson—not that she needs it—and then I'm off to help Claudia for the afternoon. Those strokes left her pretty weak. It's hard for her to use her whole right side right now."

"When is she coming home, though," I asked.

"It will be another week." Liza sighed. "I'm going to work here in the mornings and then stay with her every afternoon while she's in hospital. I wish Cole would do more shifts, though; he barely visits."

"Oh," I said, suddenly hit with an amazing idea. Maybe I didn't have to tell Liza about Folly at all. Maybe if I was very careful to hide the evidence, I could ride Folly in the afternoons after she was already tired from her workout with Liza in the morning. If I hosed her down and made sure she was spotless then Liza might never find out. I would just have to convince Cole not to tell her.

I was still cleaning stalls when Liza started tacking Folly up herself. I kept looking over nervously just in case I'd left an incriminating mark on her somewhere or left slobber on her bit or something, but Liza seemed totally unaware. Folly, too, seemed to have gotten over her trauma from yesterday, but just in case, I made sure to stay far away from her.

Just as she was heading to the arena, Cole came sauntering in, coffee cup in hand. "What are you doing with *my* horse,

Liiizzza," he sang out, a wicked glint in his eye. He was practically dancing toward her. Nothing would make him happier than to tell her that she couldn't ride Folly anymore.

"Cole," I interrupted loudly. "Can I talk to you for a second? My dad wanted me to ask you something."

Liza sent us a weird look and then shrugged, continuing on to the ring.

"What's up, buttercup?" Cole grinned at me. "You're ruining my surprise for Liza."

"Please stop being so mean to her, Cole," I said. "She really loves Folly. Anyway, I have an idea."

"Okay, I'm listening," Cole said, crossing his arms over his chest.

"I can't ride Folly like she is, Cole. She's way too much horse for me and you know it. And you also know that *you* don't want to ride her."

"I ride lots of horses I don't like, Astrid, it's not a big deal."

"Yes, but it's a big deal to Folly. I heard what she was like in Germany. That's why you could buy her so cheaply. My dad is totally going to sue you if she kills me, Cole."

He raised an eyebrow at me. "Fine, what is your plan, then?"

"Let Liza keep riding her in the mornings, at least for this week. I'll ride Folly in the afternoons once Liza is safely out of the way. That way, hopefully, she'll be tired and won't be so difficult for me to handle."

"You don't think Liza is smart enough to figure out that someone is riding her, I mean *my*, horse?"

I sighed. This was a flaw in my plan. "She might, but I'll try to keep it from happening as long as I can. She's distracted, worrying about your mom right now. She might not notice."

Cole shook his head, a small smile played around his mouth. I could tell that the idea had taken hold. "Okay, you win, for this week. Good luck with keeping your secret."

As soon as he'd gone to get Montego, I ran upstairs to the viewing area to watch what was left of Liza's ride. From now on, I would have to study how she handled Folly as closely as possible. I wanted to duplicate her ride as much as I could.

It was hard to see what she was doing, though. Liza sat like a statue on Folly's back, a slight slack in the reins and a smile on her face. I could barely detect any aides at all. Folly moved forward rhythmically around the arena, ears flopping to the sides and a look of happy concentration on her face.

"Okay, I'm going to have to try to use my core more than my reins," I murmured. "Cole is wrong about all that hard contact. That's what she hates."

It was easier said than done, though. I had the best of intentions, but when I eased Folly over to the mounting block that afternoon, she was already tense with worry, her coat damp with sweat, despite her morning ride. I sat as lightly on her back as possible while she jigged and tossed her head. I didn't dare ride without stirrups today, which was odd since I usually felt *more* secure without my stirrups getting in the way. I concentrated on my breathing and visualized my weight sinking downward, and for a few steps, Folly did seem to deflate and relax. But it didn't last. She shied at every corner, ears swivelling around in alarm as she grew more and more tense.

Cole watched us circle him with a frown on his face. "Okay, we won't be as firm with her as we were yesterday then, but she still has to listen to you, Astrid. You're the brains and she's the brawn, right. You're the captain of this ship. So shorten your reins and make her move forward into your contact."

I shortened my reins about a millimeter and held my breath, waiting for the explosion.

"Move her into a trot, circle around me at this end, and we'll start with transitions. You were right about having Liza riding her; she's in a much better frame of mind than yesterday."

The best thing I could say about that lesson was that it hadn't been as horrible as the day before. But Folly still hadn't really listened to any of my aides and my shoulder throbbed from having her drag me around the ring. She wasn't as upset as she had been yesterday, but she was drenched with sweat and exhausted, and so was I. Despite how tired she was feeling, she jigged beside me on the way to the wash stall, knocking into me and nipping at my arm.

"Hey, you stop that, Folly," I said in astonishment. I hadn't seen her act up on the ground in a long time. "We'll just give you your bath and turn you out in the pasture for a while. Then you'll feel better."

She relaxed as the warm water ran over her body and she even let me practice some massage work on her back and hips.

Once she was nice and dry, I stuffed a carrot in her mouth and headed with her back out toward the pasture.

She followed me nicely all the way out, but when I stopped to unlatch her gate she just kept walking, crushing her huge chest right into me, pressing me into the gate so I could hardly breathe.

"Hey!" I said, squeezing myself free just before she flattened me like a pancake. "What are you doing, Folly? Back up." I jerked the lead rope toward her chest to get her to back up, but she didn't move, even when I pushed on her shoulder as hard as I could. She just stared down at me with a horsey look of condescension stamped on her face. Then she nudged me with her nose, hard enough that I stumbled again.

"Ow, cut that out, Folly. I'm just trying to put you out in the pasture, you stupid horse." She turned and looked off in the distance while I fumbled with the gate and swung it open. As soon as the gate was open, she pushed past, dragging me a few feet until she finally stopped and let me take off her halter. Then she spun around, barely missing me with her flying back feet as she took off across the pasture at a full run.

I shut the gate quickly and took a deep breath, fighting back tears. Was it always going to be this difficult with Folly? She behaved beautifully for Liza, so what was her secret?

That night I got the text I'd been dreading.

Hey, Astrid, do you know what's going on? Dad was pulled out of his office by the police and interviewed. He won't tell us anything. I don't know what's happening. S

Damn, damn, damn. I stuffed my phone under my pillow and closed my eyes. *I know nothing*, I told myself, *I am just a kid and this is my Dad's business. It has nothing to do with me.*

I lay there, staring at the ceiling wondering what the Lings would do if their dad was thrown in prison. No, not just imprisoned. *Wrongfully* imprisoned. How would I face them if my dad walked free and theirs didn't?

I tossed and turned, feeling sick.

* * * * *

The next day was a little worse. Cole had to hold her still so I could even get on, and the whole time I was getting settled in the saddle she nipped at his hands with her big, yellow teeth. Some parts of our ride were bearable, but when I applied my leg a little harder than I'd meant to, she lashed out viciously with her right hoof, splintering the side panelling. She limped a few steps and then stood in the middle of the ring snorting unhappily.

"Senseless cow," Cole said, striding over to examine the break in the wood. "Serves you right if you've hurt yourself. Get her moving, Astrid. I want that bloody horse working so hard she doesn't know whether it's night or day. Move it!"

Folly sprang into a jerky canter, and I did my best to steer her around the ring without her breaking anything else. But afterwards, I had to walk her for nearly an hour before she cooled out and her sides stopped heaving. She held her head down during her bath and rested the hind foot she'd hit the wall with, not looking at me at all.

When I turned her out to pasture, though, it was a different story. She squealed and pulled out of her halter before I'd fully unbuckled it, then whipped around, hooves whistling through the air about a meter from my head. She took off across her pasture, bucking and squealing angrily.

"Folly!" I yelled, both shocked and angry. *Well, at least she's not hurt*, I consoled myself. *That foot doesn't seem to be bothering her now.*

By the next day, Liza was definitely suspicious. She ran her hand down Folly's hind leg and examined her hoof carefully before standing up to look Folly over.

"Hey, Astrid," she called, bending to look at the corner of Folly's mouth.

I groaned silently, picturing the small, hairless spot that the bit had rubbed the other day. "Yes, Liza?" I called from depths of the stall I was pretending to clean.

"Have you noticed anything weird with Folly? She has some marks on her and she's sore on one hind."

"Um, no," I gulped. "Well, she was tearing around pretty hard in her pasture yesterday. Maybe she pulled something.

"Hmm," Liza said, narrowing her eyes as she ran her hands over Folly's side. "Well, maybe I'll give her the day off today, just in case."

Just great, I moaned to myself. *Well, if she's hurt then Cole will have to agree to give her the day off, too.*

But unfortunately, he didn't see it that way.

"She's fine, Astrid. We have work to do. It'll give us a chance to see how she does with just one ride a day. Liza's going to find out soon enough that you're riding her. You might as well prepare for the inevitable."

Reluctantly, I led Folly to the ring, and Cole again held the cheek piece of her bridle tight so that she would let me get on. This time, Folly barely let me get seated before she half-reared in the air, knocking Cole sideways with her shoulder and bolting across the ring, bucking and snorting.

By some sort of miracle, I held on. Desperately, I grabbed my left rein in both hands and hauled on it as hard as I could, yanking her head sideways until her chin was nearly resting on my knee. She squealed angrily, but was forced to come to a stop long enough for me to kick my feet free from the stirrups and leap to the ground.

"Folly! Whoa!" Liza's voice rang out across the arena and immediately the horse stopped dragging me sideways. Her ears pricked forward and made a desperate little nickering sound at Liza that nearly broke my heart. She jerked her head sideways; my hands slipped from the reins, and Folly trotted over to Liza and buried her head under Liza's arm.

Cole, for once, was speechless. He sat on the mounting block, still looking dazed and took a big swig of his coffee. "You okay, Astrid?" he asked, finally.

"I...I think so," I said, my eyes fixed on where Liza was still standing stroking Folly's forehead, ignoring us.

"Liza," I said tentatively, taking a step toward them.

"Don't say it, Astrid," she said bitterly. She looked up and shook her head. "I don't know what's going on here, but there is nothing you can say to make this better. Folly's terrified. Can't you see that?"

"Of course I can!" I practically wailed. "I'm trying my best, Liza. I didn't have a choice—"

She held up a hand to cut me off. "Oh, stow it, Astrid. Don't say that you didn't have any choice because you know it's a lie. Folly is too much horse for you. If you get hurt, it'll be your own damn fault, you understand? You're just a beginner, Astrid. You ride so well because Claudia's an amazing teacher and Quarry has been babysitting you all along. Without them, you are going to fall apart so fast it will make your head spin. And who will be there to pick up the pieces when that happens? Or when you and Cole have ruined a perfectly good horse? Not me, that's for sure."

She turned and marched Folly out of the ring without looking back.

"Well, I guess the cat's out of the bag," Cole said humourlessly. "I think I'll call it a day."

I left the arena without looking back. I didn't want to run into Liza, but I didn't know what to do with myself, either. I was so mixed up and upset about everything. Finally, I grabbed my backpack and I hid myself away in a corner of Quarry's stall to have a good cry. He was lying down again, resting his foot, so I curled myself into the shavings near Quarry's head where I could stroke his face and arrange his mane. I alternated between crying, reading my homework, and eating my lunch.

"Wow, what's wrong with everyone?" Sadie said, coming over to peer into Quarry's stall. "You're hiding in here, Liza's throwing stuff around the tack room, pretending she's reorganizing, and I can't find Cole. He's supposed to give me a lesson. Is anyone actually working today? Did the horses even get lunch?"

I nodded my head miserably. "Yes, they had lunch earlier. I'm sorry, Sadie, I think Cole went home already. Liza's angry because she hates me now."

My lower lip began to tremble again, and before I could stop myself, I poured out the whole story in a series of choking sobs.

Sadie whistled low under her breath. "Wow, that sounds awful. Why on earth would Cole have you ride Folly? She can be dangerous in the wrong hands."

"Oh, I *know*." I sniffled. "I was supposed to show my dad how far I'd come in my riding, but then Quarry was hurt, so Cole volunteered Folly. But I'm not nearly good enough to ride her. She's not a beginner's horse."

"No, she's not. Did you tell your dad this?"

"I tried, but he wouldn't listen and Cole didn't help. He kept talking about her bloodlines and her untapped potential, and I couldn't get a word in."

"Huh?" Sadie raised an eyebrow. "So they picked you up and put you on that horse? They tied you on her back?"

"Well, no," I said slowly. "No, but you don't understand the pressure my dad puts on me."

"Oh." Sadie snorted. "I think I understand pressure. Try being the first woman in your family to go to law school. I think my parents, aunts, and uncles sat down and decided I was going to be a lawyer when I was in third grade. I just wanted to be a scientist and study bugs. Their expectations nearly buried me alive sometimes."

"That's awful," I said. "So how did you avoid being a lawyer then?"

"Well"—she coughed—"actually, I *am* a lawyer, but not a corporate lawyer like they'd planned. I became an Environmental lawyer so I could protect the planet and the animals that I love from extinction. I found a way to make that dream my own, to take what life handed me and change it to fit my own purpose. I love my job. I feel like I make a difference every day."

Great, I thought, *she's probably one of the lawyers helping to prosecute my dad. Pretty soon she'll figure out who I am and then she'll hate me, too.*

"So, you think I should ride Folly even though she's dangerous?"

"No, what I'm *saying*," Sadie said in irritation, "is that you need to take responsibility for your own your life's journey, Astrid. You can't be a passenger in your life. You need to be in the driver's seat. If you think Folly is too much horse for you then you need to put your foot down and say that. Stand up for yourself. Nobody is going to respect your opinion if you don't respect yourself. Right?"

"Um, right," I said, in what I hoped was a convincing voice. Maybe it worked that way for Sadie, but she was strong and beautiful. Life didn't work that way for me.

I was still hiding in Quarry's stall when I heard Cole breeze back into the barn. Almost right away, Liza and Cole began to fight.

"Come on, Liza, you know it's the best solution for everyone. You keep riding Folly in the morning, and give Astrid some tips on how to handle her on the ground. At least that'll keep the kid from being killed."

"Get away from me," Liza snapped. "I'm not having anything to do with your money-grubbing scheme. You're ruining Folly, and that girl is going to get seriously hurt at some point. What do you think her family is going to think when they realize that you pushed a totally unsuitable horse on their kid?"

"Liza," he said in his most patient voice. "The fact is, Folly is not your horse. You are welcome to buy her from me if you like, if you can scrounge the money up somewhere. But, for me, she's an investment—a bad investment, honestly—and I'd like to get at least some of my money back. The horses I'm going to need to be really competitive aren't cheap. Even if mom gives me Marcus...."

Liza snorted loudly, but Cole went on as if he hadn't heard her. "I can't make it with just two horses. Montego is practically shot. He's only going to last a few more years. I need to have some good, young horses waiting in the wings.

"Liza, Folly will perform much better if you're involved. You ride her in the mornings like always, and I'll give Astrid lessons in the afternoon. This thing is happening with or without you, Liza. It's your choice whether or not to make it easier on that horse."

His boot steps headed toward the door.

"Wait!" Liza called out. "Fine, I'll do it. Not for your sake, Cole, or for Astrid's. Just for Folly."

The next day, Hilary was finally back from her choir trip. I'd never been so glad to see a friendly face. But, as I poured out the entire story to her during morning chores, her colour changed from white to red, and she had to bite her lip to keep back whatever emotions were raging inside.

"Damn that Cole," she said finally. "Liza was doing such a good job with her, too."

"I know," I said miserably. "But it's really not my fault that she lost the ride. Cole said he was going to sell Folly one way or another. It would have happened eventually."

"Yes," Hilary said slowly, "but it probably hurts her more that it was *you* and not a stranger. You know, because you were her friend and you sort of, well, you hurt something she loved and then you lied to her."

"I just didn't want to hurt her feelings! I thought I'd get out of riding somehow before she even found out it was happening."

Hilary nodded. "I guess that's not how Liza would see it, though. She probably feels like you broke her trust. Especially when she caught you red-handed."

"I know," I said, looking down at the pitchfork in my hands. "But I overheard her agreeing with Cole to help me, so I guess she'll forgive me eventually."

"Hmm," Hilary said. "We'll see."

There was no laughter in the barn that morning. Hilary remained caught up in her own thoughts, and Liza stomped around not speaking to anyone, especially not to me.

The sick feeling in the pit of my stomach grew worse with each passing hour. Only spending time with Quarry eased my dread. Today was the first day he was allowed out of his stall for a short walk, so I took him out on the lawn for some grazing time.

When I got back, Liza was tacking up Folly. She looked at me coldly and frowned. "Meet me in the ring," was all she said.

I sat in the bleachers while Liza led Folly to the mounting block and nimbly slipped onto the mare's broad back. Folly stood calmly, obediently, with a mild expression on her face. She looked like a different horse than the one who'd terrified me yesterday.

Liza walked her around quietly on a loose rein and then moved into a stretchy trot, still not picking up her rein contact. Folly responded instantly, moving forward without any hesitation or resistance. Finally, Liza brought her down to a walk again.

"Astrid," she said, not looking at me. "Folly is like a Ferrari, like an expensive, highly-tuned temperamental race car, or maybe like a space shuttle with thousands of little buttons that only an expert with years of training knows how to work. You, Astrid, are like a beginner driver…no, I don't think you're in the car yet, you're on a bicycle pretending it's a car. And when you get off your bicycle and into this Ferrari, or space shuttle, you start flailing around and accidently pushing all those little buttons. Do you know what would happen if you started pushing all those buttons on the space shuttle, Astrid?"

I didn't answer, just stared at her with my face flushed and tears springing to my eyes.

"No? Eventually you'd push the wrong one and you'd blow yourself, and the shuttle, up. That's what you're doing to Folly, Astrid."

I looked down at the arena footing, melting with embarrassment. "But Quarry is a Grand-prix horse and I can ride him," I said stubbornly, my voice rising into a whine.

"Quarry," Liza spat, "is a freaking *saint*. And you had Claudia holding your hand every step of your rides with him."

She looked at my crushed expression and her eyes softened just a hair. She took a deep breath. "I'm not saying you're not doing great for a beginner. You have a light, sensitive seat and are developing real feel. There's nothing wrong with being a beginner. That's where we all start. But you are way, way over your head with Folly. She can't forgive mistakes like Quarry can. She's too sensitive and too emotional. When you hit the wrong buttons, it literally drives her insane. The slightest flexing of your seat bone, your calf, the curl of your big toe, signals her to do something, Astrid. If you're not in complete control of every inch of your body, and of your mind, at all times, you are sending her a million conflicting signals that just shut her down.

"When I ride Folly, my aides are like tranquillizers; my seat, my hands, my breath all tell her that it's okay to relax because I'll be right there to take care of her."

"So, what am I supposed to do?" I wailed.

"Nothing," she said sharply. "Ride a horse at your ability level for the next five years and then get a horse like Folly. Then you wouldn't be scared of her; she'd be the greatest ride of your life."

She turned away from me and rode toward the door without looking back.

"Give her the afternoon off," she said abruptly over her shoulder, "she's still tender on that hind. And tell Cole exactly what I told you today. See what he says."

I sat there alone a long time after she left.

When I talked to Cole about it, he was strangely thoughtful. "Hmm, tranquilizers, that's an interesting way to put it," he said when I told him, word for word, what Liza had said. "She might be on to something there. Give Folly the afternoon off, like she said. I have to run into town for something."

I never thought I'd be so relieved to miss riding a horse.

It was nice to be able to actually enjoy my day at the stable without having the nagging terror of handling Folly hover over my head. I'd forgotten how fun it was supposed to be.

Chapter Twenty

Astrid, please call me when you get a chance. They're talking about seizing all our assets now. I don't understand how this is happening. Can you ask Marion to call my mom? She's freaking out. I don't want to lose our house. Can you call me, please? S

I turned off my phone with shaking hands and stuck it into my sock drawer. I would just say I lost it if anyone asked.

I fell gratefully into the busy barn routine. Liza taught Hilary, Pender, and some of the outside riders in the morning, and then rode Severus, Marcus, and finally, Folly.

Hilary and I groomed horses, cleaned tack, and swept just like usual, except that now Liza pretended I didn't exist. She made sure to thank Hilary directly a few times without even looking at me.

"Wow, she's really mad at you, Astrid."

"Yeah, I know. Hopefully, she'll forgive me enough to help me with Folly. I think it's the only way I'm going to survive this month. If I can just get through this then life can get back to normal. Quarry will be healed, Claudia will be home, and I'll get to go back to the archery range."

Hilary nodded thoughtfully. "I hope it works out for you that way, Astrid, I really do. I'll.... I'll be praying for you."

"Uh, thanks, Hilary." I said, feeling that slight twinge of discomfort that I always felt when she talked about religion. It was worse now that I felt guilty all the time. I had the feeling that, if there was a god, he, or she, wouldn't look very kindly on me right now.

That morning, I sat in on Liza's ride on Folly, hoping I'd absorb some of her skill through watching. It didn't help very much. Liza's aides were still mostly invisible and she ignored me the whole time she rode. Folly was lively, but obedient, her contained energy making her footsteps lofty and powerful. I watched in awe, missing my time with Quarry and wishing that I could have that same connection with Folly.

As soon as Liza was done with morning chores, she disappeared to the hospital to be with Claudia. It was a painful relief to see her go. I missed the easy friendship we'd shared before.

"We're going to bring Folly in about an hour before her lessons from now on," Cole told me casually. "Just leave her in her stall so she can relax and have an extra feed. There are some extra supplements I want her to start getting."

"Oh." I looked up from the bridle I was cleaning. "She loves her pasture time. Can't we just throw it in with her morning food?"

"No," Cole said quickly. "She needs to have them at lunch. Best not to mention this to Liza, either."

"Okay," I sighed. "It's not like she's speaking to me anyway."

That afternoon, I pulled a reluctant Folly out of her field and practically dragged her toward the barn. She stomped after me with her ears pinned, huffing angrily under her breath. She cheered up a little when she saw that she was getting extra hay and grain, though. Cole had already filled her bucket and it smelled really nice, like apples and molasses. Folly dove in before I could even get her halter off.

"Just wait, you big pig." I laughed, trying to pry her head out of the bucket. She ignored me completely and finally, I just gave up, leaving the halter on while she finished her meal.

When I went to tack her up an hour later, she gazed at me mildly and didn't snarl when I clipped her up and led her to the wash stall. She bobbed her head up and down as I groomed her and stared sleepily at the floor.

She was being so good that I gingerly put on her leg wraps, keeping an eye on her to make sure she didn't suddenly attack.

"Wake up, silly," I said as she stumbled following me to the ring. "You've had too much grass and sunshine today, ma'am."

She was so quiet that after I led her around the ring a few times I felt brave enough to lead her over to the mounting block. "Are you going to stand still for me today, Folly?" I asked, scratching her on the neck. "You seem like you're in such a good mood today."

She didn't tense up and flatten her ears as I carefully mounted. She just stood there, staring off into space as if she was thinking of something else. I adjusted myself in the saddle as quietly as I could and picked up my reins.

"Okay, buddy, we're going to just take it easy today. No more drama like before. Right?"

I asked her to walk and, after a long hesitation, she ambled forward, neck held low.

"How does she feel, Astrid?" Cole said, striding in. "A little calmer?"

"Yeah, she's a lot calmer, Cole. She feels like she's half asleep."

"Oh." He frowned. "We might have to adjust her supplements a little, then. All horses react to them a bit differently. She might need a lower dose."

"Dose?" I asked suspiciously.

"Oh, I just added some natural calmers to her diet, herbs to help her relax, all perfectly normal supplements. Look, she seems much happier."

I had to agree with that. After a few sleepy walk-trot circles around the ring on a loose rein, I began to lose my terror that she would wake up from her stupor and try to kill me at any moment. She just reacted obediently to my aides like a robot, and didn't try and fight me at all. It was wonderful, if a little strange.

"Okay, now pick up the contact, tactfully. No sudden moves."

I shortened my reins and instantly, she slid to a halt and dropped her head.

"Leg!" Cole yelled. "Don't let her get away with that. Use your leg."

I used my core first, then my seat, and finally my leg. Nothing worked until I actually kicked her with both heels. She flicked her ears back and then moved into a slow, bumpy trot.

"Good, now more rein, but add leg at the same time. She's feeling sluggish, so don't worry about booting her hard in the sides if you need to. We'll find a pair of spurs for you tomorrow."

At the end of my ride, I was dripping with sweat and shaking with exhaustion. I'd spent the whole hour just getting Folly to move forward and then, even when she was moving along at a shuffle, she'd leaned her heavy head on my reins the whole time, bearing down on the bit like a bulldozer. My shoulders ached with the effort of holding her together. I felt like I needed a handful of pain killers just to walk back to the barn.

Folly seemed fine, though. She closed her eyes as I gave her a bath and leaned her head on the cross ties as if she was too sleepy to even stand. I didn't bother putting her back out in the pasture afterward. When I put her back in her stall, she laid down right away and fell asleep in her shavings.

Cole laughed when I told him. "She got the dose she needed all right. Tomorrow, I'll adjust it and we'll find you some spurs."

By the time night feed came around, Folly was back to her old self. She snarled at me and snatched the hay net out of my hands when I went to hang it up, pinning her ears until I left her stall.

"Yeah, I like you, too, Folly," I said, rubbing my elbow from where her teeth had banged my arm. She hadn't exactly bitten me, more like smacked me with her big jaw, but it still hurt.

I watched her ride with Liza carefully the next day to see if she would act differently, but everything looked perfectly normal to me. Folly seemed happy, her steps light and lofty, communicating with her rider in some invisible way I couldn't detect.

That afternoon, our ride was better. Folly didn't stumble anymore and she was alert enough to walk, trot, and canter without falling asleep, but she also wasn't trying to kill me. It was as if she was dreaming her way through our ride. Cole had fitted me with a pair of blunt spurs that I could use to poke her a little when she felt sluggish, which was all the time now. I hated the idea of using spurs, but I could hardly make her move without them.

"They're mild spurs, Astrid. They couldn't possibly hurt her. You should see how hard horses are on each other when they play together. This is no worse than that."

Even though I had a niggling doubt about Cole's "supplements," I couldn't help but be relieved that I was no longer in danger during my time in the saddle. It wasn't fun or magical to ride her like it had been to ride Quarry, but I was gradually able to learn how to pilot her around the ring like she was a mechanical horse.

Luckily, there was nothing in our upcoming tests that required much on her part except to go in some straight lines and circles. We were entered to ride two tests at the year-end show, both at Training Level. It was easier just to focus on memorizing those than it was to worry about how different this was than riding Quarry.

Every night, though, my arms and legs ached even after I'd soaked in the shower or bath. My shoulder had begun to throb even when I wasn't riding, and I'd had to take a break from my archery exercises and my morning yoga.

I'll just hold off on doing that until I feel better, I told myself. *Once I'm used to this new way of riding I'm sure the pain will go away.*

* * * * *

At the end of the week, Claudia still hadn't come home. She'd developed a chest infection and they'd decided to keep her until she was better. Only Cole and Liza were allowed to visit, and I felt awful, knowing how much Claudia must hate being away from her beloved farm. I sent Cole with a letter to take to her including a photo of me and Quarry that Marion had taken at the horse show. Cole had assured me that she'd loved it and that it made her feel better that I was there to make a fuss of Quarry and make sure he got lots of attention. Liza, of course, still wasn't speaking to me at all.

Caprice was flourishing at our house. Marion didn't drop her off at the barn with me anymore. She kept her at home all day and had started jogging with her on the beach in the mornings.

"Well, she loves it so much," Marion said when she'd come in one morning smelling like fresh air and the ocean. "Besides, there are hardly any people out there this time of day. You should come with us sometime."

I wished I could, but the way I was feeling, it was an effort just to clean stalls and do my chores these days.

Life at the barn now seemed to have two split personalities. In the morning, Liza played classical music, rode the horses on her list, and taught her students, including Hilary and sometimes Sadie. She'd developed her own client base; mostly old friends of Claudia's who came to ride with Liza like aspiring painters to a Master. They moved quietly around their horses and spoke in hushed tones. I sometimes sat in on their lessons so I could soak up some knowledge, but was baffled by most of their esoteric discussions. They talked so much about philosophy, feel, and spirit, that it was a wonder they got any riding done at all. It was like listening to people speaking a strange language when you only knew half their alphabet.

Cole's lessons, on the other hand, were easier for me to understand. Even if I didn't always agree with how he treated the horses, he was forthright and direct. To him, horses were machines that had to operate smoothly and obediently in order for the horse-rider team to be successful. His clients were there because they were driven to succeed and he was an expert on helping them find the fastest route to the winner's circle. It wasn't that they were exactly mean to their horses, but they were exacting and disciplined, and they expected obedience instantly. It was such a sharp contrast to Liza's style of teaching that I was left a little baffled.

With Folly, any thought of brilliance in our rides had disappeared. I knew the best I could hope for was to navigate her around the ring without getting killed. There would never be any connection between us like I'd had with Quarry. I was grateful that Liza never asked about our lessons or stayed around to watch. I really didn't want her to know what was going on.

Nobody mentioned Folly's lunchtime supplements, but I saw the grave looks that Hilary and Pender sent me sometimes. Hilary didn't talk to me quite as much, and I knew she wasn't as happy as she'd been before.

Despite the fact that I now pretty much hated riding, I still loved my time at the barn. I actually really liked grooming for Liza and Cole. I knew how each horse liked to be brushed and massaged, and whose girth you could tighten right away, and who needed to be walked before you pulled the buckle up to that final hole. I read my books between chores and hung out with

Hilary and Pender. And I always took a good part of my day to spend time with Quarry. He was brushed within an inch of his life and I was taking him for longer and longer walks. Quarry was my best friend and, even though I couldn't ride him, he was still the best part of my day. Claudia was going to be so happy when she saw what good care I was taking of him.

Rob was Liza's last lesson that day. I hadn't seen him since that day in Quarry's stall, and I hadn't answered the few texts he'd sent me, either. He'd even sent Hilary a message to make sure I was all right.

"Why are you ignoring Rob?" Hilary had asked. "I thought you liked him."

"I did. I *do*," I'd told her. "I just, well, there's a lot going on right now and I don't know quite how to explain everything."

"Hmm," she said. "You could just tell him the truth."

The truth was that I didn't know why I hadn't contacted him. I liked him, I *really* liked him, but I didn't want to sort of *contaminate* him with all the bad stuff going on in my life right now. Maybe later, when Quarry was better and Claudia was back, and I didn't have to ride Folly anymore or deal with Cole or lawsuits or jail. Maybe then I could be friends with him again.

Hilary and Pender went on a trail ride after their lessons, so I was left all alone when Rob showed up.

"Hey," he said, not smiling. He'd brought both Artimax and Ferdinand for his lesson and was trying to lead them down the aisle together. I held out my hand wordlessly for Arti's lead rope and he passed it to me without arguing.

"I could give Artimax a massage while you're riding," I said shyly.

"If you like." He shrugged and led the big chestnut horse into the ring, not looking back.

I sighed, feeling awful. I must have really hurt his feelings for him to be this mad. He was usually so easy going. I put Artimax in the cross ties and worked on him for a while. He closed his eyes and napped while I went over the muscle fibres, working out any sore spots until he was practically Jell-O in my hands.

When Rob came back, he couldn't help but smile. "What have you done to my horse?" he asked in mock horror. "How are we supposed to get any riding done?"

"I can work on Ferdi next, I mean, if you want," I said, not quite meeting his eye.

"Why are you doing this, Astrid?" he asked suddenly. "Why are you pretending everything is okay? I was worried about you, you know. And, you look awful."

"Oh, please don't talk about this," I said desperately. "Can't we just make-believe that everything is normal? I'm trying hard to just make it through the rest of the summer, Rob. When we're back in school, it will be so much better. I just need to make it to the end of the month and then everything will be back to normal."

"Huh," Rob said, putting Ferdinand in the wash stall. "Did you ever think that maybe I could help make it better, Astrid? That's what friends do for each other."

I didn't answer. Everything was too mixed up and fragile for me to think about. I felt like talking about anything would just be like pouring salt in my carefully bandaged wound. Rob went and got Arti's bridle, wraps, and a fresh saddle pad, and we silently got ready, pulling the saddle off Ferdinand to put on Artimax.

"I'll take care of Ferdi," I said, pulling out the hose and adjusting the warm water.

"Okay, thanks," Rob said, heading back to the ring.

Ferdi was washed, dried, and massaged by the time he came back.

"Great job today, Rob," Liza said, ignoring me completely. "Ferdi's really doing well in your program. The jumping seems to suit him."

"He loves it." Rob smiled fondly at his horse. "He'll be ready to settle down in a few years to some serious dressage, but right now he's rocking the cross-country field."

"See you next week," Liza said. "I'm off to the hospital."

She brushed past without even looking at me and then was gone.

"I have to go bring Folly in for lunch," I said as soon as the sound of her car faded away. "I'll be right back."

"I thought they already had lunch," Rob said in confusion.

"Folly gets extra," I said, anxious to get away. She needed at least an hour before my lesson for the supplements to kick in fully. Otherwise, she was awful to tack up. Liza had run late today, and it put me behind schedule.

I grabbed some carrots and crossed my fingers that the horse was in a good mood.

She wasn't really, but she liked carrots and she liked getting a special extra feed in the middle of the day. She marched back to the barn, towing me along in her wake. She snarled when she saw Rob and his horses in the wash stalls and barged into her stall, not even waiting for me, sending me crashing into the sharp edge of the door. She dove into her waiting lunch like a dragon, snorting and snuffling into her food bowl.

"Holy cow, Astrid. Does she always act like that?"

"Uh, yeah," I said, gingerly rubbing my arm where it had smacked into the door. "She wasn't too bad today, though."

"Um, no. That was the opposite of good. You're going to have to get a handle on her soon or she's going to hurt you."

Tears stung my eyes and I had to turn away before he could see my face. Damn it, why was he still here? Why didn't he just leave?

"Astrid, are you okay?"

"Yep," I said brightly, staring into Folly's stall. "Totally fine. I guess I'll see you next week."

"Hey." He'd come up behind me without me noticing and laid a hand on my shoulder. "You don't have to be like this. I can help you deal with her, if you like."

He peered into Folly's stall and stopped suddenly, hand tightening on my shoulder until it hurt.

"Astrid, what is she eating?"

"Supplements," I said, shrugging out of his grip. I held my breath and willed him to go away and just stop asking questions.

"Yeah, I can see that. What type?"

"I…I'm not sure, something Cole picked up in town."

"Huh, well, it smells a lot like Ace to me. Are you guys drugging this horse?"

He suddenly turned me around to face him. He looked so disappointed and so angry that I wanted to melt into the ground and disappear.

"No! It's just something to take the edge off. It helps her," I said, desperate to defend myself. "Cole says—"

"Since when do you go around quoting Cole? Like hell, it helps her, Astrid. Do you have any idea what this will do to her long-term health? I thought you were better than this."

"I don't have any *choice*," I said, my voice quavering. "I'm just trying to stay alive here. It's just until the show and then everything will be back to normal."

"Damn it, Astrid!" Rob clenched his fists. "Forget the stupid show. How many people have to say she's not the horse for you before you understand?"

"I do understand! But riding her is the only way I can get my bow back and start archery again. I just have to make it a few weeks more, Rob. Honestly, I can't wait for this to be over."

Rob closed his eyes and drew in a deep breath. "Okay, we're done here, Astrid. If you think that getting back your bow justifies drugging this horse, then I guess there's nothing else to say. Don't bother calling me."

Tears sprang to my eyes, but I didn't look up as he walked away. I kept my eyes fixed on Folly as his two horses clopped down the aisle and outside.

He doesn't understand, I told myself. *I'll explain it to him better once we're back in school. He won't be so mad once he's had a chance to cool off.*

Folly looked up, crinkling her nose into what looked like a snarl when she saw me standing there. Her dark eyes bored into me, seeing right into the dark, rotten place in my soul.

Chapter twenty-one

September came in hot and sultry without a hint of fall in the air. The heat was stifling and everyone—horses, dogs, and people—spent their time looking for shade.

The heat had only added to Folly's volatile nature. She spent her time out in the pasture standing under a low hanging tree and gnawing on a nearby fence post until it there was almost nothing left. She'd started chewing at the wood in her stall, too. Something she'd never done before.

Liza had looked grim when she'd seen the damaged post and the teeth marks on the boards of her stall. "She's stressed out, Cole," I'd overheard her say. "I think she's getting ulcers."

After that, she refused to ride her in the ring anymore. She rode out on the trail instead, trying anything to make Folly happy.

Folly was grumpy in the ring, too. She was her usual obedient, robotic self, but she kept her ears back most of the time and didn't listen to my legs unless I really stuck my spurs into her.

"At least she's rideable," Cole said, when I told him I was

worried about her. "She'll be happier eventually, once she realizes that she's not going to get out of work. She was just spoiled, that's all."

My nerves were shot, too. They got worse and worse the closer the show day came. My dad had said he'd planned to come to watch, but I didn't know if that made it better or worse. I didn't even know the rules of this game I was playing, and I was too scared to ask. If I survived today, was my grounding over, did I get to go back to the range tomorrow? Would my bow be presented at dinner tonight? Did I just have to ride Folly well today, or did I have to win a ribbon? It was all so vague. I'd bitten my nails down to the quick trying to figure out all the answers.

It didn't help that gradually everyone at the barn had taken Liza's lead and were speaking to me less and less. Nobody acted mad, but they avoided me, too, and didn't include me in any discussions or laughter like they used to.

Even Hilary had grown quiet around me, and Rob wouldn't even look at me, let alone speak to me. Only Quarry still loved me; his wise eyes never judged or demanded. He just watched me calmly and was like a safe port in a raging sea.

I had been surprised when Hilary had insisted she was accompanying me to the show to help me groom. "Somebody needs to watch over you, Astrid. It's certain that Cole won't do it."

"Oh," I said, looking at her in surprise. "I thought you all hated me."

"Nobody hates you, Astrid. But it's a bit like watching a train-wreck in slow motion without being able to stop it. We're all just waiting to see how it will turn out."

That didn't make me feel better at all.

Despite my growing dread, a shiver of excitement (no doubt left over from happier days with Quarry) danced down my spine when we pulled into the show grounds. The intoxicating smell of horses, leather, and dirt wrapped itself around me like a familiar blanket.

It was the same competition grounds we'd been to the last time, but this time it was a much bigger show being held and the whole place had been transformed. Impeccably groomed horses and their runway model riders sauntered everywhere, looking impossibly cool and collected.

Music was playing, vendor tents selling everything from art to horse trailers were set up everywhere, and there were at least four different food trucks that I could see. There was a big tent just for the competitors with champagne, fruit, croissants, and chocolate dipped strawberries to snack on.

I was riding the same Training level test as last time, plus another one that Cole had had me memorize. Unlike last time, though, there was no joy in this outing. I was only filled with a sick dread. There was no Liza or Claudia to help me like last time, and no teammates to rally around.

Cole's two horses strolled off the trailer without a care in the world. Folly, however, had spent the whole ride over banging and kicking at the metal trailer. Neighing her displeasure for everyone to hear.

"I'm sorry, you'll have to get her for me, Cole," I squeaked, peering inside. "I can't do it."

"It's fine, Astrid. Let me slide in; you open the door for me when I tell you."

He held something small hidden in one hand as he slipped inside. There was the sound of angry hooves against metal, then a moment of silence, and then the banging started again.

"Okay," he said, pushing open the door and jumping to the ground. He capped the syringe in his hand and stuck it in the back pocket of his breeches. "That went well. Give her ten minutes and then she'll be fine to bring in."

"What?" I hissed. "What did you give her?"

"A special cocktail a friend made up for show days. Don't worry, he said it should pass the drug test no problem. Her home brew wasn't exactly legal."

I leaned against the door with tears stinging my eyes and listened to the sounds of Folly's outrage slow down and then disappear altogether. Finally, I opened the door and peered inside.

"Are you okay, girl?" I asked tentatively. The trailer was hot inside and I could see that her neck and sides were streaked with sweat. "Come on, buddy. Let's get you into your nice stall. Your hay and a bucket of water are waiting for you."

She let me approach and didn't resist when I clipped on her lead rope and tugged her toward the door. She followed me down the ramp in a quiet daze and went right into her stall without protest. She lipped at the hay half-heartedly and then turned to stare out the door, listening intently. She didn't even know I was there.

After a few minutes, I left her and wandered aimlessly around the show grounds pretending to look at things. I had over an hour before I had to warm up and I just couldn't stand to stay at the barn near the horses anymore. I felt sick thinking about Cole injecting Folly with some awful cocktail. What if it hurt her?

I reached the competitor's tent and flashed my badge that had my name and number on it to a smiling, red-headed lady at the entrance.

"Come on in, dear. It's air conditioned and we have juice and snacks to keep up your strength."

The wonderful, cool air hit me, and I closed my eyes and held out my arms a little so it could hit me everywhere. Then I headed right to the chocolate strawberries, loaded up my plate, and then grabbed two croissants and slathered them in a thick layer of butter and jam. Food was going to be the only good thing about this day.

"Ooh, champagne, Mina, let's have some to take the edge off. My nerves are shot and I don't ride for hours."

I looked up to see two impossibly tall, thin girls already dressed in show clothes pouring champagne into little plastic cups. They loaded their plates with cheese and bread and then disappeared outside.

My hands shook as I ate the chocolate strawberries and one croissant after the other. I licked my fingers and then stared hungrily back at the table. I was still famished. It felt like nothing was ever going to fill that unhappy, hollow space inside of me. I looked around to make sure the lady at the door wasn't watching and then went back for seconds.

I paused, looking over at the champagne table. Maybe a small glass would help my nerves. It had certainly done that at the Ling party.

Yes, and look how well that *turned out*, I told myself. Still, one glass wouldn't hurt. Would it?

I filled my plate, edging closer to that end of the table until I stood right next to the bottle. I lifted it with shaking hands and filled a plastic cup to the brim. Then I moved quickly back to my table and hunched over my plate.

The first sip was tangy. It stung my throat and the bubbles tingled in my nostrils. It wasn't exactly delicious, but the warmth that flowed down through me was exactly what I'd needed. I drained the whole glass and went back for another.

"What are you doing in here, Astrid?" Hilary said quietly, watching me from the door.

I spun around so fast that the drink dropped to the dirt floor, liquid bleeding away into the ground. "Hilary!"

"Cole sent me to find you. It's time for you to get Folly ready."

"Uh, just having some juice here," I said, my voice too loud. "It's pretty hot out there, hey? Good thing they have this tent to cool off in."

Hilary stared at me intently and crossed her arms over her chest. "Don't do this to yourself, Astrid, there's still time...."

She broke off as my dad and Marion pushed into the tent.

"Astrid!' My dad said jovially, clapping me on the arm in what I'm sure was an affectionate way. "Almost show time. Cole says you've done some amazing work with this horse. She'll soon be giving you a run for your money, hey, Hilary?"

Hilary blanched, her eyes wide. I could see her trying to find something polite and appropriate to say to my dad, who she clearly did not like.

"Um, I guess so," she said finally. "Okay, Astrid, well, I suppose I'll see you back at the barn then."

She spun around and was gone.

"Shouldn't we be getting Folly ready, darling?" Marion asked. "I want to take some pictures of you two."

"Okay," I sighed, curving my lips into a smile so I didn't seem ungrateful. I wasn't going to ruin my chances of getting back into archery now after all the hell I'd been through in this last month. I didn't want my dad thinking I was spoiled.

Folly was still a bit sweaty when we got back, but she'd eaten some of her hay and the water bucket had been drained. I refilled it for her and gave her a pat on the neck, which she didn't even acknowledge.

"Go get changed, Astrid," Hilary said with a small smile. "I'll get her ready."

I fumbled into my show clothes. Outside, I could hear Cole schmoozing with my dad and Marion, talking up all of Folly's good points and conveniently leaving out the part where she had to be heavily sedated before I could even sit on her.

"Darling, you look wonderful. Stand beside Folly so I can take your picture. You, too, Cole and Hilary. I want you all included."

Cole threw an arm around my shoulders and grinned into the camera. I didn't look at Hilary's face, but I was pretty sure she wasn't smiling.

By the time I mounted up and made it to the warm up ring, Folly was slick with sweat and her breathing sounded a little funny.

"Is she okay, Cole?" I whispered urgently. "She doesn't feel right."

He looked in her eyes and then flipped her lip up so he could check her gums. "Yes, she's okay. It's just this heat. Lots of the horses here are sweating. When you're done riding, just give her a good bath. She'll be fine."

Chapter twenty-two

I let her walk around the ring, and then moved her into a shuffling trot. She seemed to perk up a little bit, and I breathed a sigh of relief. Cole was right, it was probably just the heat.

"We'll be up in the stands watching, Astrid," my dad called out. "Break a leg out there."

Folly felt better and better the more we moved. She was actually listening to my leg now instead of me having to use my spurs. Her head was up and she moved proudly, with purpose.

"Okay, just canter a couple of times and then you're good to go in. Hilary's on deck to call your test."

Shifting my leg back a millimeter, I asked for a canter depart in the softest way I knew, not sure how she was going to react. Her shoulders came up for that first stride but, instead of moving forward, she let out a strange deep sigh as if all the air had left her body, and then she collapsed like a stone beneath me.

It must have happened so quickly, but for me, that moment lasted an eternity. I could see the whole thing unfolding in slow motion—the strange dead feeling as Folly dropped away beneath me, her red neck twisting sideways as she fell. The faded shout of someone standing at the rail. The sky tilted over my head and I had just enough time to kick my feet free from the stirrups before the ground came up to meet us with a mighty roar. I heard Folly groan, an awful sound that shouldn't ever have come out of a horse, as she crashed face first into the ground.

The impact threw me forward over her head, and I landed hard in front of her, the jarring crunch knocking the air from my lungs. I lay there, unable to move, gasping desperately for oxygen, arms flailing. From where I lay, I could see Folly was half on her side and struggling badly. The air suddenly roared back into my lungs, but before I could move, one of her thrashing front hooves struck me hard on the cheek so that my teeth clicked sharply together and then another hoof smashed hard into my shoulder. There was a sharp cracking sound, and I screamed in agony, clutching my arm and curling into a ball on the ground. *Get up, get up now*, an inner voice said. I struggled painfully to my knees. There was blood in my mouth and my whole side clenched with pain. Folly rolled her eye wildly toward me, white rimmed with panic, before flailing again. *Why are you doing this to me?* Her face seemed to say. Then her hoof hit me squarely in the face with an audible crack. My head snapped back, vision blurring, and stars danced in front of my eyes. Everything went dark.

There were voices all around, horses neighing, and a man's voice shouting. Someone touched my shoulder and I struggled back to consciousness with a groan. My face was wet and my nose throbbed. I touched my cheek gingerly and whimpered when my hand came back red with blood.

"Don't move," a voice commanded. "You've had a bad fall.

We're going to the hospital."

"Folly," I said, half-sitting up. "I have to help Folly, she needs me. This is all my fault."

Faces hovered into view. Marion and my dad stood beside my stretcher, faces white with horror. Two emergency attendants stood at my feet, strapping my legs down to the board I lay on.

"The vet is looking after your horse. Your trainer is with her now," the attendant said kindly. "We have to get you to the hospital now."

"No!" Despite the pain I struggled upright. "Get him away from her. She was drugged. He tried to kill her. Get away from her, Cole!"

"Astrid," my father stammered, his face white and wide-eyed. "The horse is injured. The humane thing to do would be to—"

"No," I said. I sat up and kicked my feet free of the stretcher, pushing Marion aside, "You get the hell away from her. This is your fault, Dad, yours and Cole's...I've never asked one thing of you, Dad, never, but I'm asking you something now. You make sure Folly lives or I will never speak to you again."

Sickness rolled in my belly and I twisted around so I could throw up onto the grass. No matter what I'd just said, it wasn't just my dad and Cole's fault that Folly was hurt; it was mine, too. I never should have agreed to have anything to do with her. If she died, it would be just as much my fault. When I looked back to where my dad had been standing, he was gone.

A circle of people stood around Folly, blocking my view. I could hear her breath coming out in ragged gasps and the thud of her feet knocking against the ground. She was dying.

"Oh, Astrid," Hilary wailed, appearing beside me. "What is happening? What happened to Folly?"

"Hilary!" I said, grasping her clean hand in my mucky one. "Call Liza, call Claudia. Call anyone you can, just don't let them put down Folly, understand. She needs to live."

"Astrid," Marion said soothingly, laying a hand on my arm. Her eyes pooled with sympathetic tears, but I shook her off roughly. I didn't have time to worry about hurting her feelings.

Hilary stared between me and Marion in horror, and then whipped out her cell phone without asking another question. I closed my eyes in relief. Maybe there was hope, after all.

"Astrid!" Rob surged through the crowd, pale and breathless. I hadn't even known he was here watching. "Are you okay?"

"Rob, you have to do something." I knew I was hysterical, but I couldn't stop. "Listen. Folly was drugged. It was supposed to make her calm, but it's killing her. Cole knows what the drug is, maybe there's an antidote or something. Tell the vet that."

"Astrid, you need to get to the hospital, *now*," Marion said firmly. "Folly will be taken care of."

"Marion, they're going to kill her," I said frantically. "I know it. She's insured and they don't care about her. Please!"

She looked at me hard and then turned to Rob.

"Robert, here is my credit card. Please let the vet know that Folly is registered in Astrid's name, and that Astrid wants to do everything medically to save her. As long as it's in Folly's best interests, of course. Would you look after this?"

Rob looked stunned, but before he could say anything, I was hoisted into the ambulance and the doors slammed shut. I burst into tears and buried myself under the blankets. Too upset to even look at Marion, I wanted to die. If Folly was injured I might as well stop living now. How would I go on with that guilt hovering over me my whole life?

I threw up twice in the ambulance on the way to the hospital and was so weak with pain, sickness, and worry that I just lay there limply while they did X-rays, and poked and prodded me. I cou.ld only think about Folly, who had only been my enemy this last month, but whose life had now become more precious to me than anything.

They had to do surgery on my arm. It really was broken this time. The upper arm bone, the humerus, had been snapped in two and needed a pin to hold it in place. My nose and right cheekbone had been broken, too, and they had to do surgery to put the pieces all back together. But of course, I only found that part out afterward.

The moment they let me drift down into darkness was a blissful relief. For a long time, I drifted in and out of consciousness, too numb to take in anything around me. My thoughts were fuzzy and indistinct, memories of the happy hours riding Quarry and working at the barn, images of the moments when it was just me and my bow all alone on an empty range.

On the third day, I woke up in the dark, alone, and instantly wished that they'd put me under again. Everything hurt, my whole body ached, but my arm and face were sharp stabs of pain.

"Oh, are you awake, dear," a grey-haired nurse said. "I'll let your family know and I'll get you some more pain meds. You've been through quite the ordeal."

As soon as the pain killers hit my system, I was gone again, pulled down into sleep. When I woke the next time, I felt much better. The pain had receded to a dull ache. I had a bandage on my face and a cast on my arm, but other than that, I was just stiff and sore.

"Oh, honey," Marion said from where she'd set up camp beside my bed. She was curled up in a plush chair with a blanket on her lap and a book in her hand. There were dark circles under her eyes and her usually immaculate hair stuck up in all directions. She put the book down on the little bedside table and leaned toward me.

"Darling, how are you feeling?"

"Okay," I croaked. I stared at her, silently willing her to answer the one question that had lodged in my head. Was Folly alive or dead?

Marion dropped her eyes to the floor and sighed. "Astrid, you need to speak with your father."

I gulped. That didn't sound good at all. And if bad news was coming, I certainly didn't want to hear it from *him*.

Marion moved smoothly to the door and peeked out into the hall. A moment later, my dad followed her inside, looking so deflated and exhausted that I hardly recognized him.

"Dad?" I said uncertainly, shocked by the change that had come over him since I'd seen him last. He looked like a shrunken shadow of his former self. He moved toward me and then sat down on the edge of my bed, staring into my face as if he were actually seeing *me*, not just a disappointing memory of my mother. To my surprise, he reached out and took my hand. I almost pulled away; he hadn't touched me since I was a little kid and my instinct was to put as much distance between us as possible. He looked so defeated, though, that I didn't have the heart.

"Astrid." He sighed then looked down at our lightly clasped hands, shaking his head. "Apologies don't come easily to me." He paused, searching for the words. "I have not always been a real father to you. I…I have a temper and I know I'm not always fair to you or to your stepmother. I want to let you know that I'll be getting some help with that."

I was too stunned, and confused, to answer; I just stared at him and waited for him to get to the part about Folly. What had happened to Folly?

He seemed to see the question hovering between us. He squeezed my hand and sent me a small smile. Probably the first time he'd smiled at me in months. "Folly's alive," he said suddenly. "But she's not well, Astrid. She'll need months to recover. She may never be the horse she once was; her career is quite possibly over."

I sagged with relief, tears springing to my eyes. I didn't care about her so-called career. I just cared that she was alive.

"Oh, thank you," I whispered, "thank you so much. Where is she?"

"She's still at the vet hospital. She had, if I understand what the vet said correctly, the equivalent of a horse heart attack, and when she fell, she sustained some broken ribs and a lot of soft tissue and ligament damage. Your friend, Liza, has been with her almost the whole time. She's been well taken care of.

"But, Astrid, now that we've gotten Folly out of the way, there is something more that I have to tell you. I think you've heard a little about my recent legal difficulties. I know I haven't always made the best decisions, and now it's caught up with me. The court cases against me are piling up, and I don't know for sure how it's going to end. Bankruptcy is probably the best case scenario at this point."

"Bankruptcy," I said in surprise. "What does that mean?"

"It means that we might lose everything. Everything I've worked so hard to build up. The business, the condo, everything. Astrid, I'm so sorry."

I sat back against my pillow. "Folly? Will they take Folly?"

He shook his head. "She's in your name, and I'm afraid she's not worth anything at this point. Folly, your education fund, and a few other assets have been put in your name. We set aside enough to support your archery training for the next few years. Just in case."

I looked into my dad's sad face and felt tears spring into my eyes. I still had everything I needed. He and Marion had made sure I was taken care of, but what about them? I hated living in the condo, but it was my dad's pride and joy. And he loved his business. What was it going to do to him if he lost everything?

"Dad," I whispered. "I'm so sorry about...well, just everything."

He smiled at me tiredly. "I've been expecting something like this for the last couple of years, Astrid. The worry nearly killed me, but now that it's actually here, I feel a sense of relief. I know I've been an awful father to you. I'm ashamed of myself and I promise you now that when this is over I'll try to do better. You're a great kid, Astrid, you've always been a great kid. Don't ever forget that."

I stared at him with my mouth open, and then surprised myself by leaning forward and wrapping my good arm around him in a tight hug. He hesitated and then gingerly hugged me back.

"Astrid," he said gently. "There is a chance that, in the end, I might have to do some time in jail." He sighed and looked down at the floor. "The choices I made did lead to making some people very sick. I did break the law and there are consequences for that."

"But, what about Mr. Ling?" I asked hesitantly, not really wanting to know.

"He's all clear." My dad sighed. "I took the blame. Astrid, there's a lot of publicity around this and I don't want you to be dragged down in a media circus. When Folly is well enough to travel, your aunt has offered to take both you and the horse back to her ranch, if you like."

"Aunt Lillian? But I don't even know her."

My dad cleared his throat uncomfortably. "It's my fault she's not in our lives, Astrid. We had a…a misunderstanding after your mother died. But, I know she'd like to have you stay with her. It would be good for you to reconnect. And it would be a good place for Folly to recover. There are hundreds of acres there. You can come home any time if you don't like it. What do you think?"

I lay back against the pillow, too overwhelmed to speak. I didn't want to abandon my dad and Marion just because things were getting difficult at home. I finally felt like we could be a real family, and I didn't want to walk away from that.

My dad seemed to guess my hesitation. "Astrid, you'd be doing me a favour if you went up to the ranch. I wouldn't have to worry about you if I knew you were safe and happy, and that would make it easier for me to focus on the case. Your stepmother and I are going to be consumed with this court case for a long time. Marion won't have time to devote to your care."

I stiffened. He was talking like I was an infant who needed 24-hour monitoring.

"Besides," he went on, not noticing my disapproval, "you won't be able to ride or practice archery until your arm heals so you might as well focus on your recovery, and focus on Folly's recovery."

He smiled at me tentatively and it was the strange, new fatherly concern in his eyes that finally made me decide. If they needed me to do this, then who was I to argue?

"Okay, and Dad?"

"Yes?"

"I'm so glad about Mr. Ling. You did the right thing."

He frowned and for a second I thought I'd made him angry. Then he seemed to sag a little, shoulders hunched. "I hope so," he said, "I really do."

* * * * *

The pain meds they had me on were so strong that I could only stay awake for about an hour at a time before I drifted off again. The line between sleeping and waking blurred and sometimes I couldn't tell what was real and what wasn't. Which was why I started laughing when I opened my eyes to find the ghost of Claudia at my bedside. She was in a wheelchair and had a tube stuck under her nose and she had on an awful flower patterned hospital gown.

"Claudia." I giggled. "Why are you dressed like that? Aren't you supposed to be riding?"

She smiled faintly and realization dawned on me; this wasn't a joke. Claudia was really here and that...that thing she was wearing on her nose was there to help her *breathe*. She was so much sicker than I'd thought. I immediately burst into tears.

"Oh, Astrid," Claudia said, taking my hand in her thin one. "Don't be silly." Her voice was weaker than it had been but she was still the same Claudia. "Sit up and stop crying."

I hiccupped and obediently pushed myself painfully into a sitting position.

"Claudia, I'm so, so sorry about Folly. I made such a mess of everything."

"Yes, darling, you certainly did." Claudia smiled to take the sting out of her words. "But the main question now is, what are you going to do to make it better?"

I gulped. "My dad wants me to take Folly up to my aunt's ranch so we can both heal. She has hundreds of acres so Folly can just go out on pasture and get better."

"I see." Claudia nodded thoughtfully. "And after she heals physically, *if* she heals physically, then what?"

"I...I don't know."

"Were you planning to ride her?"

"No!" I shook my head emphatically. "Never again." I looked at her closely, wondering what she was getting at. "Why?"

"I have a favour to ask of you, Astrid. Pretty soon I'll have to make a decision to downsize the farm. It's too much for me right now and I'm going to have to concentrate on my health. Rob's father has agreed that Marcus and Quarry can come and live at his place when the time comes; it was part of the deal when I sold them Ferdinand."

"Oh, that makes sense."

"Rob has the perfect set up at their small farm, although we'll be lacking the spectacular indoor arena. Liza will stay on to take care of our two special boys and will still travel to teach lessons."

"But, what about Jerry and Rabbit and the other horses? Where will they go?"

Claudia blinked back tears. "That is yet to be determined, I'm afraid. But nothing is happening right away. There is still plenty of time to figure everything out.

"The thing is, Astrid, Liza and Folly have a really special bond, I truly believe that Liza is the only person who can bring out the best in that strong-willed horse."

"I know." Tears stung my eyes. "I really am sorry."

"So, Astrid, take Folly with you to this ranch to heal. Liza has too much on her plate right now to take on another horse and we won't have the room for Folly when we move to the new barn. Hopefully that won't be for a while yet, but I have to stay practical; it might be sooner rather than later. But, when she's ready to start being worked with, please consider selling her to Liza at a fair price. The mare won't be of any use to you."

Relief flooded over me. "Oh, Claudia, I will. That's a perfect idea. Can you tell Liza for me? I don't think she'll speak to me for a long time, if ever."

Claudia squeezed my hand and smiled. "I will. You're a great girl, Astrid. And I know in time you'll be an amazing rider. And thank you so much for taking care of my wonderful boy, Quarry. I knew he was in good hands with you."

* * * * *

I couldn't leave the hospital for another week because of the head trauma, but between the drug-induced napping and the constant visitors, the time passed quickly.

Marion stayed by my bedside almost the whole time and my dad visited nearly every day. Slowly the awkwardness between us eased into a tentative friendship and one day I finally got the courage to ask him about the photo I'd found, the one with he and my mom and Marion smiling together.

"You said you'd met Marion long after mom died, Dad. How did you know each other?"

He sighed and looked down at me. "Astrid, I'm afraid I've done your mom a real injustice by keeping the truth from you. I was so hurt by her inability to handle the addiction that ultimately killed her that I feel like I've made her into some sort of monster. She wasn't a monster. She was loving and funny and full of life. But she had a dark side, too—we both did—and I guess I wanted to protect you from that.

"Your mom and I met in AA, Astrid. Marion introduced us, actually. She was our sponsor."

"What does that mean?" I asked, confused.

"It means that, a very long time ago, Marion had a problem with alcohol. She beat it and moved on, but she also wanted to help other people, so she became a sponsor. It's sort like a support counsellor for other people who struggle with addiction. She took on both me and your mom, and ran a small AA group."

"Marion did?" I asked in disbelief. "She doesn't even like to leave the house."

"She was different then, Astrid, she was braver. She helped so many people and she helped me. We all became good friends, but when, years later, your mother relapsed and there was nothing anyone could do to save her, it sort of damaged Marion inside. She'd only had successes up until then. It was an awful blow for everyone when your mother died. She'd touched so many lives."

I lay back on the pillow and stared up at the ceiling, wondering what else people had been keeping from me all these years. Still, it was a start that they were including me now.

"Thanks for telling me, Dad," I said finally. "That means a lot."

* * * * *

The next day everyone from the barn showed up to have an impromptu party in my room. Everyone except Cole and Liza that was. Pender had brought pizza and we all dove in; I practically inhaled my piece of the first real food I'd been allowed since my accident. Ally had just arrived back from the Caribbean, looking tanned and perfect and very disappointed that she'd missed all the drama.

"And for Cole to just pack up his horses and leave like that overnight, with Claudia being so sick in the hospital. It's just crazy. That boy is so selfish." Ally's eyes were shining.

"Oh, I don't know," Hilary said thoughtfully. "He felt pretty bad about Folly after the show. He was crying and I know he spent the day with Claudia before he left so he must have told her everything. He's banned from showing for a while so he's just gone to lick his wounds. I bet he'll be back one of these days."

"I feel awful about the whole thing," I said softly. "It wasn't just his fault about Folly. I was to blame for pretty much everything. If I had been a better rider…."

"Oh, pshaw," Sadie said. "Cole's a grown man, he should have known better. He just left because his reputation's been damaged. He'll come crawling back as soon as he can, I guess."

Rob lingered behind after everyone had left. "I'm sorry you're going away. I'm going to miss you, Astrid."

"Me too," I whispered. "I'm so sorry that we fought, Rob. You were right about everything. I handled it all so badly."

He shrugged. "Oh well, you'll know better next time. Just say no to drugs."

He winked at me and I couldn't help but laugh.

Chapter twenty-three

As soon as I had permission to leave the hospital I begged Marion to take me to the barn to say one last goodbye to Quarry.

When we got there, the place seemed deserted. The barn was swept clean but stood empty; all the horses had been turned out to pasture. I walked around, feeling desolate, wondering if I'd ever be able to call this wonderful place home again. Marion waited in the car for me while I slowly walked down to the paddocks.

Quarry came striding over to the gate as soon as he saw me, whickering low under his breath.

"Wow, you look good, buddy," I told him, slipping into his paddock and offering him a carrot. "Maybe soon Claudia can come home and ride you again. You'd like that, wouldn't you?'

He crunched the carrot happily between his teeth and then lifted his nose so he could gently touch the bandages on my face.

"I know, I'm a mess, I look like a freak, don't I?"

He dropped his head to sniff my cast, lipping it carefully as if seeing what it was made out of. He stopped and looked right at me with his big, wise eyes.

"Yes, I broke that, too. Oh, Quarry, I've made so many stupid mistakes." Suddenly, I was crying. I wrapped my good arm around his neck and pressed my face into him, inhaling that rich horsey scent that had somehow become a part of my whole being.

He stood stone still until I was done and then gave me a small push with his head, turned, and walked off into his pasture as if to say, "there now, you'll be okay on your own. I've done my job."

And strangely enough, he had. I went back to the car feeling lighter than I had since that first awful day I'd ridden Folly.

* * * * *

We waited another two weeks until we were certain Folly was well enough to make the journey up north. She hobbled out of her stall at the vet's and onto the trailer like an old woman, and she leaned heavily against the padded divider when it was snugged up against her. We'd hired a shipping company for her with a roomy, air-ride trailer and my dad had somehow convinced them to let me ride along.

"Are you sure she's okay to make the trip?" I asked anxiously for the third time. We had eight hours of roads and ferry crossings ahead of us, and Folly didn't look like she'd make it out the driveway.

"Drive slow and carefully," the vet said. "She'll arrive just fine."

Despite the fact that we had to leave at 6:30 in the morning to catch the early ferry, Hilary and Rob had come to see us off. Hilary's eyes watered as she went over to peer in the trailer at

Folly. "Bye, girl," she said sadly. "At least you're going to a nice place."

She came back and gave me a careful hug. "I'm going to miss you so much, Astrid," she said. "Email me every day and tell me how you're doing. I want to know everything."

"And don't let any of those cowboys chat you up," Rob said, coming to stand next to me, so close that I could feel the heat coming off him. "You just tell them that you're already taken."

"I doubt anyone will want me like this." I laughed. My nose and cheek were still bandaged and I had bruises everywhere. I was not what you'd call a real prize.

He reached out and brushed a stray curl behind my ear. "Maybe I'd want you," he said, and then leaned down and softly kissed me on the lips.

"Wow, that must be love if you're willing to kiss her around all that bandaging," the truck driver joked as he passed by. "Safety check is done and we're all packed. Time to hit the road, missy."

I pulled back, dazed and stared up into Rob's smiling face.

"See you," he said softly.

"Okay, see you."

I walked toward the truck, staring straight ahead, still stunned. *I just had my first kiss*, I thought, coming out of my stupor. I looked back to see Rob staring at me with a lopsided grin. I turned away quickly, a blush stealing up my neck. *Huh.*

"Are you sure you don't want me to drive you there, Astrid?" Marion said anxiously. "I hate to think of you making that long trip by yourself. Did you pack enough food? Do you have your medication?"

"Marion, I'm fine," I lied, suddenly already homesick. Right then I wanted nothing more than to go back two months in time and have everything be the way it was before I'd ever gotten on that rope swing. Well, almost everything. I reached over to hug her. "Thank you so much, Marion. Take care of Caprice and let me know what happens with...well, with things." I paused, my lower lip suddenly trembling as I thought of Claudia still sick in the hospital and my dad fighting to stay out of jail.

"Of course," she said smoothly. "I will talk to you every day. You just concentrate on getting better and healing that horse."

One last hug and then I was climbing into the truck beside Allan, the driver who my dad had hired on Claudia's recommendation.

The big truck started with a rumble.

It's not too late to change your mind, I thought. But I didn't move. I watched Marion head back to her car and then craned my neck around and waved at Rob and Hilary until they were just a blur on the retreating horizon. Then I turned to face the front, my eyes fixed on the road ahead of me, looking only toward the future.

If you loved reading Defining Gravity then stay tuned for the next two books in Astrid's series. Be sure visit the website www.genevievemckay.com for updates on new releases.

Authors love to hear from their readers. Drop by the website, join the mailing list or consider leaving a review on any of the platforms where these books are sold.

Genevieve Mckay is a four-time novelist and horse enthusiast living with her family on the wet and wonderful West Coast. She is an excellent horse-mom but a terrible archer.

All About Books

If you enjoyed Defining Gravity I'd love if you'd take a moment to write a review on any of the platforms where it is sold.

You can stay updated on new releases, contests and freebies by joining my fun newsletter list, All About Books. I like to promote other authors too so if you write YA books about horses or fun-loving zombies feel free to drop me a line.

Visit my website at www.genevievemckay.com
Follow on Twitter @Geners_Mckay
Or join my Facebook author page:
https://www.facebook.com/authorgenevievemckay/

Astrid's Series

Defining Gravity
Flight – coming Summer 2017
Freefall – coming Winter 2017

The Strange Adventures of Carolina Brown

The Opposite of Living
An Aching in the Bone
Wayfarer's End

Made in the USA
Las Vegas, NV
19 November 2020

11152176R00187